W9-ALN-073

Also by Maggie Marr

Hollywood Girls Club

SECRETS OF THE *Hollywood* GIRLS CLUB

SECRETS OF THE *Hollywood* GIRLS CLUB

a novel

MAGGIE MARR

Crown Publishers • New York

This is a work of fiction. Names, characters, places, and incidents either are the product of the author's imagination or are used fictitiously. Any resemblance to actual persons, living or dead, events, or locales is entirely coincidental.

Published in the United States by Crown Publishers, an imprint of the Crown Publishing Group, a division of Random House, Inc., New York.
www.crownpublishing.com

CROWN is a trademark and the Crown colophon is a registered trademark of Random House, Inc.

Library of Congress Cataloging-in-Publication Data
Marr, Maggie.
Secrets of the Hollywood girls club / Maggie Marr.—1st ed.
1. Women in the motion picture industry—Fiction. 2. Motion picture industry—Fiction. 3. Hollywood (Los Angeles, Calif.)—Fiction. I. Title.
PS3613.A7687S43 2008
813'.6—dc22 2007038919

ISBN 978-0-307-34631-5

Printed in the United States of America

DESIGN BY ELINA D. NUDELMAN

10 9 8 7 6 5 4 3 2 1

First Edition

For Chad Henderson

You are my everything

M.M.

Rule 1

There Are No Secrets in Hollywood

Kiki Dee, Publicist

Kiki Dee thought she knew where all the Hollywood bodies were buried—even the ones she had killed—because secrets were her business. Celebrity secrets. Kiki was a secret keeper. As a publicist, Kiki shifted the bright white spotlight away from everything her celebrity clients needed to hide. And their gratitude to her for covering up their indiscretions took the form of a check, or cash, whichever they preferred. Kiki collected secrets the way some people collected diamonds or cars. Each naughty tidbit could potentially destroy Hollywood careers. And of course, along with the indiscretions came the clients. Kiki promised to lock the secret in "the vault," also known as her brain, for a weekly fee. Some called it extortion. Kiki called it commerce.

And Kiki didn't keep just one secret per client. She'd discovered that once a star accepted that she knew their most depraved act or hidden kink, suddenly all the crimes and misdemeanors came pouring out. Kiki listened to all her clients' confessions. It was good to have collateral.

But *this* secret, the one Kiki witnessed in Dr. Melnick's office . . . well, this secret was platinum. This secret could sink movie studios, destroy high-power industry marriages, and ruin one of the biggest celebrity careers in Hollywood. With this one amazingly well-kept secret, Kiki and her publicity firm, KDP, which had suffered a precipitous slide into the abyss of B-list stars, would be back on top. This secret potentially affected dozens of Hollywood heavyweights. Not to mention the little lovely who was rapidly sleeping her way up the A-list. Kiki would sign two big stars based on this peccadillo. Failing to have Kiki in their corner would result in the release of this salacious bit of gossip to the press. And if the truth reached the masses, the two stars could kiss their careers and their paychecks good-bye.

Kiki had proof, and she figured it was worth at least seven figures. But Kiki cared little about the money. No, she desired prestige. The prestige obtained by representing the biggest stars in the world. Prestige and access were priceless commodities in Hollywood, and for Kiki, prestige, access, and power made her job almost worthwhile.

Kiki would be thrilled . . . if she weren't so nauseated. Her discovery almost made the torture of her lipo, tummy tuck, and eyelift worth it. Almost. She gritted her teeth as the Lincoln Town Car came to a fast stop on Wilshire. How had *this* luscious deceit remained quiet? People must know. But Kiki had rummaged through celebrity lives for twenty (okay, twenty-five) years, and she had *never* sniffed a whiff of this treat. She carefully leaned back against the supple black leather of the backseat. The trip was a short four blocks from Dr. Melnick's office to the Peninsula Hotel, but with stitches around her face and the super-tight spandex body glove around her stomach, the ride felt like miles. She knew from experience.

Although painful, the spandex body glove prevented her belly from rupturing. She turned her gauze-wrapped head toward the window and attempted to block from her mind the lipo procedure that Dr. Melnick had just completed, otherwise she'd be sick. She clutched the paper airsick bag that Dr. Melnick's receptionist (who herself had bovine-fat-enhanced lips and perfectly Botoxed brows) had handed Kiki before the nurse wheeled her out the back exit of the office to her awaiting car and driver.

Boom Boom, Kiki's ever-faithful and ever-suffering assistant, sat in the backseat holding a BlackBerry in one hand and a cup of ice chips in the other.

"She said it was urgent," Boom Boom said and scrolled through the e-mails. "Here, look."

She held the BlackBerry within inches of Kiki's nose, but Kiki couldn't read it. *God, Boom Boom could be an idiot. You couldn't wear glasses right after an eye-lift. Where did Boom Boom think they put the stitches?* Kiki leaned her head to the left. She could barely speak. Her lips were swollen with ass or bovine fat, she didn't even remember at this point, and her jaw hurt.

"Read it," Kiki mumbled, trying to move her lips as little as possible.

Boom Boom pulled an ice chip from the cup and managed to wedge it into Kiki's mouth. "Fine. It says, 'Kiki, my luv, we need to talk. Urgent news, don't want to e-mail, call me.' "

Kiki looked at Boom Boom. That was it? That was the e-mail Boom Boom appeared so worked up about? Kiki had worked the public relations gig for a long time, and *urgent* to one of her stars could mean a broken nail without a manicurist on set. This was nothing, especially compared with Kiki's recent discovery. But still, the e-mail had come from one of her biggest stars.

"When?" Kiki whispered, then winced as the Town Car bounced over a pothole. She remembered that bump from the last face-lift, six months earlier.

"Three hours ago," Boom Boom said. She put on her headset. "Want to roll some calls? We've got twenty-five to return."

Kiki glared at her assistant. She felt doped up on morphine and hadn't yet taken her Vicodin.

"Lydia called. She needs an answer about press."

Kiki shook her head and motioned for the pad and pen resting on Boom Boom's lap.

"Jen wants to know about the CDF fund-raiser," Boom Boom

continued. She handed Kiki the pen. "Also Natalie asked about your trip to the ashram, wants to know if it's one or two weeks?"

Kiki's head pounded. She put pen to paper.

"Galaxy just FedExed dailies from the *Take No Prisoners* set and wants you to let them know about the Oscar campaign."

Kiki finished writing and turned the monogrammed notebook toward her young, wrinkle-free servant. Boom Boom continued to chatter about appointments and calls. Kiki tapped on the pad, and then again with more force, finally requiring Boom Boom to silence her yammering and look at the paper.

A small gasp escaped Boom Boom's lips as she read Kiki's short but effective note.

"I'm just trying to be helpful. You don't have to get bitchy about it," Boom Boom said.

Kiki turned toward the window and tried not to smile, as smiling would tear the stitches clamped to the skin behind her ears. Business would have to wait until she wrapped herself in the luxurious sheets at the Peninsula. She relaxed as the limo finally turned into the private entrance to the hotel. Kiki glanced at the notepad in her lap. Two very effective words were emblazoned across the pad: *Fuck you.*

Rule 2

Never Let Them See Your Next Move

Celeste Solange, Actress

Cici's leg muscles felt like they were ripping away from the bone.

"That's great, just two more! Come on, Cici, you can do it!"

"That's what you said eight reps ago," Cici said through clenched teeth.

Celeste Solange glared at her trainer, Liam. The only exercises she enjoyed were sex and shopping, and this endorphin-producing endeavor was neither.

"Almost there," Liam said.

Easy for you to say, Cici thought. She glanced at Liam's abdominal muscles, poking through his T-shirt. She guessed his body fat to be around 1.5 percent on a bad day. Cici cringed and extended her legs one last time. If her fans could see her moaning and sweating like a sumo wrestler, they'd never again believe the I-can-eat-anything-I-want-and-never-gain-a-pound sound bite.

Cici's legs collapsed under her. Her thighs burned.

"Great job!" Liam grabbed her by the forearm and pulled her up. "Nice workout. Walk that off and then we'll stretch."

"Water."

Cici limped to the Fiji bottle, lifted it to her lips, and guzzled greedily. She glanced in the full-length workout mirror. Her profile looked good for thirty (fine, thirty-six), though right now her blond hair frizzled around her barrette and sweat dripped down her face.

Tall and lean, with the kind of thinness that curvy women fight to maintain, once Cici had passed the big three-oh she worked nonstop to keep the pounds off her five-eight frame. The camera didn't add ten pounds. Try twenty.

Great film roles were sparse each year, and everyone (Angie, Jen, Nicole, and Sandy) wanted them. After actresses hit thirty, their agents and managers slugged it out to secure great roles for the ladies. Sure, everyone said that forty was the new thirty, and often a forty-year-old appeared on the cover of *Us, People,* or *Star* . . . but how many roles did Julia actually score in the last year?

"Okay, let's stretch," Liam said, sitting on the exercise mat in front of Cici.

Between the daily six A.M. workouts (Liam was truly a sadist), visits to her nutritionist, whose mantra was "Raw, baby, everything raw; it'll turn back the clock ten years," and Dr. Charles Melnick's magic Botox needles and microderm, Cici remained stunning.

But for how long?

Cici glanced into the long exercise mirror in front of Liam. Maybe she should consider the knife. A small shudder passed through her. She didn't want to end up the spawn of Dr. Spock, with slanty eyes and Vulcan ears, as had so many women in Hollywood. How could these women fail to recognize one stitch too many? Cici leaned over her outstretched legs, her nose touching her knees. Charles Melnick did excellent work and had performed her breast-lift. But her face? Did she really want Melnick to stretch the skin on her cheeks up to her ears? No, she didn't. But time marched on, and Cici didn't want the boot marks under her eyes. She exhaled and sat up, raising her arms over her head.

At her last appointment for Botox, she finally brought up the big *F.* Charles Melnick worked on the majority of female faces that flickered across the silver screen and was used to the face-lift discussion.

"Cici, my darling, how could I possibly improve on perfection?" he'd asked.

He held her jaw with his hand and turned her face gently first to the left and then to the right. "You eat right, you exercise, and most important, you hydrate."

"Water, water, water," Cici said.

"Yes, that and sunscreen. Those two things alone could put eighty percent of the plastic surgeons in L.A. out of business. But I know the demands on a face such as yours."

Cici glanced past Melnick to her reflection in the full-length mirror behind him. *God, fluorescent is unflattering,* she thought. *Are those bags?*

"It's part of your burden as a celebrity to be an archetype, if you will; a testament to beauty. A goddess." Dr. Melnick traced a line under Cici's eyes with his index fingers. "Like porcelain."

He rolled back his chair and turned, meeting Cici's gaze in the mirror. "So, my darling, what is it? What is it that you think my feeble talents can do for you?"

Cici stared in the mirror. The press often touted her as the modern-day Marilyn Monroe. She still looked beautiful, but a gnawing sensation ate at her insides. She had lost her ex-husband, Damien Bruckner, to a seventeen-year-old. What did Cici have if not her beauty and the illusion of youth?

"I'm worried about the lines. Here and here." She traced a finger along her forehead and mouth. They were creases that Ted Robinoff, her billionaire boyfriend and the owner of Worldwide, told her were invisible to everyone but her (and of course Dr. Melnick).

"Darling, these are completely under control with the Botox and collagen or Restylane."

"What about this?" Cici asked and tapped the hint of sag under her eye. "And this?" She touched the bone under her highly arched brow. She had noticed the beginning of an extra fold of skin touching her eyelids.

"Well, there are a number of options, but the best and the longest lasting is, of course, a bit of surgery."

Cici's heart caught in her throat. The idea had been at the back of her mind, but her face was her most precious commodity.

"But, darling," Melnick continued, "you don't need it. Most women don't do it until thirty-two, and you've just turned thirty."

Only Cici knew the truth—she was thirty-six, soon to hit thirty-seven. So she was actually four years past due. No wonder younger actresses looked so good.

"No. I think it's time," Cici said. "Better too soon than too late."

"Well, that does make these procedures less noticeable. If you keep up the maintenance while you age," Dr. Melnick said. He continued appraising Cici's face in the mirror. "Working on a face such as yours is like trying to repaint the Sistine chapel. I just cannot do it any better than the original master. But if you insist, Connie can schedule you for, when? Next week?"

Cici's heart thumped. Surgery next week?

"I've got press and a photo shoot. You know, this whole month is bad. Can we wait until next month? The end of next month?" She wanted to put it off in case she changed her mind.

"Done. Connie will call to confirm. You'll be here, in the office. Same-day service; in and out."

Cici stood and reached for her bag. Nausea threatened to overwhelm her, from the thought of Melnick slicing into her face.

"You know, I have a lovely deal with the Peninsula for recovery time," Melnick said. "Back door to back door service. And I do house calls to the hotel for post-op follow-up. So easy." Dr. Melnick pulled open the exam room door. "Next month, my darling," he said and followed her into the hall.

That was almost a week ago. Now Cici stared into the workout room mirror searching for the flaws that she and Dr. Melnick had discussed.

"Okay, then. Finished," Liam said. He jumped up from the mat and grabbed his gear. "Cici, you do me proud," he said and kissed both her cheeks. "Hard work and sweat. All natural all the time. See you tomorrow."

Cici waved and glanced into the mirror. *Yeah, all natural all the time.*

* * *

Cici pulled her sky blue convertible Jag, a recent gift from Ted (selected to match the color of her eyes), into the parking lot behind the Nail Hut. No one would guess this nondescript shop on Wilshire Boulevard housed the best manicurists in Beverly Hills. Ever since *Seven Minutes Past Midnight,* Cici kept a standing once-a-week date here for a mani-pedi with Mary Anne Meyers.

Cici enjoyed her time each week with Mary Anne, who had become a close friend while Cici was filming *Seven Minutes,* almost four years before. Cici felt she could be her true self with Mary Anne. *Her true self?* Sometimes Cici feared each character she played stole a piece of her true self and in return left an indelible mark on her personality. After decades of playing pretend, Cici felt unsure about how to know who her true self was. But somehow Mary Anne grounded her, perhaps because she was the least "Hollywood" of all Cici's Hollywood friends.

Cool manufactured air hit Cici in the face as she opened the back door. She walked toward the celebrity suite, where she and Mary Anne could gossip privately; another lovely perk to the Nail Hut. Well, semi-privately: Two manicurists would be listening, but Jessica Caulfield-Fox, Cici's manager, required everyone who worked on Cici to sign a confidentiality agreement.

"Cici!" Mary Anne called from her pedicure throne, one of four in the room. "Were you followed?"

Cici pulled off her hat and sunglasses. "Not today."

She reached for a chilled Diet Coke from the crystal ice bucket sitting on the marble table next to the door, and stepped up to flop into the chair next to Mary Anne. Cici looked at her good friend. Mary Anne was more than pretty, but not necessarily the first woman you'd notice when entering a room, perhaps because at first glance she looked like someone you'd met before at the grocery store or the mall, not that Cici ever went to the mall anymore. Mary

Anne's beauty, in part, came from the fact that she had no idea that she was beautiful. Tall with fair skin, the kind that burned easily, Mary Anne had blue eyes with specks of green and freckles dotting her nose. The freckles, Cici believed, helped Mary Anne appear ageless . . . what a gift.

"Good to see you," Cici said, feeling comforted by the presence of her friend. "How was the West End? I hear Adam's play is spectacular."

"I love it. The West End, I mean."

"Incredible isn't it? But the press in London is even more intrusive than here. Really, the only place to get any peace is Paris. Or maybe Africa."

"I'm only a writer, not nearly as sexy as you. A photo of me exiting a grocery store isn't worth thousands of dollars," Mary Anne joked.

"When did you get back?"

"Yesterday."

"For how long?"

"For good."

Cici eased her feet into the warm water and glanced at Mary Anne. The response surprised her. She assumed Mary Anne would be in town just for a visit before returning to London to stay with Adam for the entire run of his play. Prior to leaving for London, Mary Anne and Adam had lived together for two years and were inseparable.

"I thought you'd stay in London with Adam."

"So did I," Mary Anne said.

Cici hesitated. She wanted Mary Anne to offer up the details without her having to ask, but Cici had never mastered patience. After a minute and a half of watching rose petals swirl around her toes, Cici finally asked. "So what happened?"

"He's . . . busy. I left London two weeks ago and went to Ireland and Scotland."

Cici hated the thought of Mary Anne traipsing around the Scottish moors alone. They were a romantic place when with a lover, but so forlorn and cold when single.

"And?"

"And"—Mary Anne paused—"we're finished."

Cici contained the shock she felt and watched Mary Anne's face wrinkle into a frown.

"I see," Cici said.

She glanced at Mary Anne, trying to read her feelings. She didn't know if Mary Anne wanted to wallow or rejoice, but Cici was willing to follow Mary Anne's cue and do either. Mary Anne gazed into the water swirling around her toes, her mouth turned down and her brows pulled tight.

"The relationship hasn't been right for a while. I mean, it's been almost seven months since . . ." She let her sentence drift off without looking up at Cici.

"Since?" What could Mary Anne and Adam postpone for seven months that had caused the apparently perfect couple to break up? Cici gasped. "Oh my God, you haven't had sex with Adam in seven months?" She saw Mary Anne cringe. "Sorry," Cici whispered. "Seven months? How did you go seven months? I can barely go seven days."

Mary Anne sighed. "We're both so cerebral, and that part of our relationship was never quite right."

Cerebral or monastic? Cici wondered.

"But it's good," Mary Anne continued. "I'll be busy. Lydia wants me to do a polish on a script she's putting into production."

"What's the script?"

"*The Sexual Being*. Sean Ellis is attached to direct; he's supposed to be good."

"Isn't Holden Humphrey starring in that after he finishes *Collusion?*" Celeste asked. She watched a blush creep across Mary Anne's face. "And the production work?" Cici asked.

"Lydia wants me to do that, too."

"I see." Cici gazed at Mary Anne, who wore her brown curly hair pulled back in a ponytail. Even after almost fifteen years in Los Angeles, Mary Anne still looked like a little girl from Middle America.

"What?" Mary Anne finally looked at Cici. "The rewrite is a lot of money, I like the project, and I couldn't say no. We go into production in about eight weeks. So, I'll be in L.A. and then Brazil for three months." She paused. "He's coming to L.A. tomorrow."

"Holden? But he's on set in Toronto, isn't he?"

"He's got a break in his schedule, so he's flying into L.A."

"To discuss *Sexual Being* with you?"

"Uh-huh."

Celeste was surprised at Mary Anne's naïveté.

"Where?" Cici asked.

"Excuse me?"

"Where? Where are you meeting Holden to discuss the script?"

Cici had worked in film for almost twenty years, and she knew you could often determine the intent of a meeting by the scheduled location. Different expectations came with a lunch meeting at The Grill than, say, drinks at L'Ermitage.

"Shutters on the Beach," Mary Anne said.

Even sweet-faced Mary Anne had to realize that when a former lover flew from Toronto to discuss script notes at a beachside hotel, certain *things* could happen. Cici gave Mary Anne a questioning look.

"What? Holden and I spent *one night* together," Mary Anne said.

"But quite a night. From what I heard."

"Holden and I are meeting because of business," Mary Anne said. "Lydia and Jessica set it up. Holden has concerns about the script and wants to talk with me before I start the rewrite."

"Makes perfect sense," Cici said. She gave a little shrug and a toss of her hair, deciding to let it go and play along with Mary Anne's charade.

"So, how's Ted?" Mary Anne asked.

"He's in Japan."

"Japan?"

"All the time, lately. Frankly, I'm a little bored by his absence. Something to do with film finance and DVD sales."

Mary Anne leaned across the chair toward Cici. "Have you told him?" she whispered.

"About?"

Mary Anne placed both her hands on her cheeks and pulled upward. Cici let a giggle escape her lips, first because of the way Mary Anne looked and, second, to ward off the pang of fear that suddenly pierced her gut.

"It's only an eye-lift."

"Sure. And what did Ted say?"

Celeste cocked one eyebrow.

"You still haven't told him?"

Cici glanced down at her toes. Some secrets were better kept than shared.

"You *are* going to tell him?" Mary Anne whispered, "Cici, there is no way you can hide this from him. You'll be lucky if you can hide it from the entire world. Celeste Solange, America's sweetheart, getting her face done? That's big news."

Cici glanced at the two women scrubbing hers and Mary Anne's feet with pumice stones.

"I'm going to tell him," Cici said.

"What are you waiting for?"

"He's distracted. Plus, I've got a photo shoot at the end of the week for *California Girl.*"

"The one sheet?"

Celeste nodded. She disliked photo shoots. Tedious affairs, they became boring long before the photographer finished.

"Who's the photographer?" Mary Anne asked.

"Some guy from London. Nathan Curtis, I think."

"I've heard of him. You know he used to be paparazzi. Got his big break when he shot one of the royals coming out of a strip club."

"Really? I don't like the sound of that."

Cici wondered why Worldwide would hire a former paparazzo to shoot one of their biggest stars. Maybe she should mention it to Ted or Lydia.

"He must have gone legit if he's working for Worldwide."

"Must have. Anyway, back to you and Holden," Cici said.

"There isn't a me and Holden."

"But there could be."

"Cici, I remember you once told me that the worst thing a girl could do was to date an actor. Do you remember that conversation?"

"Who said anything about date? I'm just saying . . . Brazil, *People*'s Sexiest Man Alive, best sex of your life, end of seven months' abstinence? Sounds like the perfect ingredients for a post-breakup affair."

Mary Anne sighed and shook her head. "I don't know."

"I'm not suggesting anything serious. I'm merely pointing out that while you're in South America, thousands of miles away from everyone, it might be a great opportunity to have a little fun."

"I wish I could be more like you and Lydia when it came to sex."

"Lydia? Not anymore. Ever since she and Zymar got together, she's so monogamous it hurts. And I haven't slept with another man since Ted and I moved in together after *Seven Minutes Past Midnight.*"

Cici leaned back and closed her eyes. *Seven Minutes* had almost ended all their careers. Lydia and Jessica had secretly screened their controversial film at CTA, a bold move that saved everyone's jobs and made Worldwide hundreds of millions of dollars.

"Where is Arnold, anyway?" Mary Anne asked, referring to Arnold Murphy, the former president of Worldwide Pictures who had tried to sabotage the movie and destroy Celeste, Lydia, Jessica, and Mary Anne.

"I think he's working for a theater in New York." Cici had neither seen nor heard from the "little leprechaun," an "affectionate" nickname Lydia had given her arch-nemesis. "Ted bought out Arnold's contract and gave him an incredible severance package."

"And Josanne?" Mary Anne asked about the leprechaun's sidekick and minion.

"She moved to New York and represents filmmakers."

"I'm surprised they're not back in the business out here."

"Oh, they'll be back. I'm sure of it. Arnold has a history of scurrying away to lick his wounds and then creeping back to L.A. Where else can he go? Please. He couldn't actually function in any business aside from entertainment." Celeste and Mary Anne both knew that quirks, eccentricities, and huge egos—liabilities anywhere else—were character traits rewarded in Hollywood.

"You're from a red state. Can you imagine Arnold trying to do business in South Dakota?"

"Minnesota."

"Whatever. My point remains the same. He can only function here. We haven't seen the last of Arnold."

"Bet he's pissed at Lydia," Mary Anne said as the manicurist uncapped Chanel's Vamp to start polishing.

"Pissed? Oh yeah," Celeste said. "Lydia'd better be ready, because when Arnold Murphy returns to Hollywood, he'll be gunning for her."

Rule 3

Never Let Them Know You're Afraid

Lydia Albright, President of Production, Worldwide Pictures

Lydia Albright disliked her job. She sat in her office atop Worldwide Pictures tower of power looking at her desk, which was piled high with scripts and the other paperwork that consumed her time. She wondered when her disdain for studio films began.

She loved making movies. She had arrived on her first film set at six months old, and then spent little time anywhere else. Until now. She had accepted Ted Robinoff's offer to become the president of production at Worldwide Pictures, and now she didn't make movies as much as put out fires, spending all the hours of her day dealing with people and problems. Since accepting the job, Lydia spent no time actually on set, making films. Her deal with Ted had allowed her to run Worldwide Pictures while maintaining her production company at Worldwide, which made her, arguably, the most powerful woman in entertainment. But Lydia didn't feel powerful.

Lydia pushed her chair back from her desk and stood to look out the window of her corner office on the thirty-sixth floor. Far below her, on the studio lot, she could just make out the bungalow that housed her production company, Albright Films. The little building with three tiny offices and an overstuffed couch felt like home—unlike this swank office. And down there, in that tiny office, she hadn't had to deal with this new problem.

Lydia caught her reflection in the glass window. Her thick chestnut hair was tousled and her brown eyes appeared weary beneath her tightly knitted brows. She glanced again at the letter in her hand—it was the third one, and she had received it this morning.

Should she tell studio security? She wanted to pretend that nothing had happened, wanted to ignore these threatening notes. She turned her back to the window and looked at the letter again. Much like the other two, it was typed on handmade ecru paper. Although the rhyme was horrid, the threat contained enough hints to force Lydia's mind to reel with the possibilities.

> *Hickory Dickory Dock, Lydia sat on top.*
> *The star turned tricks, the director's a dick,*
> *Hickory Dickory Dock.*

Lydia had received the second letter—same paper, same typing, same horrendous take on a nursery rhyme, this time Humpty Dumpty—the night before, at her home in the Hollywood Hills. She had been sitting alone on the back patio reading when the phone rang. The static sound of the front gate crackled over the line. Lydia went to the front of her house and peeked out the window to watch the Excalibur Messenger Service van pull into her drive. The driver parked and skipped up the steps to the door. The envelope was the right size to contain movie scripts, but when Lydia took it from the messenger, the package felt light.

"That it?" Lydia asked. She was expecting four scripts from the studio.

"Yes, ma'am. Please sign here."

Lydia dutifully signed and then shut the door. The typewritten label didn't have a logo and there was no return address. *Unusual,* she thought. Everyone in entertainment realized the importance of a good picture logo. Lydia walked toward the slate patio at the back of the house, where her still-warm cup of tea sat on the wicker table.

She slid her finger under the lip of the envelope and the glue gave way. She reached in and pulled out the thick, soft stationery. The note was typed, not handwritten, and the author had typed the numeral two in the top left corner of the page. *Strange,* she thought.

Then Lydia read the rhyme:

> *Lydia Albright sat in a tower*
> *Lydia Albright had all the power*
> *All Ted's attorneys and all of Ted's men*
> *Couldn't put Worldwide back together again.*

Although Lydia had read plenty of horrible writing—she'd worked both as a producer and a studio head—this rhyme not only offended her literary senses but also caused her heart to drop. This awful little take on Humpty Dumpty changed the mood of the evening . . . and, potentially, her life. She felt a sinking sensation, like watching a rock drop into a pond and descend to the darkened depths. Lydia glanced at the letter again, and the numeral two in the upper left corner finally registered in her mind. She realized with a jolt that this must, in fact, be the second letter . . . meaning that the first letter remained elsewhere, floating in the world.

Lydia stood and walked into the house. Vilma, her housekeeper, always placed Lydia's mail in the Waterford bowl on the marble counter in the kitchen. Lydia rifled through the advertisements, requests for money, and bills. Nothing. It must have come to the office.

She picked up the phone and pressed three, speed-dialing the home number of her assistant, Toddy.

"Hello," Toddy answered, her voice thick with sleep.

"You're asleep?"

"Yes, Lydia, some of us do sleep at night."

"But it's not even eleven."

"Can I help you? Fourteen hours a day isn't enough?"

"Do you remember me getting a letter?" Lydia asked. Her pulse quickened with the thought of letter number one out there somewhere.

"Could you be more specific? You get approximately three hundred and ten pieces of correspondence each week. All of which, by the way, I open, sort, and file," Toddy said.

"This one would go under *crazy,*" Lydia said. "And it might rhyme."

"Those I usually send to Briggs Montgomery."

An image shot through Lydia's mind of an uptight guy, mid-forties, with graying hair and steel gray eyes. She had spoken to Briggs, head of security, a couple of times since starting at the studio.

"Do we keep copies?"

"No." Toddy paused. "You know there was one letter I got the day before yesterday, and I didn't send it down to security. It rhymed, like a poem written in couplet form? I read the first line and put it on your desk. I thought it was some sort of joke and that when you read the note, you'd laugh and know who sent it."

"Ecru paper? Heavy ecru paper? The kind you'd get from Soolip?"

"Yeah, soft, like suede."

Lydia's chest tightened.

"I put it on your desk," Toddy said.

"Thanks, Toddy," Lydia said, relieved that the first piece of the puzzle was on her desk. She hung up the phone and reached for her keys.

A half hour later, Lydia exited the elevator onto the thirty-sixth floor of Worldwide's executive building and felt the hair on her arms rise. The nighttime lighting cast a fluorescent pall over her floor. During the day it buzzed with the movie business, but tonight cold silence greeted Lydia. The emptiness gave her the creeps. *How ridiculous,* she thought. She traveled everywhere in the world for location scouts, oftentimes alone, and here, in a secure high-rise, in the second biggest city in the United States, she felt afraid? She slid her keycard through the electronic lock to the outer suite door and then the main door to her office. Lights from the San

Fernando Valley and the Hollywood Hills twinkled through her office window.

Lydia surveyed her office. Her file folders lay askew on her desk. She lifted a stack and set them on the floor next to a pile of scripts. A dozen letters she'd yet to read sat beneath the files. Lydia tried to maintain a twenty-four-hour turnaround time on all correspondence coming into her office. The first letter on the pile was from an independent producer begging her to reconsider financing his film. The second letter, sent by an Academy Award–winning screenwriter, thanked Lydia for her excellent notes on his script. The third was an invitation to Jennifer's birthday party in Malibu—sure to be overrun with A-listers like herself. Finally—the sixth letter in the stack. Lydia lifted the handmade paper. The note was typed, a numeral one in the upper lefthand corner. Lydia's eyes flew over the words:

Secrets, secrets everywhere
When in Hollywood don't despair

Corporate heads and stars galore
Create a beautiful well-moneyed whore

The secret, much too big to keep
I think my price will make you weep.

Lydia exhaled with the memory from the night before and closed her eyes. Someone knew something. But what? She'd worked in the movie business a long time—she had secrets, as did everyone. These rhymes could be about anything, anyone. She slipped into her office chair. Her mind quickly made a list of the most damaging of the secrets she herself kept. As a long-term resident of Hollywood, she'd swept plenty of dirt under the proverbial rug. And as president of a studio, she had a multimillion-dollar stake in preventing that dirt from ever mucking up Worldwide's films.

The heavy handmade paper felt soft between her thumb and forefinger. A tiny voice in Lydia's head urged her to shred the letters and pretend she'd never seen them. Perhaps she could will the correspondence into nonexistence and bring back the world from a day before, where secrets remained secrets and no one was threatening to reveal them. She felt the fear implanted in her gut take root, its tendrils spreading through her body. She picked up the ecru paper and scanned the third letter once more, just to ensure she'd made no mistake when she read the rhyme the first time. No, this was real. She would have to take action.

"Toddy," Lydia yelled to her number one assistant who sat outside her office door, "get me Briggs Montgomery."

* * *

Lydia watched Briggs Montgomery, head of Worldwide security, read the final letter. His chin rested on his chest and his brow furrowed as his steel gray eyes traveled across the typewritten lines. Briggs kept his hair, the color of burnt charcoal, closely cropped. A white starched collar held his cobalt blue necktie. He looked up at Lydia as he finished the third letter.

"Do you know what they're about?" he asked.

Lydia had a few suspicions, but none she wanted to share with Briggs.

"Not for sure."

"But you have ideas," Briggs said.

Lydia felt Briggs studying her face. She knew that while in the military he had trained in psy-ops. She wondered if he was analyzing her now. Watching for subtle signs that would give away any lies.

"I run a studio. There are a million possibilities."

She felt Briggs's eyes release her as he glanced back down at the letters lying before him on Lydia's desk.

"Are there copies?"

Lydia shook her head.

"Two were delivered here and one to your home?"

"Yes. Well, not delivered. The first and the third came by mail. The second was messengered."

"To your home," Briggs said.

His look was intense. Lydia understood Briggs's implication. The arrival of the letter to Lydia's Hollywood Hills doorstep violated her sanctuary from the world.

"And her?" Briggs asked. He nodded his head toward Toddy sitting at her desk on the other side of the glass partition surrounding Lydia's office.

"Opened the first and the third," Lydia said.

Briggs arched his eyebrow and cocked his head to the side. "Do you trust her?"

Lydia paused. Good question. She trusted Toddy with her Social Security number, her bank accounts, and the keys to her Hollywood Hills home, her cars, her vacation home, and the beach house. But with her career? Her Hollywood career? The career Lydia had spent the last twenty years bleeding and sweating to obtain, the career that defined her life? Hollywood was a cutthroat town, loyalty a priceless commodity.

"As much as I trust anyone," Lydia said.

"That much," Briggs said. A hint of sarcasm laced his voice. He understood Hollywood. Before Briggs accepted his job at Worldwide he had worked another studio gig, and before working studio security he had coordinated personal security for five of the town's biggest stars. You didn't complete that rigorous tour of duty in the Hollywood war zone without learning when to look the other way and keep your mouth closed.

"If Toddy wanted to sink me she could have done it a hundred times before and a million other ways," Lydia said. No, Toddy wasn't the culprit.

"I need you to make a list," Briggs said.

"Of?"

"Enemies."

"That's a long list," Lydia said.

"For people with power it usually is," Briggs said. "Plus, this is Hollywood."

Lydia knew what he meant. The letter writer could be any screenwriter whose script she'd passed on, a jobless director whose reel she'd forgotten to watch, or a valet she'd forgotten to tip.

"How do we deal with this? The notes don't ask for anything? Are they threats? Are they blackmail?"

"Until we find out who's sending them, or the person finally asks for something, we have to treat these like a serious threat," Briggs said. "I want to put a security detail at your home."

"Isn't that a bit extreme?" Lydia heard the bitchy edge in her voice, but her home was the only place she didn't have to be mega-producer-president-of-production-über-successful-superwoman. At home, on the weekends, she could leave her makeup off if she wanted, not take a shower (although Zymar kidded her mercilessly), and pad around all day in sweatpants and an old T-shirt.

"Delivering the second letter to your home was a message."

Briggs's request annoyed Lydia. She made movies; she didn't carry national security codes.

"And I want access to your schedule. I need to know where you are and when. A precaution, until we determine if any of this is real."

"What next, a bodyguard?"

Briggs looked Lydia in the eye, and she realized that her flip remark was about to come true.

"Listen, Lydia, I know you like to lead a private life when you're away from the studio. I also know you've fought hard to keep that life private. I work for you and a studio head who is pretty much a recluse, or was until he started dating Celeste Solange. So I get that your privacy is valuable. But until I sort this out, we need to work under the assumption that there is a wacko out there with a vendetta against you and possibly the studio. Whoever wrote these thinks they know something. Something that could destroy you and possibly Worldwide." Briggs looked at Lydia. "I need the names of your family and close friends. Everyone close to you." Briggs paused. "Anyone a crazy person might try to harm to hurt you."

Lydia felt like somebody had hit her hard in the chest. Briggs finally verbalized the unspoken fear that was now growing upward and pushing against Lydia's diaphragm, forcing the air from her lungs.

"Zymar and Christina Darmides, Jessica Caulfield-Fox, Mary Anne Meyers, and Celeste Solange." She watched Briggs scribble the names on a pad of paper. "They're my family. All of them."

"Celeste is easy. We already have security on her."

"You do?" Briggs's comment surprised Lydia. Cici appeared larger than life in public, but she, like Lydia, protected her privacy.

Briggs paused his pen and looked up at Lydia. "Yes, why?"

Lydia again felt Briggs's eyes searching her face.

"I'm just surprised that Cici allows it," Lydia said and shrugged.

"Well, it's not up to her." Briggs resumed his note-taking. "What are you doing for the rest of the week?"

"In about an hour, I'm flying to Toronto. Zymar and Jessica are up there working on *Collusion*."

"Taking the jet?"

"Yes."

"I'll have Jay meet you at the airport. Just think of him as your driver. No one needs to know that he's security unless you want to tell them."

Briggs stood and walked toward Lydia's office door. She felt herself relax ever so slightly as she collected the three letters from the far side of her desk, her fingertips brushing against the paper. Holding the pages in her hands stunted the growth of fear within her. She looked up and saw Briggs watching her from the doorway.

"You have a safe?" Briggs asked.

Lydia nodded yes.

"Lock those up," he said, pointing at the letters.

* * *

Snow blanketed Toronto. Lydia shivered and leaned forward in the backseat of the Town Car. Her new security detail, Jay, drove.

"Jessica's directions say to turn left here," Lydia said.

They pulled into the parking lot of a nondescript brown building with a blue neon sign that read BOYS CLUB. Jay pulled to a stop at the front entrance. Lydia glanced at Jay, unsure whether to go inside alone or wait for him to park. He glanced into the rearview mirror.

"Go on in, I'll park." Lydia must have looked worried. "Don't worry," Jay said. "Like I said, you won't even notice me. I'm discreet."

Failing to notice Jay, Lydia believed, was impossible. He had an athletic body and walked as though he'd spent the majority of his life either running down a football field or studying martial arts. His smile was dazzling white, his skin a lovely shade of mahogany. Lydia watched the muscles in Jay's shoulder tense as he turned to look at her in the backseat.

"Really. Go, Lydia."

She reluctantly slipped out of the car.

Lydia pulled open the front door to the Boys Club. *What is this place?* She wondered. The scent of liquor, cigarettes, and testosterone wafted through the air—it was obviously a bar. A gorgeous six-foot-tall hostess wearing a tank top and Farrah Fawcett running shorts greeted her. Lydia checked out the statuesque blonde's figure: Her breasts sat high, her stomach carried not an ounce of fat, and her ass looked firm and round like a fully ripened peach.

"Jessica Caulfield-Fox," Lydia said.

"You must be Lydia. Zymar told me you'd be here tonight. Follow me."

Of course; Zymar, Lydia thought. Before she and Zymar began dating, Lydia's director boyfriend was a notorious collector of exotic tail. He *would* have discovered the bar with the most gorgeous woman in Toronto working the door. Lydia followed the hostess down the long dark hallway to a private room at the back.

"Ms. Caulfield-Fox is already here, and Zymar's just called. He promised only thirty more minutes."

"Thanks."

Lydia entered the VIP room. Red velvet couches sat near the entrance and a round leather booth with a dark hand-carved table sat at the far end of the room. Jessica Caulfield-Fox, Lydia's best friend and most trusted adviser, sat in that single corner booth chattering away on her cell phone. A Harvard-educated attorney, Jessica had graduated magna cum laude after editing Harvard's *Law Review*. She began her film career in the mailroom, eventually became an agent, and until starting her own company had worked at CTA, repping A-list actors. After the clandestine screening of *Seven Minutes,* Jessica founded Caulfield Management, and now, only four years later, she was managing the careers of a handful of high-end clients and employing ten other managers. She maintained a first-look deal at Worldwide and a full slate of films. Her small boutique company had quickly become an entertainment powerhouse. *Some women,* Lydia thought, *have a knack for success.*

Jessica closed her cell phone and scooted around the half-moon booth to hold out her arms. She pulled Lydia into a hug, and Lydia felt the anxiety inside her melt.

"That was Mike. He made me promise we wouldn't get too drunk—our call time tomorrow is seven A.M." Jessica turned to the blond goddess who still stood to Lydia's right. "Tilly, will you bring Lydia a Grey Goose and tonic, and I'll have another pinot."

Lydia watched Tilly retreat to the door.

"Great tits, great legs, great ass? And I thought all the pretty girls had moved to L.A.," Lydia said.

Jessica grinned. "So, tell me," she said. She picked up her wineglass and swallowed the last sip.

Sitting next to Jessica, Lydia suddenly felt that her problem was surmountable, as most problems are when you're in the presence of a trusted friend. But Lydia wondered if she should tell Jessica about the notes. Briggs had failed to give Lydia specifics on how much information to provide her friends and family. He had only told her that while he searched for the letter's author Lydia remain discreet.

"My news can wait, at least until Zymar gets here. But you tell me all the gossip from the set."

Before Jessica could respond, Lydia's BlackBerry buzzed. She glanced at Jay's number flashing across her BlackBerry screen.

"I'm sorry, Jess, I have to take this," Lydia said. She placed the BlackBerry against her ear. "What's up?"

"The tranny at the front door won't let me in," Jay said.

"Tranny?" Lydia was surprised. It certainly didn't make her very comfortable that Worldwide's security team couldn't differentiate between men and women.

"The Amazon goddess at the front door. The one with the bad dye job."

"Jay, you'd better have your eyes checked."

Lydia glanced up at the tiny five-foot-four Latina dropping off drinks to her and Jessica. A bustier and black silk corset held her tits tight. Lydia glanced down . . . *was that a codpiece?*

"Thanks, Mikey," Jessica said to the waitress.

Lydia ignored Jay's yammering in her ear and turned to Jessica. "Is that a man?" she mouthed.

Jessica nodded. "Welcome to Toronto's Boys Club," she said, raising her glass to toast Lydia.

Rule 4

Always Remember Whom You're Dealing With

Mary Anne Meyers, Screenwriter

Mary Anne Meyers sipped her third glass of cabernet and watched Holden lift the Foster's to his lips. Holden's eyes matched the Pacific. *How strange,* Mary Anne thought, *he doesn't have on sunglasses.*

The early evening sun sank toward the water. Electricity buzzed between Mary Anne and Holden Humphrey, one of the top male actors in the world. Mary Anne felt wildly aroused. Her mind flashed to the only one-night stand she had ever experienced. That torrid night, filled with the hottest sex Mary Anne ever had, had been spent with the perfect male specimen sitting by her side.

Holden's skin crinkled into tight sun-kissed folds as he smiled. "I mean, can you believe it? After our thing, she left shit in Tupperware on my bed."

"She's cuckoo," Mary Anne said.

"Right?"

"I met her before you did," Mary Anne said. "She slept with my boyfriend."

"Idiot," Holden said and shook his head.

Mary Anne felt her stomach plummet. Maybe he was right. Maybe she *was* an idiot. But how could she have known? She and Viève were neighbors and, Mary Anne also thought, friends. She'd never suspected that Viève would sleep with her completely geeky boyfriend.

Holden was looking at Mary Anne's frown. "What? No, Mary Anne, not you. The guy! The ex-boyfriend. What an idiot. I mean, come on, you or Viève? That is a no-brainer."

Mary Anne relaxed and let out a small sigh. "Has she shown up naked in your room yet?"

"No, why?"

"I heard on her last film she tried that with Bradford Madison," Mary Anne said.

The script for *Sexual Being* lay on the table next to Mary Anne's unopened laptop. Lydia and Jessica had scheduled this meeting because Holden wanted to discuss script notes about his character with Mary Anne before she began the rewrite, but the sun lay low on the horizon and neither she nor Holden had yet to mention the script.

Maybe the way Mary Anne had first met Holden made her feel bold with him. She had picked him up at a club. Actually, she had snatched him away from Viève's clutches. Out of character for Mary Anne, definitely, but the payback—stealing Viève's lover after Viève had slept with Mary Anne's—had felt surprisingly good. Mary Anne remembered Holden's forlorn look when after their rendezvous he had offered up his number to her and she'd declined. Not because of him—he completely turned her on—but because she didn't want any attachments. Not long after, though, she'd met Adam.

Until now she'd believed that her amazing night with Holden would remain a Hollywood memory. A story perhaps to share with her grandchildren—of course in an edited form.

Holden reached out his hand and placed it on the small of Mary Anne's back, where her jeans played peekaboo with her thong.

Mary Anne sat up straighter and felt a tingling between her legs. Holden slipped his hand down the back of her jeans. Holden

Humphrey was now cupping her ass at Shutters on the Beach. Mary Anne took a quick look around the patio—if she weren't tipsy, she might be concerned. Holden leaned forward, and his lips brushed her earlobe.

"You know, I did something," he said and moved closer, his breath warm on her neck.

Mary Anne tilted her head.

"Just in case . . . I wasn't assuming anything but . . . I thought maybe . . . if I had a chance? I got a room."

Mary Anne tried to play it cool, but the sexiest man alive, according to *People* magazine, rented a luxury hotel room *just in case* she would repeat their one-night affair.

"You did?"

"I haven't forgotten our night together." Mary Anne felt Holden give her ass a firm squeeze.

"That was a long time ago," Mary Anne said. But she let herself sink into the sensation of Holden rubbing her backside.

"The best sex ever," Holden whispered into Mary Anne's ear.

Mary Anne closed her eyes and relaxed into the naughty thoughts that filled her brain.

* * *

They barely made it to the suite. Holden fondled Mary Anne's breast under her shirt with one hand as he struggled to open the hotel room's door with the other. *Thank God I wore good underwear,* Mary Anne thought as she rubbed her hand over the bulge in his jeans.

"Damn door," Holden muttered. He tried to insert the key card without letting go of Mary Anne's breast.

They stumbled into the oceanfront room. Mary Anne looked around. Flower-filled vases decorated the room, and a bottle of Veuve Clicquot chilled in a bucket next to French doors that opened onto a deck overlooking the Pacific.

Holden lifted Mary Anne onto the bed, unbuttoned her shirt and unsnapped her Agent Provocateur bra. Mary Anne's breast toppled out, and Holden's mouth left hers and found her nipple. She let out a small moan and grabbed for the button at the top of his pants. She felt excited in a way she hadn't felt in a long time, which made her aggressive. She unzipped his fly and reached into his pants. *No underwear! Of course, how could she forget?* She pushed his jeans down over his hips.

She touched his cock, moving her fingers in circles, and a moan escaped his lips as he worked his way from her nipple down her stomach. He pulled off her jeans, and she arched her back as his tongue roamed over her.

"Give me your cock," she whispered.

His tongue never left her as he moved himself to straddle her face. Mary Anne hungrily took him into her mouth, and for a few minutes they moaned into each other.

She arched her hips with pleasure and knew she was going to come. Pulling him from her mouth, she reached up and grabbed the back of his head. "Fuck me," she hissed.

Holden flipped her onto all fours. He reached his fingers around her to massage the wet, now engorged spot between her legs.

"You like that, baby?" he panted. Then he inserted himself from behind and started to move.

"Harder. I'm going to come," she moaned.

Holden pushed into her. She felt him stiffen and let out a loud grunt just as she felt the pleasure shoot through her in waves. Her toes curled, and a small squeak escaped her lips. He gave one last thrust, pulled out, and collapsed beside her.

"That was so good. Just like last time," he said.

Mary Anne blushed. Something about sex with Holden allowed her to be dirty. When she slept with him, she felt a wildness that she'd never experienced in bed before. She suddenly felt embarrassed by her aggression.

"You're blushing," he said and smiled his million-dollar smile. She turned her head and buried half her face into the plush pillow. "Could you be more adorable?" he asked and wrapped his arms around her, pulling her close and giving her a peck on the nose.

"I could try," Mary Anne whispered.

Rule 5

Be Unpredictable

Jessica Caulfield-Fox, Manager-Producer

Film sets, Jessica discovered in her transition from agent to manager-producer, were boring 99 percent of the time. Accomplishing anything on a film set was an exercise in tedium that always took a minimum of forty minutes. Changing a light took forty minutes, setting a take took forty minutes, adding an actor took forty minutes . . . nothing, except the expenditure of money, moved quickly on a movie set. Jessica stood behind the monitor on the set of *Collusion* (her biggest production to date) and watched Zymar talk to his DP about a shot, a minor task that was now twenty minutes into the requisite forty minutes.

Jessica tried to be patient. She developed many skills while she worked as an agent and ran CTA, but she had failed to learn patience. She finally mastered the skill when she became a mommy to Max Fox and a wife to Mike.

Jessica glanced at Holden Humphrey. Returned from his script meeting with Mary Anne Meyers in Los Angeles, he now stood in front of the camera waiting and stomping his feet, trying to endure the cold. Holden was the picture of professionalism, a producer's dream. He arrived to set each day on time and with his lines memorized. If only Holden's costar and former lover, Viève Dyson, could be so pleasant. But no, Viève became the one wild child tormenting the cast and crew from preproduction until now. Ten days remained in their shooting schedule, and then the cast and crew could return to Los Angeles. *Ten days,* Jessica thought. *Only ten more days.* Jessica had survived law school, pushed a mail cart, run an agency, started a company, and produced films . . . but Viève Dyson exceeded any of the Hollywood eccentricities that Jessica had previously witnessed.

* * *

Just before *Collusion* went into production, they lost their female lead; the young actress took a role in a Scorsese film—and who could blame her, really? It was *Scorsese.* With production scheduled to begin in twelve days, they had scrambled to find a new female lead.

Jessica watched Viève's entire casting session unable to place her. *I know that I know this girl,* Jessica thought, sitting on the couch next to *Collusion*'s casting director, Skylar Harris. With brilliant green eyes, red hair, and translucent skin, Viève appeared innocent and fragile on camera, but gave powerful performances. The tiny creature created a character for the role in *Collusion* that exuded innocence and strength, with a hint of dirty-girl spiciness.

As Viève finished delivering her lines, Jessica finally remembered how and when she'd first met her. Holden Humphrey. This little nymphet had dated Holden years before, when Jessica still presided as president of CTA. The three of them—Jessica, Holden, and Viève—had eaten lunch together at the Ivy. Well, Viève hadn't *eaten;* she drank water while Jessica and Holden ate. Jessica supposed any actress had to forgo some meals, and live on laxatives, to remain a size zero.

"Excellent, just excellent," Skylar said, that day at the casting session, shooting Jessica a look that seemed to say *is there really any question here?*

"Thank you," Viève whispered.

"Viève, I think we've met," Jessica said.

"Yes," Viève said. Her green eyes appraised Jessica's face. "At the Ivy with Holden."

"You have a great memory."

"I never forget a face," Viève said.

Jessica felt a shiver run down her spine. As fragile as Viève appeared, Jessica felt as though the actress's comment was somehow a warning. Viève's eyes, now that she finished her scene, appeared eerily vacant. Almost as though the character she created filled her completely and now, with no lines to read, the girl appeared empty.

"There's one more meeting, a chemistry read. Have you done one before?" Skylar asked.

A chemistry read was part of the audition process that most male stars and producers looked forward to. It determined if sexual energy existed between the male and female lead, and watching one was much like watching badly lit soft-core porn.

"Yes," Viève whispered. She looked toward the ceiling. "I have. They feel so dirty."

Jessica and Skylar exchanged a glance. Suddenly Viève seemed so vulnerable.

"I know, chemistry reads seem like such a setup," Jessica said. The chemistry read felt unnecessary in this case, especially since Viève and Holden had dated years before. But there could be baggage that might interfere with the sexual nature of their on-screen relationship.

"Holden's coming in at two. Will that work for you?" Skylar asked.

"No," Viève said. "Two won't work."

"Okay . . ." Skylar said. Viève's response surprised both Skylar and Jessica. "What about three-thirty?"

Viève paused, looking toward the door.

"Yes, three-thirty will work," she said in a hushed tone.

"Great," Jessica said, "we'll see you then."

***

The chemistry between Holden and Viève smoldered. Their sexual tension bated your breath with anticipation—exactly the kind of anticipation that, in a sexually charged thriller, kept the audience interested and aroused. Holden and Viève had a hot history, or so it seemed by the sparks flying in the room. Jessica felt anger emanating off Viève as she read opposite Holden. Jessica remembered the story: Holden had blown off Viève for a one-night stand with Mary Anne Meyers (of course, that was after Viève had slept with Mary Anne's live-in boyfriend). But Mary Anne wouldn't be working on *Collusion,* and if Viève and Holden could maintain their civility and their sexually charged chemistry, then *Collusion* would be one hot thriller.

After the chemistry read, Jessica had made two phone calls. First she called Lydia, both because she was her friend and because she was the president of production at Worldwide, the studio financing *Collusion.*

"It's fine, cast her. But are you sure you want this mess on your set?" Lydia had asked.

"Holden says he can work with Viève."

"And what about Viève?" Lydia asked.

"She tells me she's over Holden."

"Uh-huh. I hear she's crazy. You ever deal with crazy?"

"Lydia, this is L.A. Who hasn't?"

"It's your film. I just write the checks," Lydia had said before hanging up the phone.

Worldwide business affairs had then closed and papered the deal, and Jessica had flown to Toronto for filming with cast and crew. Her excitement about casting Viève as the female lead in *Collusion* quickly turned to regret. Once Viève landed in Canada, she turned on Jessica like a wounded wild animal you fed for months and nursed back to health only to have it bite off your finger. First, Viève demanded that the studio fly in her pets. *All* her pets. The menagerie consisted of three dogs (all weighing less than two pounds), her Persian cat, and a pet bunny. As soon as the pets arrived, the hotel informed Jessica that they were happy to house *Collusion*'s crew, director, and production staff, but not Viève's zoo. Jessica needed to find another home for the elf and her animals.

Jessica rented a three-bedroom house within walking distance of the hotel for herself, Max, and Max's nanny to live in during production. This house, Jessica soon realized, was the only place for Viève to live. But once outside the confines of a hotel that included housekeeping, a concierge, and room service, Viève demanded an entire staff . . . which had all been very slyly prenegotiated by Viève's agent, should Viève be moved from her hotel.

"Jessica. See section three, paragraph four, line C," Tyler Bruger, Jessica's former colleague at CTA, barked over the phone when Jessica originally said no to Viève's list of demands. A subservient twit with a very bad coke habit and a penchant for malnourished redheads, Tyler, Jessica soon realized, enjoyed screaming his demands. A biting anger lodged in Jessica's chest as she grudgingly hired staff for Viève and took Tyler's calls. *All* of Tyler's calls. Tyler complained on behalf of Viève about the staff, the sheets, the special rabbit food that the studio flew from Los Angeles every third day.

Jessica surrendered the three-bedroom house to Viève and her pets. Meanwhile, for herself, Max, and Max's nanny Jessica found a tiny two-bedroom condo farther from the set *and* the hotel—meaning she was farther from her son. Jessica hoped that Viève would be happy. But for Viève, happiness was not in the cards, or at least that's what Viève's tarot adviser had told her.

* * *

Jessica glanced at Zymar. His conversation with his DP had finally finished. According to Jessica's slim Rolex, the PA had called Viève to set twenty-seven minutes ago. Jessica knew Viève's driver had dutifully delivered the tiny creature to set on time, as he did every day, after the multiple stops for prescriptions, chai tea, and hair care products. But as always, Viève, like a tiny mouse, had scurried to her trailer and slammed the door. Each day, Viève barricaded herself inside her trailer with her pets and her personal makeup artist and hairstylist, both flown in from L.A., as no local hires could satisfy her. "See section two, paragraph two, line D in her contract," Tyler had bellowed over the phone. Viève was never seen until she'd been called to set a minimum of four times, was thirty-five minutes late, and Zymar, the ever-patient, ever-comedic Zymar, was spouting epithets and hurling chairs.

"So, Jess," Zymar said as he walked up beside her and glanced at his watch, "I see we've got at least twelve more minutes before the little twat opens her trailer door."

Jessica nodded as her PA, Matt, walked toward them.

"I've tried three times," Matt said. "I think it's your turn."

"Even 'e's ready," Zymar said and pointed over his shoulder at Holden, now hopping on one foot to keep warm in the Toronto snow. "And I'm ready. Why isn't she ready?"

"I think I heard tears," Matt said.

"Oh, for fuck's sake. Not this again." Zymar stomped toward the monitor.

Although Jessica felt a stab of anger in her chest, she sighed and put on her oh-isn't-this-lovely face, the face she'd learned watching her friend Lydia Albright produce films before Lydia became president of production at Worldwide. Jessica handed her coffee to Matt and walked toward Viève's trailer door.

She heard the wailing before she got to the Star Wagon's stairs.

"Viève," Jessica called. She tapped on the door. "May I come in?"

Jessica heard Viève's crying turn to sniffles. "Yes," she said.

Jessica took a deep breath and forced down the irritation that bubbled in her throat. She pulled open the door and there, per their daily routine, sat Viève cross-legged on the couch with her three teeny tiny dogs perched on her lap, her bunny beside her, and her Persian cat pressed against her neck as though it were fur trim for her shirt.

"Sweetie," Jessica said, approaching slowly as one might approach a wounded wildebeest. "We're ready for you on set." She bent forward and put her hands on her knees so she could be eye level with the star.

"I can't," Viève hiccupped through the beginning of more tears.

Geez, this one is worse than yesterday, Jessica thought. She glanced at the prescription bottles and homeopathic remedies strewn across the trailer floor. "Oh, sweetie, yes you can. You're beautiful and you're brilliant and the camera loves you. We all love you," Jessica said. She inched forward slowly, so as not to frighten the beast.

"You don't understand." Viève clutched the white Persian so tightly to her neck Jessica saw the cat's eyes bulge.

"No, darling, we don't. It's a lot of pressure, but you're doing an amazing job."

"He hates me."

"Who hates you? No one hates you," Jessica said. She stepped closer. She could think of no one who admitted to hating Viève, although she guessed most of the crew harbored a desire to string the little harpy up by her toes.

"Yes he does!" She jumped up and all three dogs scrambled from her lap.

"Darling, no one—"

"What the fuck do you know?" Viève hurled the Persian to the floor. "He's awful to me! He hates me!"

Jessica stood up straight and put on her parental I've-had-enough face. She felt anger rise in her throat. "Viève, who hates you? I can't help you unless you tell me who hates you."

"Holden. Holden Humphrey hates me."

Jessica put her hands on her hips. Holden might dislike Viève—because, at this point, who didn't?—but on set he appeared completely respectful toward her. "Viève, Holden doesn't hate you. He respects you. He talks about how talented you are."

"Respect?" Viève spat like a snake spitting venom. "Respect? I don't care about respect."

Obviously, Jessica thought. With this tiny gnome, none of the rules of logic applied. "Then what is it? What did Holden do?" Jessica asked.

"Fuck me," Viève sobbed. "He won't fuck me."

* * *

'E won't fuck 'er? Oops," Zymar said, pointing to Jessica's son, Max, who giggled.

Jessica sat next to Zymar at the dining room table, across from her husband, Mike.

"He won't remember," Mike said, glancing from Max to Jessica. "Well, he might repeat it, but he won't remember."

Jessica looked first at Max and then at Mike. The feeling of calm she always felt when sitting with her two men was absent. She had failed to regain her sense of equilibrium after her encounter today in Viève's trailer. Usually Jessica shrugged off Viève's tantrums as behavior from an overindulged child. But today Viève's lack of self-respect and her insistence that her costar bed her had forced Jessica to ask herself the question: Why? Why, after she had received a law degree from Harvard did she choose to babysit petulant prima donnas? Jessica had hoped that Mike's arrival from Los Angeles two hours before, just as *Collusion* wrapped for the day, would cure her discontent, but so far she was still upset. She picked at her Chinese food, feeling anxious and irritable.

" 'Ow you like being a producer there, Jess?" Zymar asked. "Those actresses are nutty. There are reasons I never dated one."

"Wasn't Christina's mother an actress?" Jessica asked, referring to Zymar's full-grown daughter, who now worked as a VP at Lydia's production company.

"We never really *dated,*" Zymar said between bites of his kung pao scallops. "We fucked like rabbits, she got pregnant, and we got married."

"You romantic," Jessica said and picked at her sea bass. Finally she gave up and tossed her chopsticks onto the table. "She's *nuts.*"

Both Mike and Zymar paused and looked at Jessica.

"Well, she is. I can't fix this," she said. She looked first at Mike and then at Zymar. "What? I'm going to tell Holden he has to screw his costar? I know *that* isn't in Viève's contract, no matter what Tyler says."

"'Tis the lot of the producer to be dependent on the crazy creative types," Zymar said.

"Jess, it could be worse," Mike said. "Viève could overdose, or the director could run off to a Balinese brothel."

"Let's not go telling tales there, Mr. Fox. I do think I ran into you and your crew in Bali a couple years back," Zymar said.

Mike cleared his throat and looked at Jess. "So how are the dailies?"

"That's the thing. They're great. Her performances are pitch-perfect and the sexual tension between the two of them is . . . well . . . it's firecracker hot," Jessica said.

"There's your answer," Mike said.

Jessica gave Mike a confused look.

"Have Holden tell her he can't sleep with her until the end of the production," Mike said.

"What? You're kidding?"

"They have history together. He can tell her he wants to keep the tension tight, the performance hot, and not ruin it by diluting the buildup. Have Holden tell Viève he wants her, but she's got to wait until the end of the shoot."

" 'E's a smart one, your man," Zymar said to Jessica.

"I can't force Holden to do that." Jessica looked past Mike out the window, into the cold Toronto night. The fate of a $60-million film rested on an actress who maintained a tenuous grip on her sanity. But the ultimate responsibility for *Collusion* lay with Jessica. Her job as producer required her to bring the film in on time and on budget. If that meant asking her client and one of the biggest stars on the planet, Holden Humphrey, to have a false conversation with his costar to ensure the completion of *Collusion* . . . well, then Jessica had to make the request.

"It'll work, Jess," Mike said. "She's crazy enough to buy it."

"I don't doubt she'll buy it. But having the conversation with Holden? Making this request seems so intrusive," Jessica said.

"Don't worry, Jess. You'll be able to figure it out. You always do." Mike picked up a fortune cookie and cracked it open. He handed the piece of paper to Jessica.

Jessica read the fortune. *Lady Luck must be Mike Fox's lover,* she thought.

"What's it say?" Mike asked.

Jessica glanced at Mike. "Words of wisdom come your way."

* * *

"You want me to tell her *what*?" Holden asked, a look of disbelief on his face.

Jessica watched Holden's reflection in the mirror. She had created this star. She had found Holden in obscurity, when she was a junior agent at CTA, and molded his career. Aside from his very brief stint with another agent, Jessica had repped Holden for his entire career. Now she still managed him and also produced a majority of his films.

"Holden, please. You don't have to mean it. Just say it. Tell Viève that you want her, and you're attracted to her, but you can't sleep with her."

"Jessica, she's *crazy*. If I tell her that, I'll never be able to get rid of her."

Jessica sighed. She knew he was right. After their last breakup, Holden threatened a restraining order before Viève finally left him alone. But this conversation between Viève and Holden needed to happen.

"Okay, I know. But, Holden, please. We are so close to finishing. We have nine days. Nine! But she's losing it. Completely. Yesterday she had a nervous breakdown because you haven't hit on her."

"She's nuts."

"Look, I know, but—"

"What about Mary Anne?"

Jessica looked at Holden. *Why would he mention Mary Anne Meyers?* "Mary Anne? How does Mary Anne fit in? Your thing with Mary Anne was forever ago."

Holden looked at his lap. "Yeah, but she's doing the rewrite for *Sexual Being.*"

"Mary Anne's a complete pro," Jessica said. "Besides, she'll never know . . . And why would she care? She's practically married to Adam."

"Adam? Who's Adam?" Holden asked.

"Her live-in boyfriend for the last two years. They met right after *Seven Minutes*. He's in London doing a play."

Jessica watched a frown flicker across Holden's face but ignored it. "Please, Holden. Do this for the film. Do it for me. I promise I'll get Viève away from you once we're in post."

Holden looked up and met Jessica's gaze.

"Okay," Holden said. "But, Jessica, you owe me one."

* * *

Holden shivered in the cold Canadian air as he tromped through the snow. He didn't understand women. He never had. He tried, he really did. He read books about women . . . okay he started books. Rarely did he finish one. But he went to therapy, he tried to listen and understand, he even read about women on the Internet. But a firm grasp of what women wanted escaped his reach.

Most men would wonder why Holden even cared. Women wanted him. They threw themselves at him. But he'd become tired of the random sex. His mother had told him that he needed someone to love, and he guessed that she was right. His parents in Indiana had been married for forty years. Every time they spoke, his mother asked him about nice girls. What could he tell her? He lived in L.A.; there were no nice girls. But Mary Anne really was a nice girl. Or so he had thought, until he heard about Adam.

But Viève? This one? This actress? Certifiable. Holden knocked on her trailer door reluctantly. He'd tested the goods, and although the package looked sweet, the inside was rotten to the core.

"Come in," Viève called.

Holden pushed open the trailer door. Darkness greeted him. He looked toward the back of the trailer, where a single candle flickered. He could barely make her out, but there she was, waiting, curled up amid silk pillows and wearing only a thong.

"Jessica said you were stopping by." Holden watched Viève roll onto all fours and crawl toward him. "Come on, come over and sit with me," she said.

Holden moved back as if stepping away from a reptile. "There's something I need to talk to you about."

Viève stood and took a step toward him.

He watched her naked form slink closer. *Yes, Viève was quite a package.* He felt himself grow hard in spite of his dislike for her. *She has a perfect ass,* he thought. *Oh, the things I used to do to that ass.* His dick grew harder.

"Holden." Viève stood and leaned into him, pressing her breasts against his chest. She ran her hand up and down his jeans. "Don't you miss me? Don't you miss us?" She pushed him backward onto the built-in couch and straddled him, unbuttoning the top of his jeans.

Holden closed his eyes and swam in the feeling of this tiny creature rubbing herself against him. "Yeah," he said. *Her pussy was so tight,* he remembered. *But her tits were little, not like Mary Anne's. Mary Anne!* He opened his eyes and grabbed both Viève's hands just as she started to pull down his zipper. "Viève, I can't."

Viève's eyes narrowed and she pulled her hands from his grasp. "Why the fuck not?"

"Look, baby." Holden put a hand on each of her hips to still the motion of her pelvis rotating on his. "I want to." He reached up and held Viève's chin. "I've been thinking, and I want us back."

"You do?" Viève asked.

"Yeah, but right now, I'm afraid it'll ruin the film."

"What?"

"Babe, we're so hot on-screen because of all the tension. Can't you feel it?" He leaned forward and let his lips brush against her neck. "I mean, you remember what it's like, don't you?" He could feel her pushing into him, surrendering to him. Holden took two fingers and began to massage between Viève's legs. "With us."

"Uh-huh," Viève breathed out.

"It's so hot," Holden whispered. Viève's breath became shallow as he continued to gently push against her with his fingers. He watched her head tilt back and felt her hips rock against him. "Baby, I want it hot. You feel it, hot like this."

Holden felt how wet she was. She slid between his fingers as he sat there watching her arch her back.

"Fuck, yes, please, please, please," she moaned. Holden pulled his hand away just as Viève's body stiffened. "Please, no, baby, don't stop, you can't stop." Viève rolled onto the couch.

He looked at her on her back with her legs spread open to him. He had no desire for her. But he was an actor.

"Baby, I can't. It's not time yet."

"Then watch me, please, will you watch me?" Viève begged, placing her fingers on her clit. "Like you used to, baby, just like you used to?"

Holden exhaled and looked into Viève's eyes. "Yeah, baby, I'll watch."

Rule 6

Always Say Less Than Is Necessary

Kiki Dee, Publicist

Kiki Dee slipped off her Prada flats and eased herself onto her king-size bed. Pain gripped her middle, and a dull throb pulsated at the top of her head. Today was her first day home after her extended post-op recoup visit to the Peninsula Hotel. Tomorrow she'd return to her office. She slowly leaned back into the pillow on her bed. The pain in her abdomen ached worse than three thousand crunches. She glanced in the mirror on the ceiling above her bed and saw that the bruising around her eyes and nose that had turned from a deep purple to apple green two days before now contained hints of yellow. Beauty was painful.

Kiki glanced at the KDP mobile command center Boom Boom had set up in the bedroom. Three fax machines and a laser printer buzzed. Boom Boom worked at a laptop with a BlackBerry and two cell phones beside her, and Kiki's landline had been rerouted to serve as their six-line office phone. Today, Kiki had finally returned all her calls, and her phone sheet, the lifeline to all business in

Hollywood, was caught up. She leaned farther back against the pillow and picked up her copy of *Daily Variety,* the industry's trade paper.

BROCKMAN BUSTS BOX OFFICE, the headline read. Kiki smiled as she scanned the article. The bonzo box office numbers were a true testament to Kiki's skills as a publicist.

Kiki continually managed to keep under wraps something that was an open secret in Hollywood but completely unknown to the rest of the world: that Steven's marriage to an amazingly beautiful young starlet was in fact fake, and Steven really lived with his true mate for life, Billy, a former male model and London club owner. A well-planned obstetrical visit and the careful use of a turkey baster had resulted in the birth of Steven's daughter, Sylvan. If the red states knew of Steven's nonhetero tendencies, his career would be severely stunted and the studios would lose a huge amount of ticket sales. Everyone had a vested interest in keeping Steven's sexuality quiet. Double retainer for Kiki! Both the studio and the star paid her a fee.

But not even Steven's secret was as big as the one she had witnessed prior to being sucked, poked, and tightened. Despite Kiki's drug-induced fog—she didn't care what anyone said, morphine and anesthesia were the best—she knew that what she saw at her plastic surgeon's office had been real.

* * *

Kiki had first glimpsed the starlet as the publicist exited the celebrity elevator in Dr. Melnick's office. (After all, she couldn't very well go through the lobby with the unwashed masses.) Kiki saw the figure disappear into exam room three, across the hall from Kiki's assigned room, and wondered why the mini-goddess needed to visit a plastic surgeon. Kiki watched Melnick's nurse knock on the door that had just closed across the hall.

"The doctor is running about ten minutes late," the nurse called into the room.

"Okay," a voice answered.

The nurse placed the chart in the chart holder beside the door and waddled back toward the front of the office.

There was no mistaking that face. And anyway, Dr. Melnick reserved this portion of his office space—the exam rooms and one surgical suite—exclusively for A-listers and the publicists, managers, agents, and attorneys who could refer the A-listers. There were only two entrances: the elevator from which Kiki had emerged and the door through which Dr. Melnick's nurse had exited. Kiki glanced at door number three.

The chart.

Kiki wanted that chart. She salivated at the thought of the potentially glorious gossip residing on those medical pages. Perhaps the file held nothing, or perhaps it contained just enough to snag a hot client for her roster. Kiki smiled with delight. She loved knowing more about a person than that person thought she could possibly know—it gave her feelings of power and control. Smiling at a bitchy A-list actress pitching a fit over the type of water she wanted on set became much easier when you knew she had spent the last six weeks sticking a toothbrush down her throat to lose the twenty pounds she'd gained for her last role. Grinning admiringly at a cocky actor who turned up his nose at your praise was easy when you knew he'd shelled out six figures to an underage girl in a trailer park in Missouri to keep her mouth shut about an unpleasant sexual episode on his last film.

And the bigger the stars, the more powerful the information. And across the hall, only four feet away, was a secret, a tidbit, a morsel of gossip about a member of the popular crowd. Kiki needed that chart.

How could she get it? Did she dare? Of course she dared. But how could she take it and not get caught? She had been inching out of her assigned exam room toward the chart when she heard the click of the door opening down the hall.

***

Kiki finished putting on her backless robe as the nurse opened her door. Her mind buzzed with the idea of the potent info across the hall. *Almost!* She'd almost grasped the magical file. Her fingertips had grazed the edge. She longed to know what brought that particular star to the plastic surgeon's office.

"Kiki, are we ready for today?" the nurse asked.

Kiki glanced at the matronly woman and wondered if she received an employee discount and if so, why her hips looked as if she was wearing a life preserver under her pants. *Pasadena,* Kiki sniffed. No self-respecting Beverly Hills resident allowed her hips to be so, well, *round.*

"Quite ready," Kiki said.

"Good. I'll get you started," she said.

The nurse stretched out Kiki's arm and searched for a vein. The needle pinched her skin. "You should start to feel that in just a second," the nurse said.

Glorious pleasure filled Kiki. If she could live on these drugs, life would be grand. A knock sounded on the exam room door.

"Nurse?" A voice called. *The* voice, coming through the door.

"Just a minute," the nurse said. "Kiki, I'll be right back."

Kiki's brain swam in pre-op drugs, but she caught a glimpse of the celeb before the nurse pulled the door shut. If there had been any doubt in Kiki's mind about which celeb was waiting across the hall, she was sure now.

Kiki turned her head toward the sink and cabinets. She felt woozy, and her eyelids drooped. Cotton balls, Q-tips, soap, biohazard containers, files. *Files?* Next to the nurse's stethoscope on the steel medical tray were *files.* Kiki opened her eyes wide and sat up. She felt light-headed. One file lay on top of the other. The label on the top file read Dee and the other was . . . *no*! Could it be? Kiki slid off the examining room table. Yes, lying there, exposed for Kiki Dee to see was the one thing she wanted more than anything at that moment. Kiki lifted the medical file folder, flipped it open, and started to read.

* * *

When Kiki first woke from the anesthetic, she believed the celebrity revelation to be a brilliant dream. No secret this big could ever exist in the gossipy berg of Hollywood. But even with her mind muddled with drugs and her body wrapped in pain, Kiki finally retrieved the memory when her driver pulled up to the Peninsula Hotel. She remembered every word in that file. And through the pain of recuperation at the hotel, she savored this, the juiciest of all secrets. Savored, and strategized how best to inform the celebrity and all others whom the scandal affected that she, Kiki Dee, had stumbled upon this deep, dark secret.

And now Kiki Dee had a plan. A plan that, if well executed, would lead to countless dollars and tremendous power.

"Boom Boom," Kiki called from her bed, "get me Sherman Ross on the line."

"Ewww," Boom Boom said. She curled up her nose as if she were smelling eight-day-old pastrami at Cantor's. "What for?"

"Business."

"There's nothing that dirty we're dealing with now," Boom Boom said.

Kiki looked over the top of her signature Louis Vuitton glasses and peered at Boom Boom. "Get him and then get out."

Boom Boom clicked her tongue in the most disapproving of ways as she dialed. "If you lay down with dogs . . ." she muttered.

If you lay down with dogs, Kiki thought, *you better make sure that the bitch doesn't bite.*

* * *

Sherman Ross watched the blonde slide down the pole in front of him. Her tits were huge—fake, but huge. He watched her squat and open her legs before him—a cavernous maw waited to be fed; dollars or dicks, whichever the setting allowed. Sherman Ross was either a celebrity's worst nightmare or best friend, depending on who paid Sherman's fee.

He inserted a twenty under the blonde's G-string. She mouthed the words *thank you* and moved across the stage. In Sherman's opinion, the day was too young to feed strippers money, but this client always wanted to meet at the Spearmint Rhino. And why not? Sherman met clients in worse places. At least this strip club was high-end, unlike the dives in the Valley that seemed to house only strippers over forty. The women working Valley clubs wore the vacant stare of dreams lost. If you asked, most told the same story: They'd moved to Los Angeles to be film stars and had turned to porn to pay the bills. Sherman glanced once more at the girl now working the pole. At least at the downtown Rhino the tits were perky.

The locations his clients set for meetings never surprised Sherman. Clients had flown him to Europe, Asia, the Caribbean. With Sherman's clientele, money meant nothing. He worked for all the stars; Jack, Tom, Denise, Heather, Ryan, Robert, whether they'd admit to his employment or not.

And the information his clients offered him surprised Sherman. He often found himself holding up his hands to halt the flow of words from their mouths. He didn't want to be an accessory. He only wanted to provide his clients with the information they required, and then deposit his payment. Once Sherman passed along the evidence he'd gathered . . . well, what the clients chose to do with the material was their business. Sherman believed his success was testament to a simple mantra he had learned while in the military, in a slightly different context: Don't ask, don't tell. Well, the mantra plus Sherman's excellent nose for scandal; he could find any mistress, piece of ass, or Swiss bank account.

Sherman glanced around the club. The client had scheduled this meeting for 11:30 and according to Sherman's watch the time was almost 11:45. He had a lunch meeting at one in Beverly Hills. If his client didn't arrive soon, Sherman would leave and shred the photos. He leaned back in his chair and sipped his freshly squeezed orange juice. He'd worked with this client before, covering up a same-sex scandal for a high-end star. Although they never discussed it, Sherman knew the client ran security for Worldwide. He'd requested pictures of a young actress currently starring in one of Worldwide's films in a less-than-professional position with her agent. *Why?* Sherman never asked.

"Mr. Ross." A tall man with gray hair sat down across from him.

"You're late, Mr. Montgomery," Sherman said.

"My apologies. You have the file, I see."

Sherman held the file out and watched as his client glanced at the photos.

"These are excellent. And the memory card? I assume these are digital."

"I have that, too. I'm happy to provide it upon receipt of payment."

"Fair enough." The man reached into his suit jacket pocket and produced an unsealed envelope. "Exactly as you requested."

The envelope contained the correct amount in the correct denominations. "Thank you," he said, pocketing the cash and placing the memory card on the table.

"You're really quite good at this."

"Yes," Sherman replied as he stood. "Yes, I am."

"This is part of a larger problem that we're dealing with."

"You have my numbers."

Sherman turned to leave, but first he gave the stripper a final glance. She now hung upside down, and he watched as she worked the pole between her legs. Her thigh muscles twitched from the workout. She had a great ass, and Sherman loved a great ass. His mind flashed briefly to a celebrity porn tape he'd recently watched at a party. The footage was so hot it hadn't even hit the Net—as far as he knew, there was only the one tape, which was now being played by its owner exclusively at parties attended by the $20 million and above club. If the footage ever hit the street, that actress's career was toast.

The sunlight bit into Sherman's eyes as he exited the club. He handed the valet his ticket and pulled down his Armani shades. The valet pulled Sherman's Porsche 911 to a stop. As Sherman slid behind the wheel, his phone rang. He popped in his Bluetooth headset and pressed on the car's accelerator.

"Sherman here."

"Mr. Ross, I have Kiki Dee for you."

What a coincidence. The last time Sherman had worked with Worldwide, he'd also been working with Kiki. The Brockman affair had concerned both Steven Brockman's publicist, Kiki, and the studio releasing his film, Worldwide. Just as Steven finished his last film for Worldwide, a sexy young stud had started making very loud claims around town and on the Internet about his alleged relationship with Steven on set. Some photos of the young stud in compromising positions with a boy who turned out to be just underage, plus a couple million dollars, finally convinced the little player to shut up. And Steven, his wife, Kathy, their daughter, Sylvan, and Steven's lover, Billy, went about their Hollywood charade.

"Put her on." Sherman pulled into traffic and accelerated.

"Sherman, my love!" Kiki said.

"Kiki, my most favorite flack. What can I possibly do for you?"

Sherman loved working with Kiki. There was something wonderfully salacious about digging into the muck of celebrities.

"I can't really say over the phone, but it is a juicy little lead that I need you to check out for me."

"How juicy?" Sherman accelerated onto the 10.

"Juicy enough that you should cancel whatever you have after lunch and come by the house."

"It just so happens that I'll be in your neighborhood. What about three?"

"Delightful. I'll see you then."

Rule 7
Play to People's Fantasies
Celeste Solange, Actress

Celeste Solange tilted her pelvis forward and arched her back. She stretched her long lean leg farther into the Pacific and pointed her toe. She threw her head back, and her signature golden locks, highlighted two days before, sparkled in the Malibu sun. She smiled at the camera.

Meanwhile, the Chanel bikini bit into her ass and her left arm ached from the pressure of lying on her side. She couldn't feel her feet or her legs from the frigid surf, and there were sand grains between her thighs getting dangerously close to her Brazilian. She'd rolled around in the surf for almost three hours now, and she was ready to stop for the day. Besides, they were losing their light. Cici had smiled at cameras professionally for almost twenty years; at this point she knew lighting. But this photographer, some boy genius from London, would not quit.

Worldwide wanted a Brigitte Bardot/Sophia Loren look for the photos that would go on the one sheet, a marketing tool the studio would use to advertise Cici's latest film, *California Girl.* Cici had one of the few bodies left in Hollywood that could pull off the sexpot look. In a sea of anorexic waifs who looked like preadolescent boys, Celeste Solange was a full-fledged female. Her body had curves that needed guard rails.

She glanced down the beach at Ted Robinoff, her lover and owner of Worldwide. Ted walked along the beach as he talked into his phone. She wanted him to tell Nathan, the photographer, to finish. Cici watched Ted furrow his brow and make wide circular motions with his arms as he yammered away into his phone. *Why is he so riled?* she wondered. Ted usually maintained a cool exterior. He had made his hundreds of millions in real estate, and then bought into the film business. He'd purchased the last privately held studio in Hollywood, Worldwide Pictures, and, contrary to speculation, planned to keep the studio private indefinitely. Ted's purchase of Worldwide made him the last movie mogul in L.A. Cici watched him pace the beach and speak into his headset.

"Go on then, luv, get a bit more sexy with it," the UK prodigy, Nathan, called to Cici.

Cici snapped back to reality and glared at the photog, who was dry on the beach keeping warm in his down jacket. *Get naked, splash in thirty-degree water, and then let's talk about sexy,* Cici thought. *You idiot.*

"Just one more," Nathan said. He crouched on his knees, holding his camera, and crawled forward only a foot from Cici. "Come on now, you little bitch," he whispered under his breath.

What?! Cici whipped her head around, her eyes flashing with rage, just as Nathan snapped his final shot.

"That's it." Nathan gave Cici a wicked grin. "The flash of passion I needed. All right then."

He waved toward his assistant to bring Cici a towel and a robe. Nathan stood, rubbing his legs a bit from resting on his haunches. He leaned forward and whispered conspiratorially, "It's almost as good in person."

Cici felt a needle pierce her heart. "Excuse me?"

She grabbed for the towel, and Nathan stepped closer. His boldness surprised her. Most men cowered like whipped puppies when she felt enraged. Nathan's eyes roamed her body as if appraising a purchase. Cici flushed, and she felt herself tingle. A sick twist in her nature, her anger toward a man often aroused her. It was a character trait that had explained her unfuckingbelievable sex life with her ex-husband, Damien Bruckner.

Cici felt Nathan's eyes linger on her breasts. He stepped closer, and his lips brushed against her ear. She tilted her head toward him, his breath now hot on her cheek.

"I said, the filmed version is never as good," he whispered.

"And to which of my films do you refer?"

"I don't think it has a title." Nathan's eyes danced with wicked delight. "But I call it *Pussy in Paradise.*"

Cici's heart dropped. She arched her eyebrow and stepped away from Nathan. "You are terribly confused," she said. She reached for the outstretched robe and wrapped it around her.

Nathan grinned and shook his head. "No, Ms. Solange. I'm not confused," he said and backed away to give her a once-over. "In awe, yes. Turned on? Perhaps. But confused? No, I am not that."

Cici turned and walked up the beach toward Ted, a pinprick of fear growing wider with each step. *How did he know? And how would she tell Ted?*

* * *

Cici sat on the plush carpet in her thousand-square-foot custom-built closet, tucked behind a Carolina Herrera gown. She held her phone to her ear, and her stomach churned with panic. She couldn't shake the dread that crept through her body and caused a light sweat to cover her palms. After the photo shoot, she had arrived home and immediately climbed into bed. Ted hovered in their bedroom, asking if he should call their doctor. Celeste finally feigned sleep until he disappeared downstairs. She knew that he was now occupied with a conference call with one of his film distributors in Tokyo. She clutched the phone tighter to her ear and listened to it ring, anxiously waiting for Howard Abramowitz, her attorney, to pick up on his end.

Howard had handled Cici's divorce from Damien Bruckner four years ago. He had also negotiated the settlement that released to her all the video footage Damien had collected of Cici's sexual trysts with others, footage Cici had forced Damien to give to her in exchange for her keeping quiet about Brie Ellison's age and sticking to the alimony amount in their prenup. Footage, Cici now feared, Nathan Curtis had somehow viewed.

"Hello?" Howard answered groggily.

"Howard!"

"Cici?"

"Yes, it's me."

"Cici, it's twelve-thirty in the morning," Howard said.

"We've got a huge fucking problem."

"Are you in jail?"

"No."

"Hospital?"

"No."

"Have you been abducted?"

"No."

"Then it can wait," Howard said.

"No! This cannot wait," Cici hissed before Howard could hang up the phone. "Do you think I'd call you at twelve-thirty on a Wednesday night if this could wait?"

"Celeste, you are a very successful woman. And I think there are a number of people who work for you that, yes, you *would* call at twelve-thirty on a Wednesday night."

Damn him. Okay, maybe he was right, but that was before Ted.

"Howard, I am telling you, this is important," Cici whispered.

"Why are you whispering?" Howard asked, seeming more interested.

"Because I am in the closet."

"Metaphorically or literally?"

"I have a stiletto stuck up my ass, so what do you think?"

"In this town it could go either way." Howard laughed at his own joke. "Okay, okay. What's up?"

"Somebody has it."

Celeste silently waited for Howard's mind to spin through the possibilities. "No. Celeste. You destroyed it."

"Someone made a copy."

"Impossible," Howard said.

"I found out today," Cici said.

"Did you see it?"

"No, but somebody else did."

"Who? What did they say?"

"The photographer from my shoot today. He's from the UK. Nathan Curtis."

"Never heard of him."

"He claims to have seen it."

"Are you sure he's not bluffing?"

"He called it *Pussy in Paradise*—sounds like he at least knows that it was mostly filmed at the beach."

"Fuck." Aside from Howard's heavy breathing, silence was all Cici could hear coming over the phone.

"Howard?"

"I'm thinking. Have you told Ted?"

"You're my first call."

Cici covered her eyes with her hand. This was very bad. The idea of the footage going public made her feel ill.

"Okay. I know a guy. I want to find out if this is contained."

Her career would end. And more important, what about Ted?

"I'll call you tomorrow," Howard said. "I may need you to come to the office. Are you on a cell or a landline?"

"Cell."

"Neither is safe. But my office is. We just swept it three days ago. And don't panic," Howard said. "We'll take care of this. Now go to bed."

"Yeah, right," Cici said. "Like that's possible."

"I'm serious. Plausible deniability is your friend, at least with Ted. If the footage hits the street, you don't want Ted thinking you knew about this ticking bomb, do you? No, you can't have known about this. So get off the phone, wash your face, put on some lingerie, and get into bed."

"How about sweatpants?"

"A man can fantasize, can't he?" Howard asked.

"Yeah, as long as the fantasy isn't based on a digital reality."

* * *

Howard Abramowitz hung up the phone next to his bed. Celeste Solange was one of the world's biggest stars and his most profitable client. Adrenaline pulsed through his body. If there was a tape, any kind of tape, showing Celeste having sex, all the dollars Celeste made for him and the rest of Hollywood would disappear.

He put on his glasses. During Damien's two divorces, Howard saw two different DVDs containing Celeste's erotic "material." In preparation for her divorce, Amanda Bruckner, Damien's first wife, compiled footage of Damien sleeping with Celeste while still married to Amanda. Then Howard found out that Damien himself often filmed his and Celeste's sexcapades and had compiled all the footage onto a DVD. The footage chronicled a number of encounters between the couple, along with some of their multipartner trysts. Damien promised Celeste that the DVD Howard had received from him was the original and that there were no copies. Howard knew Celeste had destroyed the DVD. And according to the settlement—and Damien's claims—Damien had destroyed the original footage. So where was this DVD coming from?

Howard rolled over and pulled himself upright, hoping he wouldn't awaken his wife. She was a chatterbox and would want every sordid detail, none of which Howard felt comfortable sharing. He made his way down to his study, first stopping in the kitchen for a glass of milk.

Howard knew one person who could determine if the footage was readily available: Sherman Ross. Howard kept Sherman's number on speed dial. When you were a divorce attorney in Los Angeles with A-list clients, it was paramount that you kept the best private investigator on retainer. Some used Pellicano, but Howard liked Sherman. Besides, Sherman Ross never got caught.

Pick up, pick up, pick up, Howard thought to himself as he paced his home office. For someone like Sherman, at 1:30 A.M., the night was just getting started.

* * *

Sherman Ross leaned against the bar at Velvet Tokyo. He watched as a gorgeous Latina rubbed her way down the thigh of a very married basketball star. Sherman turned his night-vision camera, built into a disabled cell phone, toward the dirty duo and tossed off a dozen quick photos. *Hello, money,* he thought. He felt his real cell phone in his pocket vibrate. He pulled it out and checked the number.

"Hey, Howard, little late for you."

"Very. Where are you?"

"Velvet Tokyo, little surveillance," Sherman said.

"I've got something for you. Something big."

"Big money or big job?"

"Don't they go together?"

"Usually."

"And as always—"

"Discretion is key," Sherman finished Howard's sentence.

"Exactly. Can you come by my office tomorrow? Early?"

"How early? This gig may take all night."

"How's eleven?"

"Works for me. Can you tell me the client?"

Howard paused. "Did you see *Seven Minutes Past Midnight*?"

"Two times. I liked that one."

"It's the star."

"Bradford?"

"The *female* star," Howard said.

"Got it. I'll see you at eleven." Sherman snapped his phone closed.

Tonight was the third time this week he'd dealt with things close to Celeste Solange. First the sex tape Sherman had watched at a party, then shooting photos for the head of security at her boyfriend's studio, and now her attorney.

Sherman had experienced the sex tape thing several times before, with a number of celebrities. Celeste's team was obviously worried. One of her people must have discovered that the footage of Celeste in flagrante was making the rounds at high-end sex parties in Los Angeles. Now her team would circle the wagons in preparation for the media attack.

He glanced over at the NBA superstar, where a hot blonde had assumed the lap position. She pushed her breasts into the player's cheeks. Sherman snapped off more shots—he was positive that the basketball star's soon-to-be ex-wife would pay top dollar for the photos. After all, she'd much rather own the shots than see them on the cover of the *Enquirer.*

* * *

Cici glanced over at Ted. He breathed deeply and his face looked calm as he slept. Her distress made her twitchy, and she kicked her leg out from under the covers. She was envious of Ted's peaceful slumber—he was unaware of the secret that could potentially sink his studio. Cici had three pictures in the can at Worldwide, and another going into preproduction. If Nathan were telling the truth, and Cici feared he was, Ted's half-a-billion-dollar investment in Celeste Solange films would be worth pretty much zero. America's sweetheart would be seen as a sexual deviant by most of America. Celeste's secret could potentially bankrupt Ted's studio.

Even when Damien promised he gave Howard the original and only DVD, Celeste knew that the DVD was too tempting. Damien claimed no one had burned a copy, and she trusted him at the time, but she knew his divorce attorney, Janice, had kept the DVD for a short time during their divorce. Any one of her assistants, paralegals, or even an inquisitive member of the cleaning crew could have burned a DVD. But why now? And why wasn't the footage all over the Net? Celeste scoured the Internet after speaking with Howard. Three search engines and two hours later, she couldn't find any trace of pornographic footage of her. So where was this tape? How had the photographer, Nathan, seen it?

There was one way to find out. But why would Nathan Curtis tell her the truth? And why would he have told her that he had seen it—what was he after? She cringed at the thought. She doubted he simply wanted money. She had an idea of what it might take to get the horny little Brit to spill. As if reading her mind in his sleep, Ted rolled over and flopped his arm protectively across Celeste. Sex with celebrities was like big-game hunting for some men. As if the number of actresses they banged were testament to their ability as lovers. But Celeste discovered early in her celebrity career that a man's perpetual need for high-profile conquests usually meant he had a tiny penis.

She'd give Howard a small window of time, and then she'd call Nathan. She placed her hand on Ted's arm, now resting across her chest, and watched him sleep, his solid chin and lips outlined against the bedroom window. He was a good man, a protective man. For Celeste, he represented everything she had hoped for in a partner but had failed to find until now. Her heart swelled with love as she watched him. Ted couldn't know. Celeste set her mouth into a firm line. She'd do anything so that Ted never found out.

Rule 8

When You're Invited to a Party in Malibu, Go

Lydia Albright, President of Production, Worldwide Pictures

Lydia sat beside Jay as he pulled her Bentley up to the gate at the edge of The Colony. Lydia preferred staying home on the weekends, but when an A-lister like Jennifer invited you to her afternoon birthday soirée and you were president of production at a studio—especially a studio that wanted to do the actress's next film—attendance became mandatory.

"Lydia Albright," Jay said.

Lydia watched as the guard scanned the list and put a small check next to her name. He waved them through. Already a dozen cars waited behind them. Lydia knew all the vehicles were headed to Jennifer's birthday party, because after Labor Day, aside from the hard-core residents, The Colony remained empty. But Jennifer loved the beach and refused to move inland with the rest of the migratory Los Angelenos.

Jay pulled up to the valet outside the house, hopped out of the car, and dashed around to Lydia's side.

"What are you, my date?" Lydia joked.

"No," Jay said. "Just here watching out for you. I'll walk you in, and then I'll be circling."

"And when I'm ready to leave?"

"I'll know," Jay said. He held Lydia's elbow as they walked up the steps to the front door.

"Oh, you'll just know?" Lydia quipped.

Jay looked at Lydia, his joking tone replaced with a serious look. "Yes. I'll know."

Lydia tilted her head to the side and looked at Jay. For a second, a nice feeling of safety encapsulated her.

The birthday girl stood just inside the front door with her current boyfriend, greeting her guests. Her honey-colored hair caught the sun beaming through the deck doors. Lydia heard the surf pound.

"Lydia!" Jennifer threw her arms around Lydia, engulfing her in a hug. "I'm so glad you came." Jennifer eyed Jay, assessing him. "Hi, I'm Jennifer."

"This is Jay," Lydia said.

"Nice to meet you," Jennifer said. "And thank you for the gift." Jennifer looked at Lydia. "I absolutely adore Lagerfeld."

"You're sure? Because if you don't, please tell me; I can get you something else."

"Lydia, I'll be outside," Jay said and touched her on the arm.

Jennifer watched him walk toward the deck. "Could you get me one of those?" she asked. Her eyes hungrily ate up the rear view of Jay.

"He's one of a kind," Lydia said. She handed her purse over to one of the party's staff who had magically appeared by her side.

"Yes, he is," Jennifer said. She tore her gaze away from Jay. "Everything's out back: the bar, the food, most of the people. I'll be out in a few. I want to say hello to everyone, and this spot seems to be perfect."

Jen tossed her hair and smiled. A very polite dismissal.

Lydia walked through the house toward the deck, spotting several studio execs; three from Worldwide. She waved to Oliver and Owen, talking near the bar. A cool ocean breeze blew through

Lydia's hair when she reached the open deck doors. She stood and surveyed the scene. Celebs, producers, and execs mingled on the deck. Most wore heavy sweaters and still shivered under the heat lamps dotting the deck. The thermometer hovered around seventy degrees, and there was a rhythmic chill as the sun played peekaboo with the earth. The tangy smell of ganja drifted past Lydia's nose.

"May I get you something?" A waiter wearing a long-sleeved blue Lacoste shirt and khaki pants hovered, waiting to take Lydia's drink order.

"Grey Goose and tonic," Lydia said. "I'll be over that way." She pointed to the corner of the deck, where a blond bombshell was holding court on a chaise lounge. Men sat on the deck at her feet and hovered around her chair.

"Can you believe it?" Cici exclaimed as Lydia walked up to the crowd she had drawn. "He wanted me to actually *blow* the actor on camera! I said, well, excuse me, Vincent, I know in your last film the lead was okay with that, but I did not sign up for a porno."

"And what did he say?" a tall surfer standing next to Cici's chair asked.

"Not one word. He cut the entire scene. And I still believe that's the only reason the film got into Sundance. Otherwise it would've been NC-seventeen for sure, and Robert wouldn't have touched it."

Lydia watched as the crowd nodded at Cici's assessment.

"Lydia!" Cici jumped up from her lounge chair and grabbed Lydia's arm. "I didn't know you were coming." She pulled Lydia close for a hug and whispered into her ear. "Get me away from all these people; I don't know any of them."

"So did you get a chance to read that script?" Lydia asked loudly.

"I did. I left word at your office. Didn't Toddy tell you? Let's walk and discuss, want to? Excuse me, gentlemen," Cici said. She raised her eyebrow and gave the crowd her signature Celeste Solange look. "Business."

She made her way through the mass of male bodies and grabbed Lydia's hand. "Thank you," she whispered as the waiter appeared and handed Lydia her drink.

"Where's Ted? I'd think he'd scare most of them away," Lydia said. She usually heard from Ted, her boss, a couple times a week. But he seemed especially busy lately.

"Somewhere in Hong Kong. Or maybe it's Beijing? I thought you knew? Location scouting or something."

Lydia paused. This was an odd position; Worldwide didn't have a film with any Asian location sequences in preproduction. She didn't know whether to tell her friend or stay loyal to her boss. She trusted Ted to have Cici's best intentions at heart, though.

"Got it," Lydia said.

Perhaps Ted picked up a script or read a book he thought would make a great film and was trying to do a little scouting before saying yes and handing it over to his executive team to actually make the movie.

"Come on," Celeste said. "It's quiet upstairs and I have a ton to tell you."

* * *

Lydia sat on the bed, leaning against a half-dozen pillows, with a bowl of chocolate-covered raisins perched on her lap. The sounds of the afternoon party wafted up through the windows. Cici pulled out a joint. "Jennifer won't care. We used to smoke up here all the time." She rifled through the top dresser drawer and pulled out a pink enamel Zippo lighter and a crystal ashtray. "Some things never change."

Cici smiled and placed the flame to the end of the joint. Lydia watched as Cici closed her eyes and inhaled. Lydia took the joint when Cici handed it over.

"It's been a while for you," Cici said. She held her breath for a moment. "How long?" she asked, exhaling.

"Five years," Lydia said, holding her breath. Her abstinence resulted from a total lack of time. She never had the luxury of a couple of hours to let loose.

"I never do it anymore. Ted hates it," Cici said.

Lydia giggled. She couldn't imagine Ted Robinoff, her boss and Cici's lover, ever taking a hit.

"What?" Cici asked, taking the joint from Lydia's hand.

"Ted? Can you imagine?" Lydia asked as she exhaled.

"Not in a million years," Cici said. She took another hit. "I love him, but he's a little Wall Street stuffy, if you know what I mean."

Lydia did in fact know. Ted Robinoff was all business.

"With Zymar at your house, I'd think you'd light up every now and then. He always has some great stuff."

In the evenings, the aroma of weed often drifted up to Lydia's bedroom window as she lay in bed reading scripts. A final toke before Zymar ended his day.

"I'm sure he'd share. I just never ask. I'm always reading or at a meeting," Lydia said. She scooped up a handful of chocolate-covered raisins.

"I'm killing this for now." Cici stubbed the joint out in the ashtray and flopped onto the bed. She grabbed a handful of Raisinets. "These are so good, but I'll pay for them tomorrow morning with my trainer." Celeste dropped the candy into her mouth.

"So, what's up?" Lydia asked. "I feel like I haven't seen you in ages. Three weeks, maybe?"

"Press for *California Girl*. And by the way, that new photographer your marketing department used to shoot the one sheet is a complete asshole."

"Name?" Lydia asked.

"Nathan something."

"British?"

Cici nodded yes. "I have to meet with him again this week."

"Why? Once the shots are finished you don't ever have to see him again, especially if he's an asshole."

Cici rolled over onto her back and stared at the ceiling. Lydia glanced over at her suddenly silent friend.

"Cici, what is it?" Lydia asked.

"There's a problem."

Lydia's heart fluttered. *Another problem?* She'd yet to tell Cici about the letters she'd received.

"Are we speaking as friends?" Cici asked. She looked into Lydia's eyes.

In entertainment, the line between friendship and business was more ephemeral than one drawn in the desert during a sandstorm. Cici was one of her closest friends, but she was also America's biggest star. A star who did the majority of her films at Worldwide. In fact, right now Worldwide had almost a quarter billion dollars' worth of finished Celeste Solange films waiting for their release dates, to say nothing of the five other films slated for the next three years. With prints and advertising costs, Worldwide had close to a half billion dollars invested in Cici. In this town, where all your friends were also your business associates, the division between friendship and business was impossible to maintain.

"Of course," Lydia said.

"Remember the DVD that Damien had during the divorce?"

"Yes." Lydia's heart rate increased in tempo. "He gave you the original."

Cici gave Lydia a serious look. "He *said* he gave me the original."

"Oh, no."

Lydia sat up from her semi-horizontal position. Raisinets spilled from the bowl and clattered onto the wooden floor.

"Fuck," Lydia said. "Who's seen it?"

"Your Brit photographer, for one."

The fear that had been drifting through Lydia's mind since the arrival of the first letter reemerged. Were the notes about the DVD? Now Lydia remembered why she didn't smoke weed anymore; it made her incredibly paranoid. She ran her hands through her hair. She needed to find Jay, and they needed to call Briggs Montgomery. With Worldwide security and Ted's money, they could hopefully stop the X-rated footage of Celeste before it went public.

"Who knows about this?" Lydia asked.

"You, me, and Howard," Cici said.

"And Ted?"

Cici shook her head. "Plausible deniability is the term Howard used when it came to Ted. Howard didn't even want me to tell you."

"Cici, there is no way you can keep this from Ted. What's Howard doing about it?"

"He's got a snoop looking into it."

"So there *is* another person who knows."

Lydia's heart pounded. *There were no secrets in Hollywood.* Once news of a sex tape of Celeste Solange leaked, every reporter, tabloid, publicist, agent, manager, and scum-sucking porno distributor would be clamoring for the DVD. Wasn't pot supposed to be a downer? She suddenly felt hopped up on speed.

"Do *not* tell anyone else," Lydia said. "Do you understand?" Her tone was the harshest one she'd ever taken with Cici, but a sex tape was a big problem. Lydia stood from the bed and walked toward the bathroom. She needed to splash water on her face.

"Celeste, if there is even a whisper in the community about a sex tape, everyone will be after it. It could go public. It would be bad."

"I know."

Lydia paused at the bathroom door. A faint moaning emanated from the other side. Lydia motioned for Cici to come place her ear next to the door.

"Do you hear that?" Lydia whispered to Celeste.

"Somebody is getting something," Celeste said. "Want to see who it is?"

"Cici, you cannot open that door."

"Why not? If it's unlocked it's their fault."

Before Lydia could stop her, Cici pulled open the door. The superstar sat on the counter with her legs spread for the supermodel. Both smiled at Lydia and Celeste.

"Care to join?" The supermodel asked in her heavy Russian accent.

"So sorry," Cici said. "Let me lock this for you." She pulled the door closed.

"And I thought that I gave Jennifer the perfect birthday gift," Lydia said.

***

The DJ was just starting to warm up when Lydia kissed Jennifer good night. Stoned, drunk, and exceptionally happy, Jennifer lounged on the couch between her boyfriend and her supermodel.

"Let me know if you ever want to give it a try," Jennifer whispered into Lydia's ear as she hugged her good-bye. A smile played across her lips and she glanced at Jay. "Or if you both want to."

"I will." Lydia had learned never to appear surprised and always checked her judgment at the door. Besides, what was a good Malibu party about if not the people you met and the wild things you tried?

Lydia watched Jay hand the valet her ticket. He had indeed found her just as she was ready to leave. *Was he a mind reader?* After her conversation with Cici, she hoped not. Lydia had lost her buzz before she left the bedroom. First the letters and now Cici's sex tape? The two must be connected. Lydia ran through the words of the letters in her head. According to Briggs, until the author made a demand, they could do nothing but wait. And Lydia was *not* used to waiting. She spent her entire career making things happen, not waiting for people. Lydia shifted her weight from foot to foot as she watched her Bentley come to a stop before her.

"Little edgy, aren't you?" Jay whispered in her ear as he opened her door.

Edgy? If he only knew how edgy. Lydia slid into the front seat and bit her lower lip, reminding herself not to tell Jay about the DVD. Jay slid behind the wheel as Lydia's hands-free phone rang. She looked at Jay. They had a system. She nodded and he pressed the button on the wheel.

"You got it?" An unrecognizable voice filled the car.

Lydia squinted and looked at Jay. *Who was it?* She couldn't even tell if the voice was male or female. "Got what? Who is this?"

"My note."

Lydia's stomach lurched.

"Check your bag."

She lifted her Kelly bag from the floorboard and peered inside. She shivered when her fingertips felt the paper, soft as suede. She pulled the envelope from her purse. Lydia sat frozen as Jay motioned for her to speak.

"I'm sorry. To what do you refer?"

A soft laugh crackled across the phone. "Well, I sure hope it's in your purse and not someone else's. The letter could be"—the voice paused—"damaging."

Fear spread through Lydia's limbs, and she felt her chin quiver. "What do you want?" she asked. She listened to the silence, waiting for more instructions. But the line went dead.

Lydia placed her head against the headrest in the car. She exhaled. She hadn't realized that she was holding her breath as she waited for the caller to fill the silence. Her chest felt tight, and a cold sweat moistened her upper lip.

"Lydia, are you okay?" Jay asked.

She couldn't answer. The caller had failed to answer the one question to which she needed a response. How could she possibly stop this if she didn't even know what the person wanted? What could she give them? Money? Power? Prestige? Her breath became shallow. The car felt like a vacuum. She looked at Jay and reached over to open the window.

"Okay, breathe slow and deep," Jay said, turning to her. He rested a hand on her shoulder and started taking deep breaths, as if trying to teach her how to breathe. "That's right, that's right," Jay said. He glanced out the windshield and then into the rearview mirror. Lydia heard a rapping on Jay's window.

"Sir, is everything okay?" the valet asked through the window.

Jay nodded. He glanced into the rearview mirror again, put the Bentley in drive, and pulled out. Cars were piling up behind them; everyone in Malibu for the good times at Jennifer's party.

Rule 9

Never Believe Actors— They Lie for a Living

Mary Anne Meyers, Screenwriter

Mary Anne luxuriated in postcoital bliss. Holden had arrived on her doorstep three days before, and aside from a quick trip home yesterday, he'd yet to leave her bed. And she enjoyed every minute. *What was she doing?* She blushed at the thought of the last three days. Never, ever had she experienced this kind of sexual freedom. He heated her to her core every single time. Who actually had this kind of sex? Could it continue? She doubted it. But right now she didn't care.

Mary Anne looked around her room. Another question had been at the back of her mind, and was nagging at her more and more—what were they doing? Having sex, obviously. But dating? She doubted that, too.

"Babe, you're almost out of eggs," Holden called from the kitchen. She heard his heavy footfall as he walked toward the bedroom. The sight of Holden standing in the doorway took her breath away. How could anyone possibly be that physically perfect?

"Seriously, babe, we're running out of food," he said. "Better call Gelson's. They deliver."

"Deliver? You have your groceries delivered?"

"Honey, come on. It's a mob scene when I go to a low-key dinner. Can you imagine me trying to pick out a cantaloupe?"

"I'll go," Mary Anne said, throwing back the covers. "I'm not a celebrity."

"You're not going anywhere," Holden teased. He grabbed her and lifted her onto his shoulder. "You, Miss Meyers, are staying right here with me."

He flopped her onto the bed as the phone rang. Mary Anne reached to answer it. "Ignore it," Holden called from the foot of the bed, and Mary Anne paused. She listened to the phone continue to ring, then reached for it. She couldn't ignore the call; she was waiting to hear back from Jessica about her rewrite on *Sexual Being*.

"Hello." Mary Anne giggled as Holden kissed her toes.

"Mary Anne?"

"Mom?" Mary Anne glanced down at Holden and mouthed, *Stop, it's my mom.* Instead, Holden gave her a naughty smile and began kissing her calves.

"How are you?" Mary Anne asked. "Where are you?"

"Today Atlanta, tomorrow Philadelphia." A children's book author, Mary Anne's mother was more of a jet-setter than her Hollywood daughter. Mitsy spent winters in Los Angeles and summers in St. Paul.

"I just got the strangest e-mail and thought I should call you," Mitsy said.

"Uh-huh." Mary Anne closed her eyes as Holden lifted her leg and placed his lips on the back of her knee.

"I e-mailed Adam, asking if he'd be back in the States for New Year's, and he e-mailed me that I should call you."

"Uh-huh," Mary Anne whispered, barely listening to Mitsy as Holden's lips worked their way up the back of her thigh. He reached under her and flipped her onto her stomach. She shut her eyes and sank into the feeling of his lips fluttering light kisses across her ass.

"So, Mary Anne, what are you and Adam doing for the holidays?"

"Adam?" Mary Anne whispered.

Holden stopped. "Adam?"

"Who's that?" Mitsy asked. "Do you have someone there?"

"Uh, Mom." Mary Anne sat up as Holden got off the bed and walked out of the bedroom. "You know, this actually isn't a good time."

"Mary Anne, are you dating someone while Adam is away?"

"No, mother." Mary Anne sighed. "I mean yes, I'm dating someone, and Adam is away—"

"Darling, you know I'm surprised with this choice, especially after what Steve did with that little tart—what was her name, your neighbor who's now an actress—"

"Viève Dyson," Mary Anne said.

"Exactly. After you walked in on Steve with that Viève girl, I'm surprised you'd do something so damaging to Adam—"

"Mom—"

"Dating someone behind—"

"Mom—"

"His back—"

"Mom, stop, okay? Adam and I broke up. Before I came back from England. We stopped seeing each other."

Mary Anne listened to the silence from her mother. Mitsy often walked a fine line between caring and overbearing, and Mary Anne wondered on which side Mitsy would fall in this conversation.

"You know, darling, I thought you and Adam were very well matched," Mitsy said carefully.

That's a pretty good start, for Mitsy, Mary Anne thought.

"And . . . well, you just aren't getting any younger."

What? She'd just told her mother that she'd broken up with her long-term boyfriend. She wasn't expecting *Are you okay?* or *Do you need anything?* exactly, but maybe an *Oh no, what happened?* or an *I'm so sorry* would have been nice. All the things normal people who care about you say. But instead Mitsy tells her that she isn't getting any younger?

"Perhaps once Adam's play is finished and he gets back from London, you'll patch things up?" Mitsy asked.

"Mother, I don't want to patch things up. Things between Adam and me weren't, well, we . . ." Mary Anne couldn't finish. How do you discuss your dysfunctional sex life with your mom?

"What?"

"We weren't really compatible," Mary Anne said, hoping Mitsy would understand her euphemism.

"Compatible? Mary Anne, you're both writers, voracious readers, love theater, and—"

"No, Mom, I mean, it wasn't enough."

"Enough? But darling, Adam is such a kind man and he wants children. Don't you want children? Now, by the time you meet someone, it'll be at least two years, possibly three, before you start a family and—"

"I can't believe this," Mary Anne mumbled.

"And then, darling, you'll be almost forty when the children are born and—"

"Did you hear me? Mom, *did you hear me*?" Mary Anne knew her voice sounded terse, but she didn't care. Mitsy had stepped over the line into intrusive.

"What, darling? You told me right before you left for London that you wanted to start a family soon."

"Yes . . . I mean, no. Mom, you need to have sex to have a family, right? The couple? They have to engage in intercourse." Mary Anne listened again to the silence on the phone line. "Mom?"

"I see," Mitsy said. "Well, darling, since Miraval, I certainly understand the importance of sexual compatibility. If this is something you want to discuss, I am happy to listen."

Mary Anne shuddered. She did not want to discuss her sex life with her mother. "Thanks, Mom."

"But you and Adam left things on a positive note?"

"Yeah, as positive as 'I don't want to see you ever again' can be," Mary Anne said. She hopped out of bed, threw on her robe, and walked toward the kitchen to check on Holden. She didn't want to have this conversation with Mitsy now. In fact, she didn't want to have this conversation with Mitsy ever. Mary Anne wanted her love life to remain a private affair between her and whomever she dated.

"Darling, you don't want to be eighty when your grandchildren are born. You're already pushing the limits of your body by waiting this long and—"

"Mother, stop. I don't want to discuss this right now," Mary Anne said, peering into her kitchen. Holden stood with the refrigerator door open, rummaging for food. "I need to go."

"So, no Adam for New Year's, then?" Mitsy sounded disappointed.

"No, Mother," Mary Anne said.

"Fine, darling. I'm off to my signing. I'll see you soon. And should you want to discuss, just give me a call."

"Thanks."

Mary Anne placed the phone on the kitchen counter and walked up to Holden. She stood behind him and slid her arms around his waist. "So, did you find anything?" she asked.

"Not much." He pushed the refrigerator door shut and pulled out of Mary Anne's embrace.

"That was my mom," Mary Anne said, sitting in the chair next to the kitchen island.

"Mm-hmm," Holden said. "Do you have a cutting board?" Mary Anne pointed to the cabinet above her coffeemaker. "I'm making eggs with peppers. Want some?"

Mary Anne felt a distance from Holden. "Listen, she called to find out if—"

"Are you dating this Adam guy?" Holden asked with his back turned. "Because if you are and this"—he turned and pointed to himself and then to her—"whatever this is, is just a fling, then fine. I'm cool with that. But I want to know."

Mary Anne looked into Holden's eyes. He actually looked worried. Was it possible that he wanted more than just a casual fling? Was it possible that this perfect male specimen standing in her kitchen could actually fall for her? Mary Anne was surprised. She was the girl next door, not one of the sexpot screen sirens the tabloids often reported Holden wearing on his arm.

"Well, I don't know what *this* is," Mary Anne said. "I mean you and me. If there is a you and me. But I'm not dating Adam." She saw relief flood into Holden's eyes. "We broke up before you and I met at Shutters to discuss *Sexual Being.*"

"Jessica said you lived with him?"

"I did. Before he moved to London. And I went to London to visit him, but things didn't work out. Look, I'm happy to tell you all the details, if you want to know." Mary Anne looked at Holden standing next to the kitchen counter. He wore blue boxers and held a serrated knife.

"I don't need details," Holden said. "I just, I mean, we were starting something in there, when you said his name."

"I said his name because my mother wanted to know why he declined her holiday invitation."

"She didn't know that you guys broke up?" Holden asked, surprised.

"Does your mother know about me?" Mary Anne asked.

"No," Holden said, "I guess not." He began to chop red peppers. "But she'd like you. I know she would. You're just the kind of girl she wants for me."

"Really? And what kind of girl is that?" Mary Anne asked. She stood from her chair and moved toward Holden.

"A smart one," Holden said.

"Smart, huh?" Mary Anne teased. She kissed his back and reached around him to lightly graze her fingers across the front of his boxers.

"And funny," Holden said, closing his eyes.

"Funny?" Mary Anne pushed her breasts against Holden's back. He set down the knife. Mary Anne gently turned him away from the kitchen counter and kissed his chest and then his abdomen.

"And . . . nice," Holden breathed out as Mary Anne took the tops of his boxers and pulled them down toward the floor.

"Really nice?" Mary Anne gave Holden a mischievous look, then slid down and inserted his cock into her mouth. She felt him arch his back toward the counter and saw the muscles in his calves flinch. He reached down and pulled her upward, his mouth finding hers, and picked her up and set her on the counter.

"Really nice," he said and gave her a tiny smile, his eyes half closed with pleasure as he pushed himself inside her. "Really . . . nice."

Rule 10

Deliver Bad News Quickly

Jessica Caulfield-Fox, Manager-Producer

"Holden, what do you want me to do?" Jessica asked. The wind whipped through her hair as she zipped along Mulholland. She loved Los Angeles. After spending the last nine weeks freezing in Toronto, any temperature above fifty-five felt like heaven. So although it was seventy degrees, cool for L.A., Jessica drove with the windows in her Range Rover rolled down.

"She broke into my house last night."

"And?"

"And she fucking destroyed my bedroom wall. She painted her name in red. With a heart."

Right now, while Viève still thought she and Holden were getting back together, she painted hearts and left him roses. Jessica wondered what kind of message he'd receive once Viève realized she and Holden were history. The rabbit scene from *Fatal Attraction* popped into Jessica's head.

"She hid in my bushes the night before."

"Wow."

"Plus she's been sending me these crazy-ass notes. Jess, you gotta talk to her."

"Okay, okay," Jessica said.

"I don't need to see her anymore, especially now that we're back in L.A.," Holden whispered.

"Why are you whispering? Where are you?"

"Jessica, you promised this wouldn't happen. You said you'd take care of it."

"And I will. Today," Jessica said as she turned off of Mulholland.

Fabrocini, at the top of Beverly Glen, was an easy place to meet, where she, Lydia, Cici, and Mary Anne could sit outside and talk. Perhaps they'd have ideas on how to get Viève to stop stalking Holden.

Jessica couldn't find a parking space and circled the lot. She spotted Lydia's Bentley (a gift from Ted Robinoff) and Cici's Jaguar (another gift from Ted). Jessica wondered if she'd ever receive a dream car as a gift from Mr. Robinoff. In her single, non-mommy days she always arrived early and waited for everyone, but after having Max, Jessica discovered that she was always twenty minutes behind, even after she gave herself an additional half hour. She pulled into a space and checked herself in the rearview mirror. On set, Jessica got by with jeans and a ponytail, but now back in L.A. she did both her hair and her makeup. She even wore a pair of Gucci heels.

"It's about time," Lydia said when Jessica appeared at their table. Jessica leaned forward and pecked Cici then Lydia on the cheek.

"Back from the tundra?" Cici said.

"Sure am. Where's Mary Anne?" Jessica asked, sitting down. She expected all three of her friends to be there to fill her in on all the gossip she'd missed while filming *Collusion* in Toronto.

"She's not coming," Lydia said.

"Why?" Jessica asked.

"She told Cici that she's writing, but I think it's because of Adam," Lydia said.

"Adam? What's wrong with Adam?"

"They broke up," Cici said. She reached for a slice of bread and dipped it into the olive oil. "Seems he's too busy in London with his play. Good thing she leaves for Brazil next week."

"Sexual Being?" Jessica asked.

Both Cici and Lydia nodded.

"Holden actually did script notes, can you believe it?" Jessica asked and reached for a piece of bread.

"I'll bet he did," Cici said. "Don't you remember Holden and Mary Anne's night together years ago?"

Jessica paused. "When I was still an agent?"

Cici nodded.

"Cici, I seriously doubt Holden remembers that. He's had so many 'nights.' "

"Oh, he remembers. He got a room at Shutters when he met with Mary Anne," Cici said.

"What? When?" Jessica asked, surprised.

"When he flew back for that meeting you two scheduled. The one about his script notes. And it seems that a very attentive concierge, who is a friend of mine, saw Mary Anne exit the hotel the morning after their meeting."

Jessica felt a pang of guilt. Only two days after Mary Anne's rendezvous with Holden, Jessica had asked him to pretend to make a play for Viève. But how could she have known? And anyway, this was Holden they were talking about. "You don't think they'll start a thing, do you?" Jessica asked.

"According to my sources, it's already started," Cici said.

Jessica bit into her bread. She needed to call Viève, and possibly Viève's agent, Tyler, just in case there was damage control to do. She didn't want Mary Anne in another love triangle with the crazy redhead.

"Mary Anne in Brazil with Holden for three months. That's a great cure for a breakup," Cici said.

And a great way for Holden to lose one little green-eyed stalker, Jessica thought.

"What about Holden and Viève on set?" Cici asked.

"There wasn't a Holden and Viève." Jessica hesitated. "Well, aside from the fact I made him tell the nut job he wanted to sleep with her."

"Oh, Jessica, that's dangerous. Actresses are crazy," Cici said.

"Cici, *you're* an actress," Jessica said.

"Excuse me, have I ever claimed to be sane?" Celeste smiled at both her friends.

"I'll stop by Mary Anne's after lunch to check on her," Jessica said, lifting her menu and scanning it. "Lots of carbohydrates and comfort foods. Good thing you're not in production, Cici; there'd be nothing for you to eat."

The silence Jessica received after her glib remark made her uncomfortable. She peeked around her menu at her friends. Both Lydia and Cici stared at her with serious expressions.

"What?"

"We have something to tell you," Cici said.

Jessica's heart sank. *Was this an intervention?* Collusion *was a flop? One of them was dying?* "Okay," she said. She slowly placed her menu on the table.

"But once we tell you, then you become a part of it," Lydia said. "You lose your—what was it, Cici?"

"Plausible deniability," Cici said.

"That's right. You lose your plausible deniability. So you may not want us to tell you."

"You're kidding, right?" Jessica asked. She looked first at Lydia and then at Cici. They were her two closest friends; they always helped one another out of tight spots.

"No, we're not kidding, Jess. With your deal at Worldwide—"

"Lydia," Jessica interrupted, "you run Worldwide. And, Cici, you live with the guy who owns Worldwide."

"Exactly," Cici said, and stopped, her pause pregnant with innuendo.

"Like I'm saying," Lydia said, "you may not want to know this. We're giving you a choice, because once you know, you lose your plausible deniability. And we know you have Mike and Max to think of."

Jessica sat back in her chair and contemplated the somber looks on the faces of Lydia and Cici. Yes, she did now have a husband and a son to consider, but these were her best friends. She'd risked her career for them before and came out on top. If anything, she was in a much safer space now than when they'd screened *Seven Minutes Past Midnight* at CTA. Now Jessica owned her management-production company. Plus, Mike made a great living as a producer; she could always retire from film and become a soccer mom.

"Okay, I get it. I do. It's obviously a big deal. But I still want to know."

"It seems that Damien, as usual, didn't keep his promise," Cici said.

"About?" Jessica asked.

"The DVD," Lydia said.

"What DVD?"

Celeste tilted her head to the side and cocked one eyebrow.

"No. No! Not that DVD!" Jessica said.

"Sh," Lydia said, glancing around the patio. She nodded her head toward Jay, who sat in a far corner sipping iced tea and reading *Daily Variety.*

"Not that DVD," Jessica whispered.

"Yes, that DVD," Cici said. "He didn't give me the only copy."

"What's he doing with it? What does he want?" Jessica asked, confused. Cici and Damien had had little contact since the divorce, but as far as Jessica knew, it had been amicable, or at least as amicable as it could be after their bitter split.

"It's not Damien," said Cici.

"Who has it?" Jessica asked.

"We don't know yet who has it, or if it's even still out there. What we've got is a photographer named Nathan Curtis who alluded to the tape at the photo shoot he did with Cici," Lydia said.

"What did Ted say?" Jessica asked.

"Well, that's were the plausible deniability comes in," Lydia said.

"You didn't tell Ted?" Jessica asked, looking at Cici. The actress looked down and shook her head.

"Cici, you *have* to tell Ted. There is no way to keep this a secret in town. You may be able to keep it away from the general public, but there is no way Ted won't find out."

"I can't," Cici said. "At least not yet. Not until we know it's real."

"And there's more," Lydia said.

"More?" Jessica asked.

"More? What more?" Cici chimed in. She glanced at Lydia incredulously.

"I've got something that may or may not be related." Lydia pulled her Kelly bag from the back of her chair. "If anyone ever asks, you guys never saw these, never read these, never even knew that they existed. I've put them in a folder," Lydia whispered, "so my keeper over there won't know what I'm showing you."

Lydia reached across the table and handed the folder to Jessica. "They're in order of arrival."

Jessica scanned the letter with a numeral one marked in the upper lefthand corner. Her heart dropped to her feet. Celeste peered over Jessica's arm, reading along with her. "Who—"

"I don't know," Lydia said.

"Really bad writing," Jessica said.

"Lydia, when did you start getting these?" Cici asked.

"About the same time you met Nathan Curtis," Lydia said.

Jessica looked up at Lydia after finishing the fourth letter. "Where were they sent?"

"The office, the house, and the last one, I found in my purse."

"Your purse?" Cici asked.

Lydia nodded. "Jen's party."

"No way," Cici said.

"Studio security checked the guest and staff lists, but so far nothing," Lydia said.

"So studio security knows," Cici said.

Lydia sighed. "About the letters. I showed them to Worldwide security before I heard from you about the tape and Nathan Curtis."

"That explains Jay," Jessica said. She glanced across the patio at Lydia's security detail. "So you knew in Toronto?"

"I'd gotten three. The weird thing? They've never asked for anything."

"They've got to be linked, right? The letters and the DVD?" Cici asked.

"That's what I thought, too," Lydia said. She reached for the folder containing the letters and returned it to her bag. "The timing is just too coincidental."

"You know, Briggs gives Ted a weekly update on studio security," Cici said.

"He does?" Lydia asked.

"Yeah, and there's a special section in the briefing about me. Seems I'm not only a lover but an investment."

"At least you know he cares," Jessica said, feigning a smile.

"Ted's going to find out about the letters," Cici said.

Jessica looked across the table at Lydia. She could tell from Lydia's expression that they were both thinking the same thing: If the letter and the DVD were linked, then the "well-moneyed whore" mentioned in the third letter could only refer to Cici.

"Cici, listen. You need to tell Ted," Jessica said.

Jessica wanted Cici to understand the tone of the letters. The risk. Jessica understood Lydia's concern. Each letter grew increasingly aggressive, and yet none contained a demand. What could they do?

"There is no way you can keep this from him," Lydia added.

Jessica watched big tears form in Cici's eyes. Jessica felt sad for her. Cici cared so deeply for Ted, and Jessica knew the delicacy of the dance required to maintain any relationship in Hollywood. She turned to Lydia. "Well, wait. Do we know this is real?"

"Those letters are pretty real," Lydia said.

"Right, but the letters might not be connected to the DVD. Right? Maybe we're jumping to conclusions. The letters never say exactly what they're about, or what they want."

"According to Security, until whoever is writing these makes a demand or shows their hand, there is nothing to do but wait," Lydia said. "And keep our families safe." She leaned forward. "Jess,

Cici already has security at her house, and I have Jay. If you and Mike want a patrol or a guard—"

Jessica looked at Lydia, at the intense concern on her friend's face. She felt fear flutter along her insides. "I need to talk to Mike. But, yeah, I'd like to have someone around the house, I think. At least at night, with Max there. After reading these, it would make me feel better."

"Come on . . . you two are kidding, right? I get crazy fan mail all the time," Cici said. Her tone sounded light, as though she were trying to brush away the seriousness of the letters.

Jessica glanced at Lydia. She felt irritated by Cici's nonchalance about the threats. Cici didn't have a child to keep safe.

"You said Sherman Ross was working on this with Howard, trying to uncover who has the DVD?" Lydia asked.

Cici nodded.

"Everyone in entertainment wants something, and usually it's to direct a film," Lydia said. "I'll just bet our little voyeur wants that, too. Why else come to Hollywood to pursue photography? I've got an idea to try to see if we can't get Nathan Curtis under our control . . . or at the very least, under our surveillance. Cici, it's your job to get on Nathan's good side, feel him out about where he saw the DVD."

"And we don't tell Ted," Cici said.

Lydia shook her head and sighed. "Fine, we don't tell Ted. At least not yet."

"Lydia—"

Lydia interrupted Cici. "Look, if our lives are in danger, I'm calling Ted and I'm calling Briggs Montgomery. I can't promise you that we aren't *ever* going to tell Ted. But we'll keep our secrets for now . . . until we really feel threatened."

Jessica watched Cici's face as Lydia's statement registered. The possibility of real danger, Jessica realized, hadn't occurred to Cici.

"You don't think someone would actually try to hurt one of us, do you?" Cici asked.

"These letters keep getting more twisted. And when I heard that voice over the phone, it sent chills down my spine," Lydia said.

"You didn't recognize the voice?" Jessica asked.

Lydia looked at her. "I couldn't even tell if it was a man or a woman."

Cici furrowed her brow. "Okay. I'm meeting Nathan, and if this starts to get ugly—"

"We go to Ted," Jessica finished Cici's sentence.

Celeste looked at Jessica and Lydia. "Okay, then we go to Ted."

* * *

The lunch with Cici and Lydia left Jessica feeling numb. Sex tapes, phone threats, and anonymous letters? Real life was better than fiction. She guessed that everyone in entertainment had a dirty little secret somewhere. And maybe it wasn't just in Hollywood; maybe everyone in the world harbored some dark little tale. Jessica glanced into the rearview mirror as she turned onto Beverly Glen. There were even a couple of tidbits that she herself hoped were permanently hidden.

Damn Damien, Jessica thought. Cici told Jessica during their divorce that she had destroyed the original DVD. Jessica knew, even then, that there was no way to keep a lid on the footage, that there had to be another copy somewhere and that the footage would eventually leak. Too much money could be made by selling a sex tape of the biggest star in the world.

Of course, until one of them actually saw the DVD, everything was speculation. But, oh man, Ted would flip. *If he ever found out,* Jessica thought. *If. Like there was an* if. Cici was in denial if she thought she could keep this secret from Ted.

Jessica dialed Mary Anne's number and listened to the phone ring as Jessica's car twisted along Mulholland. She finally hung up and tried Mary Anne's cell, but still no answer. *I bet she's taking the breakup really hard,* Jessica thought. Unlike Cici, Jessica wasn't convinced that Holden and Mary Anne were involved. She doubted Mary Anne could fall for a guy like Holden. Physically, of course, yes. Any woman could. They may well have had a fling at Shutters, especially with Mary Anne in such a fragile state. But as smart and as well read as Mary Anne was, how could Holden possibly maintain her interest? What would they discuss? And besides, Holden had a new starlet on his arm every three days.

Mary Anne often unplugged her phone when she wrote, but she almost always answered her cell. Jessica suddenly had a vision of Mary Anne curled up in a ball on her couch with a box of Kleenex, a vat of Ben & Jerry's Phish Food, and a bottle of Absolut. Jessica hit the gas.

When she got to Mary Anne's and parked, she peeked in the front window, scanning the living room and the hall. She rang the doorbell. No answer. Maybe Mary Anne wasn't home? But Mary Anne's white Mercedes was parked in the drive. Being a writer, Mary Anne spent the majority of time at her home. She kept the spare key tucked in the planter on the front porch. Jessica rang again, waited, and finally retrieved the key, slid it into the lock, and gave the door a gentle shove.

"Mary Anne?" Jessica called.

She walked down the hall toward Mary Anne's writing room.

"Mary Anne?" she called louder.

What was that? Jessica heard a low moan escape from Mary Anne's bedroom. *God, it's worse than I thought; she's crying and hasn't even gotten out of bed!*

Jessica pushed open the door. "Sweetie, it's not that bad." And there she stopped. Before her was a mass of arms, legs, and one bare ass. *A very good-looking bare ass.*

"Oh! I, just . . ." Jessica sputtered. "Never mind!" She pulled the door shut.

How did that happen? This was the second time she'd walked in on people having sex. And why was it always surprising sex? Jessica hurried down the hall toward the front door.

"Jessica, wait!" Mary Anne called. Jessica paused and turned back toward her client and friend, who was throwing a robe on as she ran after her.

"Mary Anne, I'm so sorry," Jessica said. "Lydia and Cici told me about Adam, and I was worried that maybe . . . well, you didn't answer your phone and I just thought I'd check on you—"

"I'm so embarrassed."

Jessica watched Mary Anne pull her crazy curly hair away from her face.

"Was that . . ." Jessica leaned toward Mary Anne. "Holden?"

Mary Anne blushed and nodded.

"I see," Jessica said. "Good for you."

"We were working on *Sexual Being* and—"

"No need to tell me," Jessica said, holding up her hands.

"It just happened."

"Really?"

"Well, the other day. At Shutters. We met there for a drink, to discuss the script and—"

"It just happened," Jessica said.

"Right. And then when he got back from Toronto—"

"It just happened again?" Jessica said. She tried to hold back her smile. "Right. Well, Max and Mike are home waiting for me and you're okay, so . . ." She turned to leave.

"Jessica, please. You won't—"

"Say anything?" Jessica interrupted. "Not a word. Promise." Jessica didn't want to tell Mary Anne that it didn't matter whether she told anyone about the fun Mary Anne was having with Holden, because her friends already knew about the affair.

"Thanks," Mary Anne said. She followed Jessica to the front door.

Jessica climbed into her Range Rover and waved at the front door as Mary Anne pulled it closed. The secrets just kept coming.

Rule 11

Whatever the Client Wants, the Client Gets

Kiki Dee, Publicist

Although she was still a member of the walking wounded, Kiki's stitches had healed and her bruises were barely visible under her Laura Mercier foundation. So she was once again ensconced in her suite of offices high above Century City. Kiki watched through the huge windows from her office, called the fishbowl, as her PR minions scurried around hard at work, sporting Jimmy Choos and Chanel suits. Kiki required her worker bees to look as fashionable as the talent KDP represented, and as Kiki herself. All of the junior publicists looked as though they had stepped out of the pages of *Vogue* . . . except Boom Boom.

Kiki let her eyes drift over to the dumpy little Asian assistant sitting just outside Kiki's office. As a favor to a B-list actor friend in a weak moment five years before, Kiki had hired Boom Boom just after Kiki's partners had split, taking most of her A-list stars. Boom Boom was short (five-two), stocky (the word itself made Kiki shudder), and frumpy (today she wore a skirt that hit her awkwardly at the knee). Of course, Boom Boom was also brilliant (Yale class of

2003) and well connected (Sony). But the bottom line was that Kiki's little ugly duckling had not an ounce of chutzpah, a quality that Kiki believed all great publicists needed. Loyal, hardworking, and exceptionally organized, Boom Boom possessed all the qualities any executive in Hollywood craved in an assistant . . . qualities for which Kiki Dee hated her. She was too perfect, in all the unnecessary ways. Boom Boom still failed to act like a publicist. An assistant, yes, but a publicist? Not even close.

When would she grow a backbone? Kiki wondered. She watched Boom Boom, per Kiki's orders, pick pollen out of the lilies that Kiki had ordered for her office. Deathly allergic but loving the look and the smell of lilies, Kiki could have the flowers but only if Boom Boom tweezed away the offending pecks of pollen when they were delivered on Tuesdays. The pollen picking was the first step in what Kiki had labeled Operation Boom Boom Explodes. Kiki's dirty little pleasure over the last few months had been thinking up new and ever more twisted ways to torture her ever-patient, ever-faithful assistant. What else to do between calls?

Boom Boom had done everything from walking Kiki's dogs to walking Kiki's bowel movement sample to her doctor's office ("No, Boom Boom, you may not drive or messenger my poop; you must walk my shit to the doctor's office."). Kiki had started requiring Boom Boom to arrive at the office at five A.M. to check Kiki's voice mail in case there were European calls. But these demeaning tasks failed to offend Boom Boom. In fact, Boom Boom's response to Kiki's *fuck you* note was the tersest tone Kiki had ever heard from Boom Boom. Even through her drugged-out fog, Kiki noticed that Boom Boom had used the word *bitchy.* Perhaps Boom Boom did have some spunk.

"Boom Boom," Kiki called.

Boom Boom dropped the tweezers to the floor and looked at Kiki.

"Get in here."

Kiki watched, hopeful that perhaps today, this day, after five years, Boom Boom would have on a pair of heels. *I'll even settle for Dior mules,* Kiki thought. But as Boom Boom trotted in, Kiki stared.

On Boom Boom's feet were generic running shoes. *Generic.* Not even cute Pumas.

"What are *those?*" Kiki asked, pointing at the offending footwear.

"Shoes," Boom Boom stammered.

"In what part of the world? Those are *not* shoes. Those are athletic equipment. *These* are shoes!" Kiki said. She threw one still-firm dancer's leg onto her desk, letting her Louis Vuitton pump gleam in the light.

Boom Boom stood silent in front of Kiki. Yet another humiliation and still no back talk. *Come on, girlie,* Kiki thought. *The reporters will eat you alive. If you can't even come up with some clever repartee with me, I'll never be able to set you lose with the press.*

"I had to walk Shasta," Boom Boom said, referring to Kiki's pet teacup poodle, who sat on a silk pillow on the corner of Boom Boom's desk. "I haven't changed back."

"You walked Shasta in those?" Kiki asked, horrified. How embarrassing for the dog. "Change them," Kiki said, a wicked gleam in her eye, "and then walk Shasta again."

"Again?"

"Did I stutter?" Kiki looked up and apprised her assistant from head to toe.

"But—"

Kiki gave Boom Boom a withering gaze, forcing her to be silent. Kiki then looked at her computer screen and clicked through her e-mail in-box. She felt disappointed—she'd yet to hear any news from Sherman.

"But . . ."

Kiki looked up. Boom Boom still stood in her office doorway. Perhaps there had been some spinal cord growth in the girl.

"Yes?" Kiki asked. She peered over the tops of her Louis Vuitton glasses.

"I can't walk Shasta again."

Hmm, was that back talk or an excuse? Either way it was a step in the right direction.

"And why not?"

Boom Boom stepped into Kiki's office, glanced over her shoulder, and pulled the door shut.

"I'm waiting for a messenger," Boom Boom whispered.

"Excuse me?"

"I'm waiting—"

"Boom Boom, I heard you. There are a dozen assistants and three interns in the office; someone else can wait for a package. Go walk the dog."

"No."

"No?"

"Kiki, this is a special package. It's from Sherman."

"What? He called? When?"

"Late last night. He left a voice mail around two A.M. saying to expect something very confidential around eleven. For your eyes only."

Kiki felt her mouth begin to water. Had he found it? Proof?

"When were you going to tell me Sherman called?" Kiki gave Boom Boom the evil eye.

"When the package arrived."

"And since when do you decide which calls are important and which aren't?" Kiki clicked on her computer screen. "I don't see Sherman Ross on my phone sheet."

"No, he didn't need you to return the call—"

"That's not your decision!" Kiki screeched. She watched as Boom Boom wilted before her. "I decide who I'm going to call, not you."

"But—"

"But what?"

"I didn't think you'd want a computer record of Sherman Ross contacting you. The voice mail is bad enough, but the phone sheet automatically backs up onto the hard drive, and I didn't think you'd want that."

Kiki deflated a tiny bit. Boom Boom might be dowdy, but she was also clever. "Still," Kiki said, remaining stiff, "you should have told me." She glanced at her computer screen again. "He said this morning?"

"Before lunch."

Kiki glanced at the clock on her phone: 11:45, and Kiki had a

1:00 P.M. lunch at The Grill with the head of CTA, Tolliver Jones. Kiki had never cared much for Jessica Caulfield-Fox, no matter what Celeste Solange had to say about her, and Kiki shed no tears in seeing Jessica depart from the presidency of CTA. Tolliver truly understood the idea of "you scratch my back and I'll scratch yours." At lunch he'd most likely throw Kiki some nasty little bits about CTA's A-list stars, which Kiki would feed to Page Six or Defamer. For that favor from Tolliver, Kiki would let him know which of her clients (or anyone else's she heard about) was looking for a new agent. And Defamer or Page Six would owe Kiki a favor, repaying her by placing a piece for any of her stars the next time they needed some press. Every move Kiki made fed the publicity machine.

"Do *not* open the package," Kiki said. She looked at Boom Boom, still standing inside the office. "Do you understand?"

Boom Boom looked at the ceiling, no longer cowed and obviously annoyed. "Yes, Kiki."

Kiki heard the familiar beeping noise of two of her office lines.

"Don't stand there," Kiki said.

Boom Boom bustled out of Kiki's office. Kiki put on her wireless headset. The caller ID flashed Steven Brockman, and Kiki sat up straight in her chair. Aside from Celeste Solange, Steven was her biggest client, as well as her most difficult. He was demanding, and of course there was always Steven's little "secret" named Billy, a secret Kiki continuously worked to keep under wraps.

"Brockman on one," Boom Boom called to Kiki. Kiki cleared her throat.

"Celeste Solange on two," Boom Boom called out.

How did this always happen? No calls for fifteen minutes, and then suddenly her two biggest clients phoned within thirty seconds of each other.

"Tell Celeste I'm in a meeting," Kiki said. "I'll have to return." Cici would wait. Now what could Brockman be complaining about this time?

"Steven!" Kiki smiled, knowing that her biggest client shouldn't hear her frown over the phone. "Darling, how are you?"

"Kiki, have you seen the *L.A. Times* today?"

"Darling, no, still working my way through the trades. Up to two hundred million on your film, congratulations, my love. All the studios are slobbering to be in business with you."

"I'm not on it."

"What darling?"

"The new and hot list."

"What?"

"In the *Los Angeles Times* today, I am not on the new and hot list."

Kiki pressed mute on her phone. "Boom Boom," she hissed, "get me the *L.A. Times* new and hot list, NOW!" Releasing the mute button, Kiki forced a smile. "Darling, how can that be? You are very, very hot."

"Exactly why I'm calling you."

Boom Boom rushed toward Kiki with her outstretched hand holding a copy of the list. Kiki grabbed it and scanned it. Everyone on the list was under the age of twenty-five.

"Darling, I'm looking at the list right now, and it's obvious why you're not on it. It's completely beneath you. I mean, come on. Most of these people haven't even *been* in a film, much less starred in one. They're *TV* actors." *And they're all fifteen years younger than you,* Kiki thought.

"Kiki, I'm not getting enough exposure."

"Steven, you just did *Esquire* and *GQ*. *Vanity Fair* wants you for a cover; we're finalizing the logistics right now. Letterman was ten days ago. What else could you want?"

"But the pictures in *GQ*! Awful. Billy hated them. He tried to help at the shoot, but that asshole photographer just wouldn't listen. I ended up looking like someone's dad."

Ah, the real problem had emerged; Steven Brockman felt old.

At forty, a male star like Steven had at least another ten, possibly twenty years of market viability if he picked the right roles and gracefully moved into the older mentor character in the action flick. Women? Unless you were Meryl, Diane, or Susan, your career happened when you were young. Once you started showing age, you might do some television, or a film every three years. Some great indies. But the paydays, the really sexy roles opposite the male stars? Those plum roles dried up at around age thirty-five.

"Who did the shoot?"

"Some British asshole, Nathan something."

"I think that's the same photographer who's working with Worldwide on print ads for Cici on *California Girl*."

"She did that piece-of-shit movie? I read it. They wanted me for the male lead, but it was complete tripe. Billy hated it, too."

Billy, Billy, Billy. The reason Kiki worked so hard for Steven Brockman. Time to change subjects. "How's the baby?"

"Good. She and Kathy left to visit Kathy's mother today. Took the jet. Gone for four weeks. Poor Kathy; her tits won't ever be the same. She'll have to get a mommy makeover if she ever wants to work again."

"Well, she certainly won't have to work," Kiki said, referring to the $40-million agreement Steven had made with Kathy for her to pose as his wife, go through artificial insemination, and carry the baby to term. The contract fixed the faux marriage for ten years. And then? Well, Kathy and Steven could renegotiate, or Kathy could opt out. She'd receive the full $40 million for herself plus a bonus payment for making it to the ten-year mark and alimony on top of that. Of course Steven had created a huge trust fund for his daughter, Sylvan. He was a very doting father.

"And how is Billy?" Kiki loathed Billy, but every publicist, agent, manager, and attorney who worked for a star knew to keep the spouses close, since they were the ones whispering into the celebrity's ear.

"Peeved at the coverage in the *Times* and the pictures in *GQ*. Kiki, did you ever find out about Billy doing the *Vanity Fair* shoot?"

Oh God. The bane of Kiki's existence, Billy fancied himself a photographer instead of the trophy wife he was. A former male model and London club owner turned Hollywood spouse, Billy had started photography as a hobby. He had a book that was okay, but he lacked hustle. He hadn't done any real photography work. And now Billy wanted his first paying job to be shooting Steven Brockman for the cover of *Vanity Fair*?

"You know, they're just not into it," Kiki said. "*Vanity Fair* keeps a list of photographers they like to use, and they go to them over and over." The articles editor laughed hysterically over the phone when Kiki brought up the idea. Letting an unknown photographer shoot Steven Brockman for the cover of *Vanity Fair*? It had to be a joke.

"Then I'm not doing it."

Kiki stopped flipping through the pages of *Variety*. "What?"

"Unless they let Billy shoot the cover, I'm not doing it."

Kiki felt like someone had sucker punched her in the gut. The cover of *Vanity Fair* was a coup no matter how big a star you were, and you did not want to piss off Graydon. Kiki certainly didn't.

"Steven, you can't do that. You're locked in. We're just finalizing details."

"Then tell them if they really want me, they'll take Billy, too."

For fuck's sake! Kiki could deliver the *Vanity Fair* cover if Billy did any real work, but this demand put her in a terrible position.

"Steven, this might get tricky. Billy's book is good, but he doesn't have any paid gigs. I know it's silly, and Billy is nothing if not professional," Kiki threw in, trying not to gag, "but they want to see some print work he's done."

"What about ad work in Japan?"

"That might be okay."

"Great. We leave tonight. I'll send you the spread as soon as we're done."

"We?"

"I'm going, too. In fact, I'm in it."

"What?" Her biggest client doing print work in Asia, and no one had told her?

"Tolliver got us the deal. Good money, and it's Billy's first paying job. Perfect, right?"

"Perfect." At lunch today she would rip Tolliver Jones a new asshole. How could he not tell her details such as these?

"We'll send you the photos in a couple of days. But I'm serious about this, Kiki. I expect you to deliver," Steven said.

"No problem," Kiki said. She shook her head. "Safe travels, darling. Ciao." She pressed release and leaned back in her chair.

She hoped the package from Sherman Ross was good, because so far her morning had been most unpleasant.

Rule 12

Keep Your Mouth Closed

Celeste Solange, Actress

Cici sipped her Chianti in a back booth at Dan Tana's. As a working actress, she spent many evenings here pursuing producers for roles, convincing studio executives to green-light films, and just getting drunk. She and Damien used to eat at Dan Tana's late at night, often after a party they had attended. *Party* was the word that Damien used to describe the multiple-partner sex groups he liked and she went along with. Funny, Celeste thought, but right now, while dealing with the dirty aftermath of her lifestyle during her marriage to Damien, the word *party* didn't exactly seem to fit. Cici felt the butterflies bumping against the inside of her stomach. This meeting with Nathan Curtis was a performance. She felt like she had one shot to persuade Nathan to tell her where he'd seen the DVD.

Cici had called Nathan earlier that day, and he suggested they meet at L'Ermitage, but that location made Cici uncomfortable. L'Ermitage was a great spot for a drink, but that drink was usually a prelude to the use of one of L'Ermitage's four-star hotel rooms. Cici wondered, did Nathan Curtis believe her to be that easy?

Nathan had acted nonchalant on the phone, as if he had expected her call. But why wouldn't he? On the beach he had tantalized her with a bit of information that could destroy her career, her relationship, her entire life. The background information that she, Lydia, and Jessica had found on Mr. Nathan Curtis was helpful but hadn't led them to any conclusions about how or where he might have seen the DVD.

Through a little bit of research, the girls discovered that Nathan grew up in a rough section of London and dropped out of school at sixteen. He began his career as a paparazzo and a "celebrity friend," someone who provided drugs, press, girls, and anything else young actors and soccer players in London might want. In return, Nathan received access and photos. After his infamous shot of a young prince exiting a strip club with a barely clothed tart on his arm hit the tabloids, his name got bigger among photographers. Then, suddenly, Nathan somehow made the transition from paparazzo to fashion photographer. Cici wondered if sordid photos of a fashionista or designer had accelerated that miraculous transition. After some work in London, Nathan accepted multiple jobs in L.A.—gigs for L.A.-based magazines, PR firms, and studios. He took a pay cut from the jobs he was getting in the UK, but Cici guessed the jobs in Los Angeles were a stepping-stone. Nathan Curtis was on the path to somewhere, and Cici wanted to know his desired destination. Lydia guessed directing, but you never knew in this town.

What is he after? Cici wondered. If she pinpointed Nathan's career goals, she'd know what temptations to use. Did he want to design clothes? Direct? Just live in L.A. among stars? Have access to the rich and famous? Cici, Lydia, and Jessica, with their positions and connections, could fulfill all those desires. And would, if Cici could get her hands on the damn DVD.

"Ms. Solange." Nathan stood before her. His accent was surprisingly mild for someone who had grown up on the wrong side of London. He wore a Marc Jacobs shirt and Earnest Sewn jeans; it was too dark to see his shoes, but Cici guessed either Gucci or Dolce.

"Nathan," Cici purred. She leaned forward and let her low-cut shirt flash some breast as she sipped her Chianti and smiled. "Thank you for meeting me here. It's one of my favorites."

"Little old-school for my taste," Nathan said. He flopped down in the booth, and instantly a waiter appeared. "Guinness," Nathan barked.

"So, Nathan. What brings you to L.A.? Other than my shoot, of course?" Cici asked, curling up in the booth.

"Your shoot? I didn't come to L.A. for that. Your shoot was totally last-minute. The photographer the studio originally booked canceled."

Cici took a deep breath and smiled. She wanted to kill him.

The waiter set down his pint. Nathan took a sip and licked the foam from his upper lip, then scooted closer to Cici.

"Is that why you asked me here, Celeste?" he whispered, his lips almost touching her ear. "So I can tell you why I'm in L.A.?"

"Of course. Why else?" Cici tilted her shoulder and looked directly at him. She'd spent her entire career acting the sexpot; she could do it now, too. "Really, if it wasn't to shoot me, then what brought you to Los Angeles?"

"I'm moving to L.A. I want to work in film."

Cici leaned forward. She wanted her body language to convince him that she was hanging on his every word. "What does that mean, though? PR? Marketing? Freelance for magazines?"

"I want to direct," Nathan said. He took another swig of beer.

Score one for Lydia, Cici thought. "Really?" She feigned enthusiasm. "Do you have a project set up?"

"Not yet, but I've got a screenplay I'm trying to get financed."

"I'd love to take a look," Cici said, eyeing him. "Perhaps I could help."

"I'm sure you could." Nathan leaned in and lowered his voice. "Does your sudden interest in my career have anything to do with the footage I watched of you recently?"

Cici felt herself stiffen. "Perhaps we can be helpful to each other. Our desires might be aligned."

"Maybe," Nathan said.

"So where did you say you saw this footage of me?" Cici asked.

A smile danced across Nathan's lips. "Aren't you a clever girl? I didn't say where. But since you've inquired, I'm happy to tell you."

Cici leaned forward. *Really?* Finding out who had the DVD was this easy?

"A friend of mine had a viewing party." Nathan's eyes glanced at Cici's breasts. "It would seem from the footage that you might be familiar with such parties."

Cici felt sick. People were viewing her fucking? At parties? She forced herself to bury her feelings of anger. She needed to convey the correct emotions to Nathan. There were multiple ways to play this scene. She decided on vulnerability. Men were usually terrified of a crying woman. Celeste forced tears into her eyes and turned to Nathan. "Oh Nathan, what am I going to do?" She dropped her head into her hands and sniffled.

Nathan placed his arm around her shoulder. "Cici, please don't cry."

Celeste felt power surge through her. She was an excellent actress. She added more tears and a sniffle to her performance.

"You'll introduce me to your friend?" Cici asked, looking up.

"Well, I'm not sure, but I'll definitely ask." Nathan set his hand on Cici's thigh.

Cici felt her stomach lurch. "Nathan, how can I thank you?"

"Well, I can certainly think of one way."

"You've got your director's reel?"

"In the car. And a copy of that script."

Rule 13

You Need a Star to Make a Movie

Lydia Albright, President of Production, Worldwide Pictures

Lydia scanned the calendar on her computer screen. She had a staff meeting in an hour and a meeting with Briggs Montgomery in twenty minutes. She bent over to grab her Versace bag and pulled out *Vitriol,* Nathan Curtis's script. She'd read it the night before.

This film would normally cost the studio a minimum of $60 million to make, plus another $30 million in prints and advertising. But if Lydia cast *Vitriol* right, Worldwide would make back its money. Of course, Lydia didn't care about the profit margins on this film. What concerned Lydia was the $250 million worth of Celeste Solange films that Worldwide wanted to release over the next eighteen months. If Cici's sex tape went public, Worldwide's investment would be worth nothing.

Lydia clicked her mouse over the soundstage calendars. Worldwide's shooting schedule was booked, every soundstage on the lot full. But Lydia would make room.

"Toddy," Lydia yelled from her desk.

"Yes, Lydia," Toddy said, entering Lydia's office.

Lydia held up a copy of *Vitriol,* the script Nathan Curtis wanted to direct. "Did you read this?"

"Last night," Toddy said.

"And?"

"And I think it's an uninspired, by-the-numbers thriller," Toddy said.

"You're brilliant," Lydia said, "because that's exactly what I think, too. Do you know the writer? This Roland Rumphy?"

"Never heard of him. I tried to look up his credits on IMDB and Studio System, but they don't have him listed. He's either new or someone writing under a pseudonym."

"Well, Mr. Rumphy needs to be rewritten," Lydia said.

"Who should we get?" Toddy asked.

"The rewrite needs to be fast, and the script has to be tight. Plus this writer will deal with the dick of a director—"

"Nathan Curtis?"

"Yeah, you've heard of him?"

"I'm on your calls."

"Right. So who do you think?"

"Let's see, great writer who can deal with big egos? Hmm, who do we know with those qualifications?" Toddy asked, returning to her desk.

"Get me Jessica, then Mary Anne, then Sean Ellis," Lydia called to Toddy.

"Sean will be pissed. You bump his writer and he'll have to wait at least six months to make *Sexual Being,*" Toddy said.

"I'm not just taking Sean's writer," Lydia said, putting on her headset. Both Lydia and Toddy were now on the phone line as Toddy dialed. "I'm also taking his star."

"Holden?"

"Yep."

"Lydia, Sean is going to flip. He's already in Brazil doing preproduction."

"Yeah, but if he doesn't whine too much and waits on *Sexual Being,* I'll make his next film, too," Lydia said.

"What's his next film?" Toddy asked.

"Who knows," Lydia said. "And who cares, as long as we get Nathan Curtis's film made. Have number two make twelve copies of the script. Start messengering them. I need copies to go to Mike Fox, Mary Anne Meyers, Celeste Solange, and Holden Humphrey."

"What about the older male lead?"

"I have an idea, but I need to work on it," Lydia said. She clicked through her e-mails as Jessica's line rang.

"Jessica Caulfield-Fox's office," Jessica's assistant answered.

"I've got Lydia Albright for Jessica," Toddy said.

"One moment please."

"Toddy, you think Celeste should play the female role?" Lydia asked while they waited on the line for Jessica.

"I thought that was a given."

"I have Jessica for you," Jessica's assistant chirped. "Jessica, you're on with Lydia."

"Morning, Lydia," Jessica said.

Lydia could hear Max singing in the background. "How is Maxie?"

"Happy, and on his way to preschool."

"Did you get it?" Lydia asked. She had sent over a copy of *Vitriol* late the night before.

"*Vitriol?* Yeah. Wasn't so great."

"I need you to produce it," Lydia said.

"How did I know you were going to tell me that?"

"Because you've lost your plausible deniability and are now my partner in crime," Lydia said. "Besides, what other producer can I trust with this?"

"Do you know the writer?" Jessica asked.

"Never heard of him," Lydia said. "Guess that explains the script. I want Mary Anne to do the rewrite."

"She's working on Sean Ellis's film right now," Jessica said.

"I'm pulling her," Lydia said.

"Not like we have much choice. What do you think the budget is?"

"Maybe forty? Without P and A," Lydia said.

"Really? I was thinking more like sixty," Jessica said.

"I'm not counting Celeste's twenty-million-dollar fee. She's offered to cut her quote," Lydia said.

"Got it. So yeah, forty," Jessica said. "Who do you want for the male lead?"

"I'm thinking Holden," Lydia said.

"Go ahead and just ruin Sean's life, Lydia."

"I'm still going to do *Sexual Being;* Sean just has to wait a couple of months," Lydia said.

"So Celeste for the female lead. What about the older male role?"

"I want Steven," Lydia said.

"Brockman? You won't get him. He refuses to play any character over thirty-five," Jessica said.

"So far. But I'm going to try," Lydia said. "It's the only way Worldwide will make its money back on this bomb."

* * *

Lydia wanted to tell Briggs Montgomery about Cici's sex tape. But Briggs worked for Worldwide, and although it was semi-acceptable for Lydia, as Cici's best friend, to lie to Ted Robinoff, it was quite another for Briggs Montgomery, head of studio security, to withhold important information from his boss. Lydia knew there was no way he'd keep the secret, and it would kill Cici for Ted to find out now.

"No more letters?" Briggs asked.

"Just the one in Malibu," Lydia said.

"And that was the only phone call?"

"So far. Any ideas about who the wacko is?" Lydia asked.

"We went through the list of names Jennifer's people gave us. Interviewed the catering staff from her party, too. So far, nothing. Has anything else happened?"

Lydia paused. "No, why? Is there something I should know about?" she asked, attempting to flip the attention to Briggs and his investigation.

"Just curious. How's Jay working out?"

"Great. I mean, I hardly notice him."

"He's excellent at his job. He mentioned you've been spending a lot of time with Celeste."

Lydia sensed that Briggs was tap-dancing around a question. Lydia often forgot Jay was around, and of course he saw everyone she met with. She needed to be more cautious about how often she met with Cici and Jessica.

"Ted is in Asia and—"

"Lydia, I'm not your dad. And you don't have to tell me that Ted's been away. Technically, I'm in charge of security for Ted and Celeste's home, too."

"Technically?"

"Ted didn't want much surveillance. He has a home security system, and that was all he wanted. He didn't have a security detail assigned to the house." Briggs stood. "Well, I've got a meeting and I know you have one, too."

"Right," Lydia said. She wondered if Ted had his and Cici's house bugged.

"So I hear you've got a new script going into production?" Briggs said, walking toward the door.

"*Vitriol.* A sexual thriller," Lydia said.

"New director?"

"From London."

"Celeste starring?"

"With Holden Humphrey."

"That's quite a cast. You'll get me all the director's info once the deal closes," Briggs said.

"You might have it, or the marketing department does. He did photography for *California Girl.*"

"That guy's directing now?" Briggs asked.

"You know him?"

"Mr. Robinoff mentioned that Celeste disliked him."

"And you remember that?" Lydia asked.

"Lydia, I get paid a lot of money to remember everything. Details are the key to my business. I'm surprised Celeste agreed to work with him."

Life would be so much easier if Lydia could tell Briggs about the

DVD and enlist the studio security team's help. Lydia felt a tiny knot of anger form in her chest. Trying to keep a secret like this was foolish.

"Cici likes the script, and I like the script. There isn't any way around working with Nathan; he controls the material and he wants to direct," Lydia said.

"And the writer?"

"Uninvolved and soon to be rewritten. Business Affairs is checking, but it seems Nathan purchased the script outright."

"You'll keep me informed? Mr. Robinoff wants us to pay close attention to Celeste and her security right now."

"Any reason why?"

"Well, the letters that you received for one."

"So Ted knows?"

"Lydia, I report directly to Ted."

"And what else?" Lydia asked.

"What else?"

"You said that there was something that Ted is concerned about."

"I'm not the only one who keeps track of details," Briggs said. "Well, he hasn't been specific yet. I'm sure I'll get more information when he returns from Asia. We've increased surveillance of their home."

"And Cici knows?"

"Lydia, that's between Mr. Robinoff and Ms. Solange. I just do what the man asks."

"Don't we all," Lydia said.

"I'll come by again when I've got more information."

Lydia watched Briggs exit her office. She inhaled and shut her eyes. She tried to force away the feeling of dread that had settled around her. *Increased security? Increased surveillance?* Both could mean that there were cameras in Cici's house, or that Worldwide security had tapped Cici's phones. Lydia rubbed her forehead. The only way to save Cici's relationship and Lydia's job would be if Cici told Ted about her sex tape.

* * *

Wooing a star required fortitude. And wooing a star as temperamental as Steven Brockman demanded fortitude, patience, and a private jet. Lydia rested her head against the leather headrest in Worldwide's Citation jet. She was flying all the way to Tokyo just to get a meeting with Steven Brockman. She'd land, meet him for dinner, and then return to L.A. It was an insane turnaround. But she wanted Steven, needed him to star in *Vitriol,* and she realized that to persuade Steven to accept the part she must fly to Tokyo, to stroke Steven's ego. Let him know that, yes, only Steven Brockman could successfully play this role.

Lydia felt the impossibility of winning this battle. So far she had an average script, a new director, and an older actor in denial about his age. She was prepared to meet Steven's full quote and even give him a tiny bump. Financially, *Vitriol* would be a good gig for him. Besides, after Lydia had helped Kiki handle the debacle on Steven's last Worldwide film, he owed Lydia. The whole affair became unpleasant. Lydia never asked from whom or how Briggs Montgomery secured photos of Steven's blackmailer with an underage boy. But the photos had forced the guy to keep quiet. Life would be so much easier if Cici allowed Lydia to enlist Briggs's help. This—keeping messy situations away from the public—was part of his job. But Lydia had promised Cici, and she'd keep to their agreement as long as things didn't become dangerous.

Her head bounced as the Citation's tires hit the runway.

"Welcome to Tokyo," the flight attendant said.

* * *

Everything in Tokyo was expensive, but the Imperial Hotel Tokyo was off the charts, even by Lydia's standards. Huge fees and outrageous perks were standard procedure for Japanese corporations, which paid exorbitant amounts for American A-list celebrities to do print work and commercials. Though it was almost unheard of in the States unless an A-lister's career was in trouble, it was fairly common for stars to jet to Japan, get treated like royalty, and make a couple extra million doing a commercial and some photos.

Steven had reserved a private dining room at Les Saisons, the five-star restaurant at the Imperial Hotel Tokyo. Lydia followed behind the host as he swept her into a large room with an intimate table . . . *for three? Of course,* Lydia thought, *Steven wouldn't make such an important decision without Billy.* Steven's constant companion for the last seven years, Billy was consulted on every decision the megastar made.

While she waited, Lydia appraised the handwritten menu lying on her plate. Steven had preselected their courses, their wine, and even their dessert. Lydia calculated the bill Worldwide would receive next week for this extravagant meal and sighed. Another part of the price the studio paid to woo stars.

"Lydia, you look lovely," she heard Steven say before she saw him. His entrance was grand: He was barefoot and wrapped in a white Versace suit.

Billy leaned forward and gave Lydia a quick peck on the cheek. Ten years Steven's junior, Billy was an exotic-looking man with black hair and dark eyes. He was stunning in a Rudolph Valentino sort of way. He always seemed to look through people. Billy quickly went to the heart of every matter and said exactly what he thought. Prior to his involvement with Billy, Steven often danced around issues, never letting anyone know exactly what he wanted. Although their life together was a secret from the world, ironically, Billy gave Steven the ability to tell people the truth.

"I went ahead and preselected our meal," Steven said. He placed his napkin into his lap. "Hope you don't mind. And Billy chose the wine."

Lydia glanced at Billy, who lit a cigarette. "It all looks fabulous," she said. An army of waiters appeared, set down plates, and poured wine.

"What time do you need to leave?" Steven asked.

"Whenever you're ready for me to go," Lydia said, giving Steven her best president of production smile.

She noticed Steven give Billy a quick look across the table.

"Good answer," Billy said in his smoker's voice. Everyone smiled.

"So, I read the script," Steven said.

Right to business, Lydia thought. At most of her dinners, business talk was reserved for dessert and coffee.

"And Billy read the script, too—"

"And we both think *Vitriol* is really ho-hum," Billy said, finishing Steven's sentence. "What's the rush on this one, Lydia? I mean, really, why are you pushing so hard?"

"I feel it in my gut," Lydia lied. "The public wants to see Steven and Cici together again."

"You're the second person to tell me that this week," Steven said, taking a bite of his ahi.

"Lydia, for Steven to start playing the older man is a big jump. Once he goes older, it's impossible for him to return to younger roles."

"Perhaps. But he'd be doing this for all the right reasons. A great part, a stellar cast, and he gets the girl. At the very least he can use the actors he's working with as an excuse as to why he agreed to play the more mature role. And personally, I think the more mature male lead is a much more interesting character than Holden's. Wouldn't you agree?" Lydia asked. She was talking to Billy. If she wanted Steven, she realized, she needed to convince Billy.

Billy nodded his head almost imperceptibly. "I agree."

"The best thing is that even though it's a more mature role, Steven's character is still a virile, sexual man. And isn't that the fundamental component to longevity in this business? Aging while remaining sexy to the audience?"

Billy cracked a smile and glanced at Steven. "Oh, he's always sexy."

"But what about this director, Lydia? I worked with him on a photo shoot, and he's a real dick," Steven said. "Made me look like my father. We hated those photos."

Billy frowned a little but didn't disagree.

"I'll admit he's a little cocky," Lydia said, lying again. She'd yet to meet Nathan, but his terrible attitude was already something she was hearing about from everyone. "But he owns the script, and his reel is good."

"So, Worldwide is just giving away features to first-time directors? I have a script, Lydia. Want to make it your next film?" Billy asked, sarcasm dripping from his voice.

Lydia felt the pressure to give them the hard sell. "Listen, I follow my gut, always have. And so far I've managed to earn over three billion in box-office ticket sales. My gut tells me Worldwide needs this film. But to make it complete, to make *Vitriol* the film that I want it to be, I need you," Lydia said and looked at Steven. "It's the only way I can make this film. Steven, the only person who can play this role is you. No one else has the gravitas necessary for this character. *You* can make him real. You and your talent will allow the audience to see beyond the limitations of the director. Your character is the linchpin on which the whole piece rests, and that's why it can only be you." She rested her hand on Steven's arm.

She was laying the compliments on thick. Too thick? No. From the look on Steven's face, he was devouring her praise.

Steven sighed. "Well, what do you think?" He looked at Billy.

"She's good," Billy said. He stubbed out his cigarette and finally took a bite of his food. "Really good." He paused. "Well, why not, if we can make a deal," he said.

"Oh, we'll make a deal," Lydia said.

"Maybe. But Lydia, there are a few extra demands," Steven said and winked at Billy.

* * *

Lydia rode in the back of the Town Car. She felt exhausted and unsure what day it was. Toddy said Friday, but Lydia's body vacillated between Wednesday morning and Saturday evening. Jay sat in the front seat with her driver.

She'd landed two hours before, and now was on her way to meet Nathan Curtis, the infamous prick and the person who, Cici and

Jessica speculated, had written Lydia's letters. Lydia wasn't convinced that Nathan was the author. The letters, to Lydia, seemed too personal to be about only Cici and her films.

The Worldwide guard waved them through. "Ms. Albright," her driver asked, "the bungalow or the office?"

"The bungalow first," Lydia said.

A sense of longing filled Lydia as the car pulled into her spot in front of her production offices. Unlike her fancy office filled with glass and chrome in the executive tower, Lydia's bungalow on Worldwide's lot was small and quaint. It had just enough room for three offices, a small kitchen, a bathroom, and a conference room. Christina, Zymar's daughter and a VP at Lydia's production company, was already there, and Mary Anne's Mercedes was in the lot, too. Jessica was right behind Lydia's car and waved as she pulled her Range Rover in beside them. Parked in the guest spot was a Lamborghini convertible. *Could that be Nathan's car?* Lydia wondered.

Jay climbed from the front seat as Lydia stepped out from the back. "Lydia, I'm going to be outside the conference room," he said. "You know we've got a couple of mics and a camera in there?"

Lydia did know but had forgotten. Briggs had told her they were going to wire her bungalow and her office at Worldwide. As a precaution, he said, so if her mystery caller telephoned on a hard line they might get the voice. Briggs wanted to wire her house, too, but Lydia had absolutely refused. Her home was still her private domain.

Lydia stood at the bungalow door waiting for Jessica.

"You look like you partied all night," Jessica said.

"Los Angeles to Tokyo, dinner with Steven, then Tokyo to L.A. in seventy-two hours. A real all-nighter."

"Commercial?"

"No. Can you imagine?"

"Today is Friday," Jessica said, following Lydia into the bungalow.

"Thanks, Toddy told me."

Jessica leaned in and whispered into Lydia's ear. "I see you still have the bruiser following you."

"It's a status thing, purely for show," Lydia said, trying to joke.

"Everywhere?"

"Except the shower."

Jessica appraised Jay from head to toe. "Not sure, but I think that is where I'd like him most."

"Zymar said no."

Lydia crossed through reception and opened her bungalow office door. Here, among the cranberry reds and deep browns, the overstuffed couches and bookcases full of scripts, was where Lydia felt most comfortable.

"Where's Zymar?" Jessica asked.

"He's on his way in right now. I offered to give him a ride, but he wanted his Harley. How's post on *Collusion*?"

"Good. I'll go by after this. We'll have a rough cut in six weeks," Jessica said.

"With Zymar that means two. He overestimates post; a little director's trick of his so he can wow everyone." Lydia tossed her Bottega bag on the chair inside her office door. She glanced longingly at her overstuffed couch. She wanted to lie down and close her eyes, but instead she pulled the office door closed behind her. She and Jessica walked toward the conference room.

"What did Billy decide?" Jessica asked. Everyone in town knew that Billy made all the decisions for Steven.

"They said yes. But it's an expensive yes," Lydia said, thinking of Billy and Steven's list of demands.

"Does it come from the budget?"

"He wants Viève Dyson to play the female lead," Lydia said.

Jessica stopped walking. "I don't think Viève as the lead is a good idea."

Lydia paused, too. "I know she's crazy. I know you just finished *Collusion* with her, and she was nothing but problems. But it's the only person Steven will approve for the role. He made that very clear."

"She's *stalking* Holden," Jessica said.

"Stalking as in showing up unannounced? Or stalking as in only-I-can-have-you?" Lydia had little patience for crazy. But the only way *Vitriol* would get made was with Viève in the lead role, so she needed the nasty little elf to hold her sanity together for twelve weeks.

"She's hiding in his bushes and breaking into his house. It's only a matter of time before she figures out Holden is sleeping with Mary Anne."

Lydia shook her head. *Vitriol* was getting messier and messier. She glanced into the conference room. She was dreading production on this film. Too much emotional baggage with Holden, Viève, and Mary Anne on set together, combined with the intrigue of Nathan Curtis and Celeste's DVD. The entire scenario made her hugely uncomfortable. Lydia felt her chest tighten. But she'd called Tolliver Jones, head of CTA and Steven Brockman's agent, on her return flight from Tokyo, and made the offer. She was in too deep to pull out now. Plus there was the DVD—they had to find out more information from Nathan.

"If Celeste would just tell Ted," Lydia muttered.

"So, wait," Jessica said. "Cici was going to play the female lead. Now Cici plays Viève's mother?"

"Right. Viève's mother, the character who's an alcoholic and hasn't aged well. Can't wait to tell Cici," Lydia said.

"And Nathan?"

"Billy approved him as director, although Steven seemed to really hate him. I haven't met him," Lydia said and glanced into the conference room. "But I've heard about him."

"It's all true," Jessica said. "Mike and I had dinner with him."

"Did you tell Mike?" Lydia asked.

"About the letters? Yes. The DVD? No. Should I?"

"Not yet," Lydia said.

"You know Mike may have some contacts in that world from his bachelor days," Jessica said.

"The world of high-end sex-tape parties?" Lydia whispered.

"I hate to say it, but yes. Mike was quite the slut," Jessica said.

"Let's wait. See what Howard can find out from Sherman before we tell anyone else," Lydia said. "Who knows, Mike might already know. Everyone could know."

They looked at each other. "So we've got a film," Jessica said.

"Yes, we do." Lydia sighed. "Now, if we can just get Nathan to give us more information," she said.

Rule 14

There Is No Such Thing As Bad Press

Mary Anne Meyers, Screenwriter

Mary Anne huddled under a heat lamp on the patio at the Chateau Marmont. Crazy—she'd spent her childhood braced against the frigid winters in St. Paul, Minnesota, and now she shivered in the slight chill on a patio in Los Angeles. She glanced at her watch, willing Cici to arrive. Mary Anne disliked the lackadaisical attitude people had toward time in Los Angeles. Perhaps it was her Midwestern upbringing, but she felt that arriving late disrespected the person you were meeting. And although Mary Anne realized Cici meant no harm, her tardy arrival still was annoying.

Cici must have called the Chateau, because the hostess seated Mary Anne at the best table on the patio. Going places with Cici guaranteed getting the best: the best restaurants, the best clothes, the best service, the best shoes, the best of everything.

Mary Anne wondered why Cici wanted them to meet. Perhaps she'd discovered Mary Anne's relationship with Holden. Mary Anne guessed yes but hoped for no. She wasn't sure why, but she just wasn't ready to talk about Holden yet. She still felt unsure how to define her affair with him. They spent most nights together, and some afternoons, but other than sex, they'd yet to really do anything as a couple.

"Mary Anne!" Cici called.

Mary Anne's eyes popped as she watched Cici walk across the patio in a tiny dress and super-high heels. Cici could pull off any outfit. Her dress appeared to be the same size as the pocket handkerchiefs Mary Anne remembered her father carrying.

"Darling, how are you?" Cici gushed.

Public encounters with Cici were sometimes a bit of a shock. Such encounters were remarkably different from meeting Cici in private. When they became friends, Mary Anne quickly realized that Cici had a public face, a persona she wore. The persona became so embedded in Cici's personality that Mary Anne guessed that Cici didn't even feel the transition from private to public personality anymore. But Mary Anne felt the shift. She believed that the persona Cici showed to the world was one Cici believed the world wanted. Cici internalized the world's definition of a sexpot superstar and made it real. The mask rarely slipped.

Cici plopped down beside Mary Anne, and immediately a server appeared with a drink for her.

"Thank you," Cici said. She took a quick sip and scoped out the patio. "So, what's this I hear about you and Holden?" she asked.

Mary Anne felt her stomach drop. Had Jessica told Cici?

"What did you hear?" Mary Anne asked, trying to play coy. Mary Anne knew she didn't bluff well. If Cici pressed her, she'd cave.

Cici leaned forward. "I hear that you two are fucking like rabbits all over town."

Mary Anne felt her face flush red.

"So it's true!" Cici cried.

"How did—" Mary Anne felt tears well up in her eyes. How did people know about her private life? She and Holden had been to three hotels, but they used aliases and never arrived or left together.

"Oh, no, no, no, darling, please don't cry. I guessed. Plus I am plugged in," Cici said.

Plugged in? What did that mean? Mary Anne wondered. Her face must have registered her confusion.

"Well, I did keep a suite at the Four Seasons for a number of years. And Shutters was one of my weekend faves."

"People are talking about my sex life?" Mary Anne whispered.

"Darling, it's not *your* sex life they're talking about, it's Holden's. You just happen to be a participant. After all, he is *People* magazine's Sexiest Man Alive. I hear that the price for the first picture of you two together just hit one hundred thousand dollars," Celeste said.

"What? Who would pay a hundred thousand dollars for a picture of me?"

"Again, darling, not *you*. You with *Holden*. Okay, if you're going to date a celebrity, you must learn the rules. You see where we're sitting?"

"Yes," Mary Anne said, glancing around the patio.

"Why did you get this table?"

"Because I'm meeting you?" Mary Anne said.

"No," Cici said.

"No?"

"I didn't call the Chateau today. You, my darling little Midwesterner, got this table because of *you*. Well, because of you and Holden."

Mary Anne leaned back in her chair, breathless. "But I'm not a star."

"Your new boyfriend is," Cici said. "One of the biggest. And in this business, dating Holden makes you valuable. Not only can you write the script, but now you can persuade one of the biggest male stars in the world to be in the movie."

"But I wouldn't do that," Mary Anne said.

"I know that, you know that, but all these people sitting around looking at us—they don't know that," Cici said.

Mary Anne loved the anonymity of writing. She could go anywhere and never be recognized—it was her favorite thing about living in L.A. And now, as she glanced around the patio, she felt that anonymity slipping away from her. She wondered who else sitting on the Chateau's patio knew she was dating Holden. It was funny—

she hadn't noticed her sense of privacy before, but now that it was gone she really felt naked in its absence.

Mary Anne leaned forward. "How do you do this?" she whispered.

"You get used to it. You learn to live with the idea that everyone thinks they know all about you, your life, your business."

No wonder so many celebrities became obsessive about their privacy. It was the one thing they couldn't buy with their riches.

"I don't like it," Mary Anne said. "I feel like I'm being watched." She crossed her arms over her chest.

"You are officially on the radar, darling," Cici said and took a sip of her drink. "Get ready for the attacks."

* * *

Mary Anne never drew attention to herself. At least not intentionally. Growing up in St. Paul, she had faded into her family's background. The older sister to a set of twins, Michael and Michelle, she quickly realized the impossibility of competing for attention with an adorable pair of children. She became the extra child in family portraits and Christmas photos—there were the twins, and then that other girl. Awkward. So instead of competing, Mary Anne became invisible. She savored her invisibility and buried herself in books. Nothing was exceptional about her at all, until the sixth grade, when Mrs. Edgar assigned the class to write a free-verse poem. And Mary Anne did.

The St. Paul newspaper and the local TV news all wanted to interview the little girl who had won Minnesota's state contest for poetry. Her grade school organized an assembly for her to read her award-winning poem. As she walked onto the stage, Mary Anne's hands felt clammy. She'd practiced reading her poem to her mother, Mitsy, for weeks, before and after school. She looked at the sea of squirming children sitting cross-legged on the gymnasium floor and at the news cameras in the back. She glanced down at the yellow notebook paper in her hand and up again at the full gymnasium.

She felt hot. A drop of sweat trickled down the side of her face, and the crinoline of her new dress scratched the backs of her thighs.

She took a deep breath and began to read.

The weeks and months of the school year had passed, bleeding into summer. Mary Anne's anonymity returned, or so she thought. Released from the confines of the classroom, she spent the humid days of summer, like most St. Paul children, at the pool. One July day, she walked toward the twins, already standing in line at the snack shack to buy sodas, and slipped in quietly beside her brother and sister, placing a dollar from their mother into each of their hands.

"She thinks she's so special."

Mary Anne heard the voice but didn't realize that the three taller girls standing behind her were speaking about her.

"Just because she won a stupid prize?"

"And was on television."

Finally Mary Anne realized whom they were discussing, and she felt sick. The line to the snack shack stretched around the pool.

"What a dork."

Mary Anne hung her head.

"Hey, dork, I'm talking to you."

She felt the rough nudge of a bony elbow in her back. *Ignore them.* Mitsy always said not to respond to impolite behavior.

"Guess she can't hear."

"Except for the voices in her head."

"What a freak."

Mary Anne felt the sting of tears in her eyes. She hadn't asked for the award. She hadn't wanted an assembly. She'd only done what her teacher required. She'd completed an assignment.

By the time they reached the front, she thought the three girls in line behind her had forgotten her presence. Mary Anne stepped up to the window and placed orders for herself and the twins. But as the boy in the snack shack window handed her the sodas and change, she felt a quick tug on her swimsuit top. The string pulled loose just as Mary Anne turned away from the window, and because her hands were full with two sodas and a candy bar, she couldn't keep her suit top from dropping to her waist. She faced the line of children in silence for a split second. Then snickers turned to howls of laughter as they noticed her nakedness. Michael and Michelle were already bounding toward their mom on the far side of the pool, and Mary Anne stood alone, frozen in front of her classmates, hands full, swimsuit fallen, and she cried.

Mary Anne remembered feeling embarrassed. Her adult self would also say violated, feelings that now, standing in the gas station and gazing at the cover of the latest *Star* magazine, she felt again.

The photographer had shot the picture from a distance, with a telephoto lens. In it Mary Anne sat on a reclined Holden, her swimsuit top hanging at her waist, after he'd pulled the string. His hands grasped her breasts. Her breasts and Holden's hands were blocked by the angle of Mary Anne's body, but it was obvious where his hands were. The headline—WHO IS HOLDEN HUMPHREY HOLDING NOW?—embarrassed her. Mary Anne flipped the magazine open to the middle section. Solo pictures of Holden and Mary Anne sat side by side. The photo on the cover, Mary Anne guessed, was the first photo any paparazzo had secured of her and Holden together. Mary Anne quickly purchased the magazine, hoping that the guy handing her change didn't know that behind her sunglasses, she was the girl on the cover.

* * *

"Mary Anne, stop crying," Cici said.

"I can't stop crying. Did you see it?" Mary Anne asked, pacing her office.

"Sweetie, there's nothing to see."

"My parents are going to freak out. My family will be humiliated. I can't believe this. How did they get this picture?"

"We talked about this. There are photographers following you."

Mary Anne peered out her office window toward her pool and the sandy cliff behind her fence. She pulled the string and let the shades drop. She loved the sunlight, but now? How could she ever write with her shades open again?

"Where was it taken?" Cici asked.

"San Ysidro Ranch in Santa Barbara," Mary Anne said, peering around the shades. "How did they know? We took separate cars, we checked in at different times, had rooms on different floors, used different names."

"Darling, these guys are pros. They spend more money bribing waiters and hotel housekeeping than I do on shoes."

Mary Anne sighed.

"Has your mother called yet?" Cici asked.

"No. She's on a book tour." Mary Anne was bracing herself for Mitsy's call. Her mother's latest children's book had been released in time for the holiday rush, and Mitsy had three more cities in her fourteen-city tour before she returned to Los Angeles. And when she did . . . Mary Anne didn't even want to think about what she'd say.

"And Holden?" Cici asked.

"Working out? I don't know. He didn't stay here last night, and he isn't answering his cell."

"Well, it won't be a shock to him. I'm sure he's used to this by now. Besides, no press is bad press when you're a star."

"But I'm not a star," Mary Anne whined, flopping into her office chair.

"You are now," Cici said.

* * *

Sweat dripped down Holden's chest and back. His post-exercise high kicked into overdrive, and he felt strong. He stripped his wet T-shirt over his head and glanced into the windows on his back patio. The push-ups that Liam, his trainer, had assigned him were really improving his pecs and upper arms.

"Looking good, bro," Liam said. "Same time tomorrow?" He grabbed his duffel bag.

"Sounds good." Holden gave Liam his manshake at the front door. He bounded up the stairs feeling powerful. A hot shower would keep his muscles loose. He glanced at his watch. He needed to hurry; Mary Anne wanted to cook lunch, and Mary Anne, Holden had discovered, became cranky when she didn't eat.

At the top of the stairs he dropped his shorts and grabbed them with the same hand that held his sweaty T-shirt. As he rounded the corner into his bedroom he faced the dirty clothes hamper and did a jump shot. Both the shorts and shirt landed inside the basket.

"Nice form, baby."

Holden stopped and looked toward the bed. Why was she still here? He walked into the bathroom and turned on the shower. She had crawled into his bed late the night before, it must have been after three A.M. He hadn't known she was there until he woke up to go work out with Liam.

"Baby, come here," Viève whined.

Holden looked into the mirror. He felt himself grow hard. The thought of sex, any sex, turned him on. He looked in the mirror. What did he want? Did he want a relationship with Mary Anne? Or did he want Viève? He decided he wanted the sex now and Mary Anne later.

"Please, baby, just for a minute?" Viève called.

Holden walked out of the bathroom. "Viève you've got . . ." He paused. She had positioned herself on all fours, her ass pointed toward him. She reached her hand between her legs and touched herself as she swayed back and forth, her perfect bare ass putting him in a trancelike state.

"I'm wet for you, baby," she whispered.

Holden wanted to walk away from her. He wanted to walk to the shower. He wanted to be on time to meet Mary Anne.

"Just slide it in for me, please, baby," her voice purred.

Sex with Viève would be so easy. Mary Anne would never know. He watched Viève's ass. But *he'd* know. Yes, physically he wanted Viève, but mentally the idea of fucking the twisted creature on his bed actually repulsed him. He couldn't. Not now, not ever.

"Viève, you've got to go," Holden said.

He pulled shut and locked the bathroom door.

Rule 15

You Can't Fix Crazy

Jessica Caulfield-Fox, Manager-Producer

Jessica looked around the meditation room and glanced at the cross-legged inhabitants. She hoped she wasn't disturbing them. Softly, she stepped around the meditators. The little redheaded gnome sat at the front of the room. Jessica bent forward and rested her fingers lightly on Viève's shoulders.

"Viève, I need you," Jessica whispered.

Viève's eyes fluttered open and her pupils slowly focused on Jessica as Viève came out of her meditative trance. "What are you doing here?" she asked.

"I've left six messages for you. I've called your agent, your manager, and your publicist," Jessica hissed.

"I know."

"You missed your ADR session for *Collusion,*" Jessica said.

"I know."

Jessica waited for Viève to provide an excuse for her no-show, but when the sprite closed her eyes to continue meditating, Jessica quickly realized that no such explanation was forthcoming.

"Was there a reason you didn't show up?" Jessica asked, trying to contain the annoyance in her voice. She needed Viève. That thought made her cringe.

"I'm upset, Jessica."

"Upset?"

"I am very disappointed with you," Viève said. Her eyes remained closed; nothing moved except her lips.

"I see, and this disappointment is because of . . ."

"Holden," Viève said.

Jessica looked around the room. She felt self-conscious. She was the only person in street clothes as she hovered over Viève, and they were causing a disruption. "Viève, I don't know what you're talking about. Your love life has nothing to do with my ADR session," Jessica whispered.

"Oh, but it does," Viève said. "And so does *Vitriol*."

Jessica's stomach flipped. *Vitriol?* How did this little troll find out about *Vitriol*?

As if reading Jessica's mind, Viève's eyes snapped open. "You're here, aren't you? And it's not because of my ADR session, now, is it?"

It's time to turn on the charm, Jessica thought. "Perhaps we can discuss this at the juice bar?"

"Perhaps," Viève said. "Once I'm finished with my session."

"And when will that be?" Jessica asked.

"About an hour," Viève said.

Jessica felt fear give way to frustration, but she forced a smile onto her face. Jessica had no choice—she needed to wait for Viève. Steven Brockman had given Lydia explicit instructions, though Jessica suspected that, once again, the instructions were really coming from Billy: Steven would star in *Vitriol* only with one actress in the female lead: Viève Dyson. If Viève said no, then Steven would fall out, and if Steven fell off the film, Lydia would have to start at the beginning of the attachment process with another A-list actor. And attaching another star could take days, weeks, months, or years, depending on the actor's schedule and appetite for the material. While Lydia tried to secure another star, Nathan would be loose in the world, unmonitored, perhaps dealing in illicit Celeste Solange DVDs, instead of on set, where he could be watched and hopefully cajoled into revealing information about Cici's sex tape.

"Great," Jessica said. "I'll wait for you out front."

* * *

Jessica had rolled calls through her first fruit juice and now was into her second, and there was still no sign of Viève. She took another sip of her freshly squeezed guava-mint-lemon-mango juice.

"Get me Tyler Bruger at CTA," she said to her assistant over the phone. She waited as Emily dialed.

"Jessica," Emily said, "you're on with Tyler."

"Tyler?"

"Jessica, so glad you called. I just got a copy of *Vitriol,*" Tyler said.

"What? From whom?" Jessica asked. Neither Viève nor Tyler was supposed to know that Steven Brockman wanted Viève for the role. If Tyler knew that Steven's doing the film was contingent on Viève's taking the role, he would strong-arm Worldwide on Viève's deal.

"Nathan Curtis sent it over," Tyler said. "The director."

"Tyler, I know who Nathan Curtis is. I'm producing the film."

"I hear Brockman won't do it unless Viève costars," Tyler said.

"What are you talking about?" Jessica asked, trying to bluff.

"Come on, Jessica. You and I both know that Billy has a big mouth and he and Tolliver are best friends."

Damn Billy! Lydia would flip. Not only was Steven's deal still not closed, but Lydia hadn't even told Cici that Viève would have to play the younger female role instead of her.

"Not what I hear," Jessica lied. "I hear Steven is dying to do the film and Lydia's not sure she wants to go that way."

"Does it matter, Jessica, who wants whom? I mean, really, all that matters is that Lydia is in a rush to make the film, and the only A-lister with a slot is Steven, right?"

The loose lips in Hollywood often irritated Jessica. "Who told you all this? I didn't think Lydia wanted to make offers yet."

"Like I said, Nathan gave me the script," Tyler said.

"Are you sure it's the right one? You know Mary Anne Meyers is working on a rewrite," Jessica said.

"That's not all she's working on," Tyler kidded. "Did you see the cover of *Star* magazine?"

"I don't comment on clients' personal lives," Jessica said coolly.

"You don't have to. That picture says it all. Do you manage everyone on this film? Holden and Cici starring, Mary Anne writing, you and Mike producing."

"I don't rep Steven and I don't rep Viève," Jessica said.

"Too bad for Lydia, isn't it?" Tyler asked. "She'll actually have to negotiate with someone other than one of her gal pals."

"Worldwide business affairs will," Jessica said stiffly. Tyler's attitude seemed worse than his coke habit. "So what's Viève's quote right now?" Jessica asked.

"You produced *Collusion* and she got seven-fifty for that."

"Right. So what do you want? A million?"

"Five," Tyler said.

"Five what?" Jessica asked. She took the final sip of her juice. "Wait, five million? Are you crazy?"

"Five million," Tyler said.

"There is no way Lydia will pay five million dollars for Viève Dyson. She hasn't even opened a film. *Collusion* was her first major role."

"She's on her way up the A-list, everyone knows it. And Lydia will pay it if she wants Brockman," Tyler said. "And from what I hear, Steven Brockman is the actor Lydia wants."

"I don't think Lydia's appetite for Steven is worth paying Viève five million dollars," Jessica said.

"She was hungry enough to fly to Japan, have dinner with Steven and Billy, and fly back," Tyler said.

Ugh. Why would Billy tell Tolliver about Lydia's travel plans?

"*Famished* was the word I was thinking of," he continued. "I'll read the script tonight and call you tomorrow."

"Great," Jessica said. Frustration ate at her insides.

"Yeah, and you might want to let your *other* client know that she's once again been bumped by a younger actress," Tyler said, "before someone else does."

"Just read the script," Jessica said. "I'll talk to you tomorrow."

Payback was a bitch. Tyler had to be swimming in self-satisfaction right now. Not long ago, as president of CTA and Tyler's boss, Jessica had chewed him out so badly he stood in her office and cried. She'd had little patience for him. He could sell used cars or scripts. Tyler's career in entertainment wasn't driven by his love for film. No, Tyler worked as an agent to provide himself with a certain lifestyle, a lifestyle with money, status, girls, and drugs.

"My agent?" Jessica looked down to watch Viève climb onto the bar stool across from her.

"Good guess," Jessica said. She placed her BlackBerry on the counter in front of her. "So you've met Nathan Curtis?"

"Ages ago," Viève said.

"Really?" Jessica made a mental note. She needed to check out how Nathan Curtis had met Viève Dyson. "He's an interesting guy."

"Very," Viève said.

"Do you want anything?" Jessica asked as she glanced at the guy working the juice bar.

"Just water with lemon. Once my chakras are clear I don't like to eat for a couple of days."

Days? She didn't eat for days? That explained the size zero. And the erratic mood swings.

"So who else is on the film?" Viève asked. "Nathan told me Holden Humphrey, Mary Anne Meyers, and Steven Brockman."

"Those are the players," Jessica said.

"And Steven's deal hasn't closed yet?" Viève asked.

"That's a question for Worldwide business affairs," Jessica said.

"Then I guess we're done," Viève said, starting to slide off her chair.

Jessica reached out a hand to stop her. "Okay, no, Steven's deal isn't closed yet."

"And it's contingent on me?"

"I don't know if I'd say *contingent* on you," Jessica said.

"Really? Because that's what Billy said."

"You know Billy, too?" Jessica asked. "Steven Brockman's Billy?"

"For years."

Suddenly Jessica felt confused. Had she missed a conversation where Billy mentioned he knew Viève, or Viève mentioned she knew Billy? How did Viève know both her director, Nathan Curtis, and Billy, the man married to her male lead? Knowing the connections between people was an essential part of being a producer and getting a film made. Her own ignorance shocked Jessica.

Viève nodded. "Billy, Nathan, and I met in London, when Billy owned clubs."

"Really? I had no idea." Jessica's spine tingled. So it was really Billy, not Steven, who had wanted Viève as the lead in *Vitriol* . . . they must have been friends back in London. Jessica remembered hearing that Nathan's success as a London paparazzo had everything to do with his connections within the London club scene. *Interesting*. She needed to call Lydia. She wondered if Lydia knew of Nathan, Billy, and Viève's prior relationship. And if not, why hadn't Billy mentioned it to anyone?

"And Mary Anne knows?" Viève asked. "About me?"

"Yes," Jessica lied.

"I'll do it," Viève said.

"But you haven't read the script," Jessica said, startled by Viève's quick yes.

"Tyler's reading it, isn't he?"

"Tonight."

"That's good enough," Viève said.

"I'll have my assistant reschedule your ADR." Jessica picked up her BlackBerry.

"There's one more thing," Viève said.

Of course there is, Jessica thought.

"I want you to talk to Mary Anne for me."

"Mary Anne?"

"You're her friend, aren't you?" Viève asked.

Jessica nodded. An uncomfortable feeling settled around her as she looked into Viève's dead eyes.

"Look, I saw the cover of *Star* magazine, but it's okay. Holden's relationship with Mary Anne is a novelty thing for him. She won't be able to maintain his interest." Viève paused and sipped her water. "You know he's very sexually creative, and I'm afraid Mary Anne may end up with a broken heart again."

Jessica forced her expression to remain blank. She felt protective of Mary Anne and resisted the urge to reach over and strangle Viève. "I really don't think it's appropriate for me to talk to you about Mary Anne's sex life with Holden—"

"Why not?" Viève interrupted. "You spoke to Holden about his sex life with me, didn't you? In Toronto?"

"It's not the same—"

"I know what you told Holden," Viève said. She twisted a lock of her red hair in her fingers. "Holden still hasn't figured out that I'm the right woman for him. But he will."

Jessica felt a chill rush down her spine. Viève's eyes were wide and her pupils were deep black holes.

"No matter what I have to do to convince him, he will."

Rule 16

Image Is Everything

Kiki Dee, Publicist

Kiki heard Sherman Ross drop onto a sofa in her living room. She pulled her head up from the massage table's padded face-holder to look at him.

"No one can confirm what you saw in Melnick's office," Sherman said.

"Then you're not looking hard enough," Kiki said.

"I've been watching, and aside from breaking and entering, so far nothing."

"Of course not. How do you think this secret has been kept?" *Was everyone who worked for her a complete moron?* Kiki wondered. "I know what I saw," she said.

Kiki sat up, her massage completed. She glanced at Sherman's face as she stood, naked, and slid into the robe her massage therapist held out for her. Kiki wanted Sherman to check out her body, but instead he looked at the floor. She wondered if Sherman's downcast eyes meant he felt revolted by her age.

"You need to get the records from Melnick," Kiki said.

"Dead end."

"How so?" Kiki sipped her lemon-infused water.

"I have a source in his office, and there aren't any records for our subject."

"What?"

"That's what she said."

"Bullshit. The records are there. I read the folder before my surgery," Kiki said.

"You were high."

"Not *that* high. You'll just have to go look for the records yourself. Or . . . how do you feel about breaking into private residences?"

"It can be done. Did you get my other package?" Sherman asked.

"Where'd you acquire that?" Kiki calmly glanced at her hands. Sherman's package had arrived days before, and Kiki had eagerly devoured the contents, her eyes eating up the sex scenes. The package could be an economic windfall for her. Another of her clients with a salacious secret to keep? Certainly Worldwide had an interest in keeping the footage hidden from the public. And while Celeste was already her client, Kiki smelled a holiday bonus coming her way. But first she had to pry some information out of Sherman about the mysterious DVD, and, with luck, get a copy of her own. She'd had her assistant try to copy it, but apparently some sort of encryption was protecting the file.

"I'm holding it for the owner. It's very high-end right now, only sex parties."

"Then what?"

"It may go mainstream."

"Or?" Kiki asked.

"Someone could buy it." Sherman looked directly at Kiki. "The owner has a cash-flow problem. Seems he's acquired some bad habits," Sherman said, touching the side of his nose.

"How much?" Kiki asked.

"At least seven, maybe eight figures."

"I see," Kiki said. She felt her palms grow moist. She now possessed two new tantalizing tidbits of celebrity information. Both could destroy careers.

"I thought you might be interested, or know someone who is."

"I'll have a conversation," Kiki said, sliding onto the couch beside Sherman.

"But I need the DVD back. It's the only copy, encrypted so no duplicates can be made. I wanted to make my own copy, strictly for my records, of course, but even my tech guy couldn't crack it," Sherman said.

"Boom Boom!" Kiki screeched. "Get Sherman his DVD."

Boom Boom entered the room holding the DVD. Sherman smiled at Boom Boom and Kiki felt a stab of jealousy.

"We've not met." Sherman stood and held out his hand. "Sherman Ross."

"I'm aware," Boom Boom said. She handed him the DVD and turned to leave.

He watched her appreciatively as she exited the room. "She's tough," Sherman said.

"Very bright. But I'm not sure she has what it takes. She's a little bit too, too, hmm . . . I guess *dull* is the word I'm searching for."

"Dull? Kiki, I'd hardly call her dull. Besides, we can't all be as obvious as you: aggressive, always looking for the next kill."

"Sherman, you say that like it's a bad thing," Kiki said as she tucked her legs beneath her. She patted the couch for him to sit. "We've known each other a long time haven't we, Sherman?" Kiki ran her index finger across Sherman's cheekbone.

The muscle in his jaw flinched. "Almost ten years," Sherman said.

"That's a lifetime in this town." She cupped Sherman's jaw in her hand and looked into his blue eyes. She bit her lower lip. "Would you like to see the rest of the house?" she asked. A massage always turned her on, and today, lucky for her, an attractive man sat in her home. *Say yes,* Kiki thought. *Please say yes.* She surveyed Sherman's physique under his tailored shirt. She wanted him. She wanted a younger man to touch her, to feel desire for her, to make her feel beautiful.

"Ah, Kiki, I'd love to," Sherman said softly, "but I have another meeting in the Palisades."

"I see." Kiki pulled her hand away from his face. "Some other time, then."

"Definitely," Sherman said.

Not long ago, when Kiki's breasts were perkier and her neck tauter, an invitation into her bed would have resulted in the quick cancellation of any meeting the invitee had scheduled. But now, no matter how hard she chased youth with a knife, it continued to elude her.

"You know your way out?" Kiki asked.

"Of course," Sherman said.

She watched Sherman retreat to the front door. He possessed lean lines and a tight ass, but no desire for her. Kiki glanced into the mirror over her marble fireplace. She pulled down her terry-cloth robe, letting it slide over her shoulders. How long since she'd slept with a man? Too long. Kiki sighed. She sat up straight and sucked in her cheeks. She could pass for under forty . . . with the right lighting. Maybe she needed a young Hollywood boy toy. Someone desirous of the access, introductions, and success she could provide. The thought of playing Mrs. Robinson to some sweet, tight-assed young Hollywood stud excited her. She turned her head from side to side admiring her profile in the mirror.

"Kiki?"

She pulled up her robe and glanced toward the foyer. *Boom Boom*. Timing, the poor girl had no sense of timing. Or style.

"Are you going into the office, or do you prefer to work from home? Your cook wants to know."

"Here is fine," Kiki said. "It's cool today. I'll eat on the west patio." As she brushed past Boom Boom she glanced down at the girl's feet. *Flip-flops?* Today was Friday, sure, but what about a pair of Chanel sandals? "Who do I have this afternoon?" Kiki asked as she mounted the stairs.

"Cici. She wants to discuss the Oscar campaign for *California Girl*, and she also signed onto a new film, *Vitriol*." Boom Boom stood below in the marble foyer with her clipboard.

"Call her and ask if she'll come to the house." Kiki watched Boom Boom scribble a note. "Boom Boom?" She paused, waiting for her assistant to look up at her. "Over lunch go get something else to wear on your feet. Those"—Kiki pointed to the offending footwear—"are for bathhouses, not my home."

"Yes, Kiki."

"And, Boom Boom, schedule a hair appointment with Frederik for sometime this week," Kiki called over the banister.

"You just had your appointment with him three days ago."

"It's not for me," Kiki called from the balcony. "No, darling, it's for you and that flop mop you call hair."

If the girl isn't going to make the necessary changes, Kiki thought, *then I'll just have to take control.*

Rule 17

Play Dumb

Celeste Solange, Actress

Cici clipped down the slate stairs behind Kiki's stocky assistant, Boom Boom, watching the girl precariously balance herself on Louboutin heels. Kiki sat at the patio table talking on her cell. She waved at Cici. Papers and black binders lay scattered around Kiki's feet. The table held only one notepad, a gold pen, a pitcher of water with lemon, and two crystal glasses.

"May I get you something to drink, Celeste?" Boom Boom asked as Cici took the seat opposite Kiki.

"I'm good, thanks. The water is fine."

Boom Boom nodded, and Cici watched the girl's treacherous ascent back to the house. She felt for her. Cici knew Kiki could be a beast to her assistants.

"My love!" Kiki exclaimed, clicking her phone closed. "You look gorgeous. Steven Brockman says hello; he's still in Asia. Can't wait to see *California Girl.* You know he loved that script. Wanted to do it, but with the baby due the same time as the shoot . . ." Kiki threw up her hands. "What can you do? I can't wait to get you two back on a set together. How long has it been? What film was it?" Kiki reached to fill both glasses with water.

"*The Lady's Affair,* almost ten years ago," Cici said.

Cici remembered working with Steven Brockman. A high-maintenance drama queen, Steven had slept with the director, the supporting actor, and two grips. She also remembered hearing rumors about a fan Steven kept as a lover for a while once the film wrapped.

"The studio made so much dough on that one." Kiki handed Celeste her water. "So, the Oscar campaign. I just got some material from the studio. I'm a bit disappointed with their choices, actually. I've seen the rough cut twice now, and I think there are better stills we can use for *Variety* and *The Reporter.* But the one thing you've got going for you, darling, is that the studio assured me they will spare no expense. We're talking parties, screenings, huge box-office promotions, print, TV, radio—all of it. You know, darling, Ted really wants this for you."

God, Cici adored Ted. He knew that she desperately wanted an Oscar. She'd won a Golden Globe for Best Actress in a Leading Role, and an Emmy for a guest-starring arc, but the Academy had failed, thus far, to find any of her film performances Oscar-worthy.

"Looks like the release date is Christmas Day. Your performance is so emotional, really; the whole film is so raw. You did a brilliant job. I know we're early in the process, but I want to get everyone on board and totally committed now, because the closer we get to awards season, the busier everyone becomes."

"I have complete trust in you, Kiki," Cici said. And she did . . . for the Oscar campaign.

"What is this I hear about a new film? *Vitriol?* I thought you were going to relax the rest of the year?"

"This project is impossible to refuse." Cici shifted in her chair. If only Kiki knew just how impossible.

"And the director?"

"Nathan Curtis, from England."

"Didn't he do the publicity shots on *California Girl* for Worldwide?"

Cici nodded.

"That's a pretty fast climb. Did he do a feature in Europe?"

"A couple of shorts, but *Vitriol* is exactly what Lydia's slate needs, a very sexy thriller."

"But, darling, Worldwide just wrapped *Collusion.* You can't get much sexier than that."

Cici sipped her water. She didn't want to share with Kiki Dee the explanation for Nathan's rapid rise to director. But Cici needed to say something. Kiki hadn't lasted as a publicist in Hollywood for this long without knowing how to dig. "Lydia asked, made my quote, and put Jessica on as a producer. So I said yes." She gave Kiki what she hoped was a convincing smile.

"I think Steven worked with Nathan Curtis on a photo shoot," Kiki said. "Steven didn't care for him much."

"Really? Why not?"

"I think Steven used the term *insufferable prick.* But who knows, perhaps Steven was describing himself." Kiki cackled. "Who's your costar on the film?"

"Holden Humphrey, and there's another role for an older male star, say forty or forty-five."

Cici wanted to plant the seed with Kiki. Even though Lydia had visited Steven in Tokyo, and Worldwide business affairs had sent an offer to Steven's agent, Cici knew that whetting Kiki's appetite for the role would help the film's momentum.

"Perhaps something for Steven?" Kiki asked. She lifted her pen and scribbled on her pad.

"Kiki, you're *such* a good publicist; most don't even think to tell their clients when they hear about a role."

"Oh but, darling, I do try. A working client is a much happier client."

"I'm not sure Steven will want the role. The film is a three-hander, and Steven's character isn't the sexy male lead, but the older, more mature voice of wisdom."

"He'll have to consider switching to older roles at some point. I'll mention it to Tolliver," Kiki said. "So, darling, anything else new for you that I should know about? Marriage, children, *scandal*?"

Cici paused. She thought she'd heard Kiki emphasize the final word.

"You know, it is my job to protect your image," Kiki said. "Make sure you're never tarnished in the public's eye. Knowing anything out there that might emerge, well, that makes my job easier."

"But there's nothing," Cici said, forcing a smile to her lips. "Everything is pretty normal."

Kiki leaned forward and placed a hand over Cici's.

"Then, darling, as your publicist, I think there is something you need to know."

* * *

Cici roared her Jaguar up Coldwater Canyon. Her hands shook and tears streamed down her face. Of course Cici had played the scene brilliantly, as though Kiki's telling her was the very first time she'd learned of the horrible DVD. She needed to call Howard, but with the tremor in her hands, she couldn't drive and use her cell at the same time.

Perhaps Kiki could be an asset in this battle? She had kept Steven Brockman's sexuality from the public for the last twenty years. But Steven's sexuality was an open Hollywood secret, well known within the confines of the Hollywood club, and Cici didn't want everyone in Hollywood to see her fucking. If she enjoyed giving public viewings of her lovemaking, she'd have stayed married to Damien.

She turned the car onto Mulholland and stopped on the side of the road at a turnout. She flipped open her phone and took deep breaths, trying to calm her shaking body.

"Lydia?"

"Cici, what's wrong?" Lydia's voice sounded panicky.

"Kiki knows."

"Oh no. Cici, I told you not to—"

"I didn't tell her. She's seen the DVD."

"What? But who? Was she at someone's party?"

"The private investigator who works for her and Howard."

"Sherman Ross," Lydia said. "He must know that Kiki reps you. He wants us to approach him."

Celeste felt her heartbeat speed up. "Maybe this is connected to Damien?"

"This seems too big to have Damien's fingerprints on it. Besides, what's his motivation?" Lydia asked.

Cici paused. Revenge? No, she and Damien had settled their differences during the divorce. Money? Damien had plenty of money and would make more if Celeste's image remained pristine. Damien owned two scripts, now in development at Galaxy and Summit, that Celeste was attached to star in. Destroying Celeste's career and public image wouldn't serve Damien's purposes.

"Hey, you okay?" Lydia interrupted Cici's silence.

"Aside from the biggest big mouth who loves celebrity secrets having seen my sex tape? Yeah, I'm fine."

"At least she has an interest in keeping it quiet. You're one of her biggest clients. Call Howard."

Cici felt an ache in her chest. She'd made so many wrong choices and bad decisions. Lydia interrupted Cici's thoughts.

"Are you still coming to the studio this afternoon?"

Cici sighed. She didn't want to go to the lot. "Can we reschedule?"

"Normally, Cici, I'd say yes, but we've got a tight schedule with *Vitriol*. We're supposed to start filming in ten days."

She knew Lydia had rushed *Vitriol* into production in an attempt to contain Nathan Curtis and the DVD. "I'll call Howard." Cici struggled to keep the terse tone from her voice.

"And I'll call Sherman," Lydia said.

Cici flipped her cell closed and pushed hard on the accelerator. Dirt and rock flew into the air from the turnout. She needed to make one more stop before going home.

* * *

Cici pushed open the front door to her ex-husband Damien Bruckner's lavish new Bel-Air home. Damien's gross profit participation on *Borderland Blue,* the super hit that Celeste starred in after their divorce, had paid for this house.

"Damien?" she called.

She walked across the rug, imported from Tibet. Damien played tennis on Fridays. Cici wondered if he was out on the court.

"Damien?" Cici walked up the stairs toward Damien's bedroom and study.

She needed to do a little recon. As Damien's former wife, she had a right to walk through his house, didn't she? She tapped on Damien's study door, hoping to find the room empty.

"Damien?" Cici called softly. No answer. She turned the handle and gave the door a gentle push. Damien's desk sat next to a wall of windows that offered a view of his pool and tennis courts. Cici glanced down toward the yard, where Damien was rushing around the court getting his ass kicked by his tennis instructor. From the looks of Damien's energetic stride, he and Dart had just begun playing.

Cici turned away from the windows and surveyed Damien's study. She pulled open his top desk drawer and rummaged. Nothing unusual: receipts, files, nail clippers, lint roller. A combination lock secured the bottom drawer. Cici punched in Damien's birth date and the lock popped open. *Not very imaginative.* The drawer contained some porn, a letter to his attorney, and a check register for a foreign bank account. She glanced out the window. Damien and Dart were still playing.

A flat-screen TV hung above the credenza across the room. A DVD shelf nearby didn't hold anything interesting—a collection of Damien's films, plus some other big-budget films. No porn or unmarked cases. The tray in the DVD player was empty. *She should be so lucky as to find her DVD in the DVD tray.*

Cici walked back across the room and took another peek out the window—still safe. She walked through the door that connected Damien's study to his master bedroom. *He still had a mirror above his bed? Geez, he was pushing sixty. What a perv.* She wondered if he had mounted cameras on the ceiling behind the one-way glass. Cici remembered the thrill she felt the first time Damien begged to film them together. Her rush continued when they viewed the tape. The graphic sounds of their lovemaking, watching Damien's face contort—it had all turned her on. Perhaps the most aroused she'd ever become was watching herself having sex.

She moved through the bedroom toward Damien's mahogany closet. In the Hollywood Hills home that Cici and Damien had shared while married, the contractor built a safe in their closet to Damien's specifications. Cici wondered if a similar safe resided in this closet. She pulled open the double doors and walked to the far end of the closet. Yep, a door with a lock. She tried Damien's birth date; no luck. *What was something that Damien always had on his mind?* She tried his monthly alimony payment to his first wife, Amanda. Voilà. Cici pulled open the door and there, housed inside, identical to the safe built into their home, sat Damien's new safe. While married to Damien, Cici had opened the other safe several times—usually after Damien had angered her by having an affair—and taken his black card out on a shoe bender. Hundreds of thousands of dollars later, Damien never changed the combination.

Inside the safe was everything Damien wanted to hide from the world. Cici remembered some of these items from their marriage: gun, fake passports, credit cards, securities, and a couple of film reels. In the second drawer she found several unmarked DVDs. *It's necessary for me to confiscate these,* Cici thought. She scooped up the DVDs and tossed them into her quilted Marc Jacobs bag.

She closed the safe and the door behind it, and walked out of the closet to glance out the bedroom window toward the tennis courts. Empty!

"Cici, what are you doing in my bedroom?"

Cici felt her fingers tingle. She was an actress. *This* she could handle.

She turned to Damien, who stood in the doorway, and fluttered her eyelashes and cocked her hip. "Looking for you, of course," she said.

Damien's eyes roved over her body. "Do you ever age?" he asked. "You still look as sexy as the day we met." He took off his shirt and dropped his shorts to the floor. "But, really, what are you doing in here?"

"No one answered the door, and I was looking for you," Cici said.

He walked naked across the bedroom and into the bathroom. "You could have called." His voice echoed off the tile walls.

"I did. How do you think I knew you were here?" She heard the water start to run.

"Want to join me?" Damien stood in the doorway of the bathroom, naked and obviously excited by Cici's presence in his bedroom.

"While I am flattered," Celeste said, "I'm still living with Ted."

"So? Marriage didn't stop you. Why should living with someone?"

"Maybe that's why we ended so badly, because marriage didn't stop *either* of us."

"Maybe. But, really, what do you need? If you're not in my bedroom to fuck, then why are you here?"

Charming, Cici thought. She felt the familiar sensation of self-revulsion. She couldn't believe that she once loved Damien, that she had allowed him to define her, that she once was the desperate woman who needed a man like Damien to love her. She became a whore for his desires. "Because, it seems, something has come up," she said. A lascivious grin danced across Damien's face. Cici rolled her eyes. "Cute. Other than that."

Damien walked back into the bathroom. "How can I help?"

Cici could see him reflected in the mirrors, leaning forward to check out his pores. "You remember your attempt to produce porn?"

"Porn? What porn?"

"The DVD," Cici said.

"Of?" Damien called.

"Me."

"I gave it to you."

"Do you remember what I said, about if it ever got out?"

"Something about collateral? That you know secrets about me, too," Damien called from the bathroom.

"Well, guess what?"

"What?" He emerged from the bathroom, a genuinely perplexed look on his face. "What are you talking about, Celeste?"

"Someone has it," Cici said.

"That's impossible. I made one DVD, which I gave to you, and I destroyed the original footage. There weren't any copies."

"Not impossible. The DVD is out there. People are paying big bucks at high-end sex parties to see me." Cici felt her anger rise. Her entire life could shatter because of Damien's perversions. "Your divorce attorney kept the DVD for a while, didn't she?"

"This is bad," Damien said. "Really bad. What are you going to do?"

"Me? Don't you mean *we*? You and your cameras got me into this mess," Cici said.

"Cici, I feel for you, really, but we're divorced. And, frankly, this isn't my problem." He walked toward the shower.

"Damien," Cici called.

He stuck his head out again, looking exasperated. "Yeah."

"You better rethink your position on helping me or all those secrets I know about you? Well, they won't stay secret for long."

* * *

Cici stood alone in the elevator and watched the numbers light up as she ascended to Lydia's office. She still didn't trust Damien, but she knew that fear and self-interest motivated him. And she knew enough dirt about him that he should be very afraid.

The doors opened, and Cici breezed by reception and directly to

Toddy, who sat just outside Lydia's door. Toddy scheduled every component of Lydia's life, and had listened to Lydia's calls for the last seventeen years. The details Toddy knew about everyone in Hollywood boggled Cici's mind. With her connections and experience, Toddy could easily sit in Lydia's chair and run Worldwide. And, in fact, Lydia told Cici that she'd offered Toddy a promotion a dozen times. When Lydia accepted the job as president of production, she offered Toddy an overall production deal at Worldwide. But each time, Toddy declined, preferring instead to manage Lydia's life, read scripts, prepare script notes, schedule meetings, and greet celebrities. Cici glanced over at Lydia's two other assistants, both barely out of graduate school, their desks askew with papers, Post-its, and scripts, feverishly working the phones. Toddy sat relaxed with one notepad and a pen. She spoke calmly into the phone. She glanced up, saw Cici, smiled, and gave her the one-second sign.

"Celeste," Toddy said after finishing her call. She stood and gave Cici a warm embrace. "She's finishing a meeting. Probably another five minutes. What can we get you to drink?"

Assistant number two sat poised like a springer spaniel ready to fetch.

"Flat water with lemon, thank you."

Toddy nodded imperceptibly, and the girl leapt up to retrieve the water.

"How are you?" Cici asked.

"Busy. Especially since she decided to rush *Vitriol* into production. We've reworked the soundstage schedule, and you can imagine how pissed Sean is since we took both his star and his writer from *Sexual Being* to get *Vitriol* going. And you? You look luscious as ever. How's Ted?"

"Thanks. Ted gets back from Hong Kong tonight."

"Hong Kong? What's he doing in Hong Kong?"

Celeste raised her eyebrow. How could Toddy, the epicenter of information at Worldwide, fail to know that Ted traveled to Hong Kong to location-scout for a Worldwide film?

"Location-scouting," Cici said.

"Oh right, right. I forgot." Toddy smiled and glanced at her pad and pen. "Here's Leigh with your water."

Cici sat in the chair across from Toddy's desk as Lydia's number two placed a crystal glass and a decanter on the table next to her.

"I think I hear them now," Toddy said as Lydia's office door swung open and Tyler Bruger, from CTA, walked out of the office.

"Cici!" Tyler said, quickly leaving Lydia and bounding toward Celeste. Cici braced herself for the full-court press that she knew she'd receive from Tyler.

"Tyler." Cici leaned forward stiffly and let Tyler kiss each of her cheeks.

"How are you? You look stunning," Tyler said. "You know I'd love to buy you lunch someday soon. We miss you at CTA."

When Jessica left to start her own production-management company, Cici had followed as both a client and a friend. She'd yet to pick up a new agency and doubted she ever would. Why should she? Unagented, she was a hot commodity in the entertainment marketplace, and every agency serviced her—sending her scripts and introducing her to their best clients—hoping they'd do such a good job she'd sign with them.

"CTA was my home for many years," Cici said, "but once Jessica left, I couldn't stay."

Tyler's smile remained, but a flicker passed through his eyes. "How *is* Jessica?" he asked. "I haven't seen much of her. You know I rep the female star of *Collusion,* Viève Dyson."

"That's what Jessica said. Very talented actress. Even if she's a little . . ." Cici let her hand wave back and forth as her words drifted off. Let Tyler sit with the idea that Celeste Solange, the biggest female star in Hollywood, thought Tyler's up-and-coming actress was unbalanced. Cici saw a bit of real anger flash in Tyler's face.

He recovered. "Have you seen Zymar's rough cut of *Collusion*? This was the first film Viève carried. You must be looking forward to working with her?"

Cici tried not to choke on her water. *What? Looking forward to working with Viève?* She bit back her response. "Oh I am. Of course. There is nothing like talent."

"Cici," Toddy called from her desk. "Lydia's ready for you now."

Cici picked up her purse. "Wonderful to see you, Tyler. Do tell Tolliver I said hi." She glanced at Toddy sitting behind Tyler.

Toddy looked up at the ceiling and shook her head as if to say, they never learn, the young ones. It takes years.

* * *

No. No! Lydia, Viève Dyson cannot play my daughter in this film." Cici paced in front of Lydia's desk. "Have you spoken to Mary Anne? You know who Viève is, don't you?"

Lydia sighed. "Cici, it's the only way I can hold this film together. Nathan wants her and so does Steven."

"Why Steven? He doesn't even fuck women."

"I think it's coming from Billy. We found out they're friends from their London days," Lydia said.

"I'm too old to play his love interest?"

Lydia paused.

"Oh fuck him. I wasn't even born when Steven Brockman started doing movies."

"He's very concerned about the public's perception of his age."

"And I'm not? Lydia, I'm an actress over thirty in Hollywood. Any film could be my last."

"Celeste, you're overreacting."

"Am I? I mean, this little tramp broke Mary Anne's heart by sleeping with her boyfriend, then Viève dated Holden, who is now dating Mary Anne."

"Should make for an interesting set," Lydia said.

"What other demands did Steven make?" Cici asked. She flopped into the chair opposite Lydia's desk.

"Billy gets to be the production photographer for a very handsome fee. And Steven wants Billy to shoot his *Vanity Fair* piece."

"How are you going to deliver a *Vanity Fair* cover?"

"I've got a call into Graydon, but it's not going to come cheap. Graydon wants an inside look on a Hollywood film set for his February issue. Perhaps following an actress? A behind-the-scenes piece as she does a major film?"

"Who'd want to do that?" Cici asked. "A film is stressful enough without some journalist following you around."

"Well, with *California Girl* being an Oscar contender . . ."

"Lydia, no. Absolutely not. Are you kidding me? Let a journalist follow me around on set? With a sex tape and your letters hanging over all our heads?"

"Look, a journalist on set is the last thing I want. But striking a deal that gets Billy and Steven the cover of *Vanity Fair* is the only way to hold *Vitriol* together. Without the *Vanity Fair* cover for Billy, Steven walks. And without the behind-the-scenes piece with you, no cover for Billy. Besides, no one works the press like you. The public adores you. Every magazine that puts you on the cover quadruples its circulation for that month. I spoke to Kiki, and she thinks it's a great idea."

Cici felt the guilt wash over her. Lydia had put her career on the line by fast-tracking *Vitriol* and keeping the knowledge of Cici's sex tape away from Ted, and Cici knew now she had to return the favor. "I get to pick the journalist."

"Kiki already did. It's Terri Seawell."

"Terri Seawell? Oh, Lydia, are you sure?" Cici asked. "You and Jessica have to contain the set, because with Terri Seawell rummaging around, she's bound to find something."

"Won't this be fun?" Lydia asked, sarcasm lacing her voice. She set her lips into a grim line.

Yeah, won't it, Cici thought.

Rule 18

Stay Cool

Lydia Albright, President of Production, Worldwide Pictures

Lydia's Lincoln Town Car pulled up to Mann Chinese Theatre. Before Lydia had accepted the job as president of production for Worldwide, back when she merely produced films, she only attended the premieres for her own films and those of her close friends. Now, unless she was out of the country, she was expected to attend the premiere of every film Worldwide released. And she no longer breezed down the far side of the red carpet, the side that spouses, guests, and noncelebs quickly jetted down, bypassing the press. No. Now, as the public face of Worldwide, she had to actually walk by the reporters and occasionally answer a question. Her job required that she appear for photo ops with the stars of all the films Worldwide released.

A Worldwide publicist opened Lydia's car door. Jay stood near her, close but not too close. Lydia had arrived dateless. Zymar had boarded a flight bound for New Zealand earlier that day, after finishing postproduction on *Collusion*. Organized chaos reigned on the red carpet. PR mavens wearing Donna Karan power suits flitted past Lydia holding walkie-talkies and sporting Bluetooth headsets in their ears. Flacks radioed drivers to alert them when to drop their celebrity cargo to ensure maximum press exposure for the star on the carpet. The infotainment journalists from *Entertainment Tonight* and *Access Hollywood* were poised to pounce on their celebrity prey. Hair pouffed, tits up, and microphones at the ready, Leeza and Lara stood side by side, waiting for their next feed. Perhaps Lydia could sneak into the theater? She didn't see any of the *Pivot and Press* stars on the carpet.

"Lydia?"

Lydia looked over her shoulder toward the voice calling her name above the hubbub. Kiki Dee stood next to her client and the star of *Pivot and Press,* Maurice Banks. Kiki held a walkie-talkie in one hand and wore a Bluetooth in her ear.

"Maurice," Lydia said. She leaned forward and gave Maurice a quick hug. "So good to see you." She quickly turned and smiled for the cameras. The bulbs flashed as the star of *Pivot and Press* and the president of production at Worldwide posed. Lydia knew that Kiki had faded into the background, as good publicists did once they got the shot for their clients.

"I'm so pleased with the film," Lydia whispered into Maurice's ear as the cameras continued to flash. "You did a great job."

"Thanks, Lydia," Maurice said and slipped away from her. "I'll see you inside."

Lydia watched as Boom Boom, Kiki's assistant, swept Maurice down the carpet to Leeza, hungry for her five-second sound bite.

"He's a great actor," Lydia said to Kiki, who approached again, since the photographers had finished with Lydia for the moment.

"He needs an award," Kiki said.

"This year big box office, next year the Oscar," Lydia said.

"I'm surprised you're so upbeat, with everything you're going through," Kiki said.

Lydia gave Kiki a quick glance. She hoped the publicist had some discretion. A film premiere wasn't the ideal place to discuss Celeste Solange's sex tape.

"*Vitriol* won't be an easy set," Kiki continued. "With Vième, Holden, and Mary Anne's little love triangle? Plus Steven and Billy? Believe *me*, I *know* Steven."

"Kiki—" Lydia followed Kiki's gaze as she looked down the red carpet toward the Town Car pulling to the curb. Photogs started flashing their cameras, lighting up the night. Kiki touched her Bluetooth earpiece. "Okay, got it." She looked at Lydia. "Looks like this is a big one."

Lydia started to walk toward the theater.

"No, no. Lydia, stay. This arrival is important for Worldwide, too," Kiki said.

Lydia watched as Holden Humphrey emerged from the car. He wore jeans, snakeskin boots, and a blue button-down that matched the teal in his eyes. He turned around to help someone out of the car.

"Don't they make a pair," Kiki said.

Lydia contained the shock she felt by freezing a smile onto her face. "Yes, quite a pair," she said. She waited as Holden and Mary Anne worked their way down the press line.

"Lydia," Mary Anne said, arriving breathless. "I'm so glad you're here."

Lydia felt Mary Anne's fingers wrap around her wrist as though Lydia were a life preserver floating on the sea of the red carpet. The threesome turned toward the press and smiled. Tonight Holden Humphrey and Mary Anne Meyers were going public with their relationship, and the *Pivot and Press* premiere had become the lead story for every infotainment show on the planet.

Lydia glanced at her friend Mary Anne, the screenwriter from Minnesota, and her heart ached for her. Mary Anne still maintained her fresh-faced charm, and Lydia could tell by Mary Anne's smile that she didn't realize what she'd done. She'd just jumped into the very deep end of the pool. The public now owned a piece of her life. Mary Anne and her relationship with Holden would become a commodity that print and broadcast infotainment would use to sell tickets, magazines, books, soap, gas, cars, and anything else their advertisers hocked. The photogs called out Holden and Mary Anne's names as the two posed, anxious for the money shot. Lydia braced herself for the questioning calls from the journalists.

"Holden! This way, this way!"

"Mary Anne, when did you start dating again?"

"Holden, what does Viève say?"

Lydia continued to smile for the cameras. "I'm speechless," she whispered to the couple, maintaining her smile. "But thrilled for you both." She stepped closer to Mary Anne as the two broke apart and Holden turned to his adoring fans. "Mary Anne," Lydia whispered, "let me have Worldwide send some security to your house." She watched a look of shock pass over Mary Anne's face.

"Security? Why?"

Could Mary Anne still be this naive? Lydia wondered. "This is a very public event. And now," she said, eyeing the hundreds of people and cameras drifting around them, "you've become a public person. This, you and Holden, will immediately be the hottest story in America. Just to be safe, please. I'll have Jay send someone over to your house now." She signaled for Jay.

"Lydia, come on. I'm fine. No one will bother me. Besides, we're not even going to the after party. Just the film and then home. Holden has to get ready for—"

"You're wrong," Lydia interrupted. Her voice felt controlled, but she realized from Mary Anne's expression that her tone was scaring her friend. "Before you get home the press will go through your garbage and trample your yard. Okay? This is a big deal. And you are unprepared." She gave Mary Anne a serious look. She wanted her to wise up. Mary Anne needed to understand the reality of the tabloid machine and how it could hurt people, even people who valued privacy.

"Lydia, I don't . . . ," Mary Anne whispered, glancing at the red carpet beneath her feet. She looked up and reached her arm out to Lydia with a look of concern. "Please—"

"Lydia," Kiki interrupted, "sorry to break in, but I need this little lovebird. *Access Hollywood* gets her first and then *Entertainment Tonight*. This is big, big, big!" Kiki was obviously thrilled by the romance between *People*'s Sexiest Man Alive and the cute writer from the Midwest. More fuel for the never-ending publicity fire.

***

Lydia worked her way toward the back of the premiere-party tent, glancing down at one of the buffet tables as she passed. Worldwide needed a new caterer. The chicken satay looked plastic, the salads appeared to be wilted, and the drinks tasted watered down. It may not have been the biggest film, or the most expensive premiere, but Worldwide's guests deserved a better selection. Lydia saw a clump of people surrounding Paul Peterson, the former president of production at Summit Pictures who, after leaving Summit, had received an overall production deal at Worldwide.

"Lydia," Paul called. He reached out to her over the bodies surrounding him. Although nothing spectacular, *Pivot and Press* was a solid film and would make its budget and P&A costs back for the studio. Because of his profitable movie, Paul would get another film made with Worldwide this year. Plus now *Pivot and Press* was getting a huge publicity bump with the red-carpet appearance of Holden and Mary Anne.

"So good to see you. Thanks for coming," Paul said. He wrapped an arm around Lydia's shoulder. "And thanks for bringing Holden and Mary Anne. Tomorrow, unless World War Three begins, we're the lead on every news show in America." He laughed. "Hell, we're the lead even if World War Three does start." He nodded at a gorgeous young man standing next to him. "Have you met Rick?"

Rick held out his hand to her. "Lydia. We've never met, but I've heard about you from Arnold."

"Arnold?" Lydia's heart quivered. Had she heard the correct name over the cacophony?

"Murphy," Rick said. "He's a huge fan of yours. In fact, I've brought him with me." Rick looked around. "Where did he go? You know he's easy to lose in a crowd. He's rather vertically challenged."

Lydia's skin tingled and her hands felt clammy. Prior to his banishment from Hollywood, Arnold Murphy had spent most of his energy attempting to destroy Lydia and her career. How had he gotten into a Worldwide premiere? When had he even arrived back in L.A.? Lydia felt anger building in her chest. Didn't Worldwide security keep a list with names of people who weren't allowed to attend Worldwide events? And if yes, why didn't Arnold Murphy top the list? Lydia had assumed Ted Robinoff's banishment of Arnold after the *Seven Minutes Past Midnight* screening would last longer. Lydia had hoped forever.

"Lyyydiiiaaa!"

Lydia felt a chill slide down her spine as the familiar voice called out to her. "Arnold." She turned, bent forward, and air-kissed each of Arnold's cheeks. "So good to see you."

"You're looking fabulous," Arnold said. He held her hand tightly and looked her up and down. "Being president must agree with you! Seems you've dropped a couple of pounds."

Lydia pulled her hand from his grasp. "Yes, I'm on the no-time-to-eat diet. But surely you remember from your tenure as president of production?"

"Ah, I missed many a meal when I had your job. No, darling, I don't envy you one bit. So, you gave my little lover his first big break?" Arnold gazed adoringly at Rick. "So talented, isn't he?"

Arnold appeared calmer, perhaps happier. But Lydia couldn't let her guard down. A mere four years before, Arnold had taken gleeful pleasure in attempting to convince the U.S. Attorney to file criminal charges against Lydia and Zymar. Lydia guessed that Arnold probably still blamed her for his ignominious exit from Hollywood.

"Arnold, I had no idea you'd returned to Los Angeles. Last I heard you were on the East Coast? Working in theater?"

"For about a minute," Arnold said. "I couldn't stand it. Too pretentious and too slow. Besides, who wants to deal with the weather? No, Los Angeles is my home. This is where I'm meant to be."

"So what are you working on now?" Lydia asked.

"Project-wise or personally? I mean, personally, I've had the most remarkable breakthrough. After getting my butt kicked out of L.A., I reevaluated my life. And what an eye-opener. I tell you, Lydia, love and meditation changed my entire outlook. And my writing? I've been putting pen to paper almost every day."

Lydia watched as Arnold and Rick gazed adoringly at each other. She almost believed him.

"Really? I've never been big on meditating. Perhaps I'll try."

"Oh, but you're so grounded in comparison to my headspace as an executive. I became so paranoid. Afraid people were watching me. Stalking me. I became almost paralyzed with fear. But you?" Arnold gazed at Lydia. "I imagine you're sailing along without a bump."

Lydia felt uncomfortable listening to Arnold. *Without a bump?* A stalker sending her letters, a sexually explicit DVD, lying to her boss, being forced to put a below-average script into production with a first-time director, and a constant security detail. Her chest tightened as she thought about all the potholes. "Arnold, such a pleasure to see you, really," she said. "Will you excuse me?"

"Sure, Lydia, not a problem. Duty calls. I remember." He gave her a knowing glance.

Lydia quickly brushed past groups of people. She glanced at Jay, five steps behind her, and nodded toward an opening at the back of the tent for the catering staff. She pushed her way through the flap. Once outside, in relative privacy, she leaned forward and rested her arm against a pole. Her heart beat so fast that she felt light-headed and unable to catch her breath.

"Lydia, you okay?" Jay whispered.

"Fine. I'm okay. I just . . . I guess I just panicked." She looked around her. No one had seen.

"It's clear," Jay said. He grabbed her elbow and gently pulled her forward. "Come on, let's get you to the car."

Lydia let Jay lead her away from the tent. She scanned the shadows as they walked together through the dark. Anywhere. They could be anywhere. Watching, waiting, and willing her to fail.

Rule 19

Never Forget Where You Came From

Mary Anne Meyers, Screenwriter

Mary Anne Meyers felt like a princess in a fairy tale. She'd found her prince, and without the glass slippers, poison apples, or nasty stepsisters. She watched as Holden slept soundly beside her. They were a couple. Officially a couple. No more sneaking around, no more lies. She now dated the Sexiest Man Alive. She watched him lying on his back, asleep in her bed—*such a perfect body.* Immediately Mary Anne felt self-conscious about the roll of flab developing around her abdomen. And her ass? Well, she'd caught a glimpse while leaving the shower yesterday, and it wasn't the ass she remembered. Today she promised to be more physical. Maybe she'd try Pilates? Jessica swore by it and had recovered her pre-baby body in record time. Yes, she'd call today for her first Pilates session . . . but after breakfast.

Mary Anne felt her tummy grumble. Holden had kept her up late the night before. She glanced at the velvet-covered paddle lying next to her bed. Mary Anne covered her eyes with her hand, embarrassed by the memories of the previous evening. They were so naughty together. She took one final glance at her sleeping prince and then got out of bed.

Mary Anne padded down the hall. She wanted her coffee so bad she thought she smelled it brewing. She turned the corner to her kitchen and stopped.

"Good morning, darling," Mitsy said. She held a cantaloupe rind and a knife. Mitsy walked over and kissed Mary Anne on the cheek. "Darling," she whispered into Mary Anne's ear, "you really should put on a robe when you have company." Mary Anne looked down at her see-through lace-trimmed tank top and tiny shorts.

"But I didn't know I had company," she whispered. *Was she sleepwalking?* She glanced at her sister, Michelle, unloading groceries onto the kitchen counter.

"Don't be silly, darling, all these people can't stay at my town house," Mitsy said.

"But what are they doing—"

"Don't you remember? Gavin's birthday? We're having the celebration out here? Disneyland? Knott's Berry Farm? SeaWorld?"

"But that's . . ." Mary Anne walked toward the refrigerator and glanced at the calendar taped to the door.

"This week," Mitsy said and tapped the box in which months before Mary Anne had written, *Meyers Family Arrives.*

"Today," Mary Anne whispered. She leaned against the counter, dazed.

"Hey, sis," Michelle said, wrapping her arms around Mary Anne. Mary Anne smiled at her sister. No one ever guessed that Mary Anne and Michelle were related. Michelle wore her blond hair bobbed, and her electric blue eyes always appeared to contain laughter. Her skin never burned and, even in the Minnesota winters, maintained a golden color.

"William wanted me to tell you he's sorry he couldn't make it. Right now is his busy time at the store," Michelle said.

"December is busy for patio furniture sales?" Mary Anne asked.

"You'd be amazed how many people give patio furniture for Christmas," Michelle said, continuing to unload groceries. "Hey, I brought you a present." She reached into the grocery bag and pulled out *Star* magazine. "Nice picture." She nudged her sister in the ribs. "I usually buy a copy if I see it in the store, but now since you'll be a regular, I'll have to get a subscription."

Mary Anne blushed, but gave her sister a tiny smile. Then she pulled open the cabinet for a coffee cup. She felt as if a pack of raccoons had attacked her kitchen as she slept.

"The coffee cups are on the kitchen table, as well as a new carafe of coffee," Mitsy said. "My breakfast quiche should be finished in fifteen minutes. Are you hungry?" Mitsy reached for the *US* magazine and perused it over the tops of her glasses "He's a nice-looking boy."

"Mitsy, where do you want these?" Marvin, Mary Anne's dad, walked in from the garage holding three pieces of luggage.

"Two in the guest room and one in the den," Mitsy said. She returned to cutting cantaloupe at the kitchen island. "Now, Mary Anne, the grandchildren are staying with your father and me at the town house. I'm leaving the adults with you."

"Michael and Sue, too?" Mary Anne asked, referring to her brother and his wife.

"I gave them a key. They wanted to stop at Costco."

"You were all over the news this morning when we left St. Paul," Michelle said, disappearing into the adjoining great room.

"Darling, do you even know what time it is?" Mitsy asked, eyeing Mary Anne's clothes again. "I thought you'd left for the studio. Don't you have some movie you're working on right now?"

"*Vitriol*," Mary Anne said. She glanced toward her great room, where she heard the sound of her plasma television being switched on.

"Look, look, there you are!" Michelle called, aiming the remote and turning up the sound. "I saw this earlier. Nice outfit, by the way. And who did your makeup? I know *you* didn't."

"Darling, that dress was a little low cut, don't you think?" Mitsy asked. "Perhaps you're sending the wrong message to the young girls in America by wearing it. Now that you're setting an example."

An example? For whom? Mary Anne thought. She was dating an actor. What kind of example could she be expected to set?

"You know, Lauren and her friends watch these shows religiously. She tells me that they look for makeup and clothing tips," Misty said.

"Right, Mother, I'm sure it has nothing to do with Orlando Bloom or Brad Pitt," Michelle said teasingly.

"Hello, hello, hello!" Mary Anne heard the familiar baritone of her brother, Michael's, voice, followed by the high-pitched squeal of her sister-in-law, Sue's, laugh. Mary Anne turned and watched as Michael entered carrying Costco bags. "There's more in the car," he said.

"Michael, where are the children?" Mitsy called.

"Pool," Michael called, just as two yells and a splash came from the backyard.

"It's *winter,*" Mary Anne said, giving her brother a kiss on the cheek.

"Not here. In St. Paul it's fifteen degrees. In Los Angeles it's summer every day."

Mary Anne remembered the first December she lived in L.A., she wore shorts all winter and couldn't understand why people gave her funny looks.

Michelle set Mitsy's breakfast quiche on the table. Mary Anne sat at the table listening to the loud banter of her family. She felt the familiar cloak of invisibility settle around her. As she listened to Marvin and Michael discuss real estate and Michelle chastise Mitsy, she felt suddenly as if she were at home and no one could see her. But then she glanced at the television and watched herself standing next to Holden as Leeza shoved a microphone in her face.

"Michelle, do you think—" Mitsy stopped midsentence, and silence emanated from the kitchen. Mary Anne looked toward her family, and there stood Holden, looking surprised and confused. Mary Anne guessed she'd worn a similar expression twenty minutes before when she wandered into the chaos of her family. His blond hair stuck out at odd angles and thankfully, he wore his boxers—though they didn't hide much, and from this angle it appeared that Holden had come to the kitchen for something other than breakfast.

Michelle leaned over to Mary Anne. "I shared my Malibu Barbie doll with you," she whispered. "Will you share your Ken doll with me?"

Mary Anne's giggle broke the silence. She walked toward Holden. "So everyone, this is Holden." She stood at his side. "And Holden, this is everyone." Mary Anne glanced around the room. "Well, everyone but the boys and my niece; they're in the pool. And, well, William, Michelle's husband, my brother-in-law; he couldn't make it. It's his busy time at the store. And—" Mary Anne stopped. She knew her nervous energy caused her to babble.

Looking at her family standing around the kitchen, Mary Anne attempted to see them through Holden's eyes. Her father, six-three and fairly thin for a man pushing seventy, stood next to blond-haired Michael, who was barely six feet, with an athletic body. Sue, Mary Anne's sister-in-law, was short and a little round but had a happy face. And then there was Mitsy, with her flat shoes, sweater set, and football-helmet hair, standing at the kitchen island with her mouth agape. Mary Anne believed that seeing a seminaked man in her daughter's kitchen had actually struck her mother speechless.

Anticipation hovered over the kitchen. Mary Anne hoped Holden responded well—you met someone's family for the first time only once, and Mary Anne knew from experience that that first meeting often set the tone for the entire relationship. She knew her family could be overwhelming, and she hadn't envisioned this morning meeting as the optimal first introduction for Holden. She wished she could have introduced him to the family after months of preparing him and warning him about the Meyerses' idiosyncrasies.

"Well, Holden, it's so nice to meet you," Mitsy said, finally breaking the silence. "Are you hungry? I made quiche."

Holden's face broke into a dazzling smile. "I love quiche." He walked toward Mary Anne's mother. "Are you Mitsy?" he asked, towering over her.

"I am," Mitsy said. She looked up, a hint of anxiousness in her voice.

"You're about the cutest thing I've ever seen," Holden said. He reached down and gave her a hug.

Mary Anne watched Mitsy's face as Holden hugged her. Her expression changed from shock to surprise to a bright shade of red. Mary Anne looked at Michelle, who started to giggle. Neither she nor her sister had ever witnessed Mitsy looking so flustered.

Holden released her from his embrace, and Mitsy inhaled quickly, patting her hair with her hand. "Well," she said. "Thank you. Now sit and I'll get you some quiche and some juice." Mitsy scurried around the kitchen. "And Mary Anne, why don't you go get Holden some pants."

* * *

Mary Anne's family reminded Holden of his parents in Indiana. He hadn't visited his mom in almost five years. She refused his invitations to Los Angeles. She didn't want to come to L.A., she told him every time they spoke; she wanted him to come home to Indiana. But there was never time. Now, after spending the last three days with Mary Anne's family, Holden realized he needed to make a trip home. And he knew that Mary Anne would go with him. She'd understand where he came from: the trucks, the trailer park, even his uncle without front teeth. After his first action movie, Holden had taken a girl home with him, an actress he'd met on set. His mom, Holden knew, had cooked and cleaned for days before they arrived. The actress didn't eat anything and threw her dirty clothes around the house as if Holden's mother were her maid. Holden finally drove her over to Terre Haute and put her on a return flight to Los Angeles four days early.

Holden parallel-parked his pickup. He wanted to do a quick run to the top of Runyon Canyon and then sprint down. This run had always worked him out better than anything Liam wanted him to do, and after three days of Mitsy's cooking he needed a heavy sweat if he wanted to be ready for tomorrow.

The early-morning air felt crisp against his legs. At six A.M. on a Sunday, he'd have Runyon Canyon to himself. He started the uphill walk from his parking spot to the beginning of the path, and just as he passed the gates and started a light jog uphill, he noticed a flash of red.

"What the fu—" Holden stopped short.

"Where have you been?" Viève asked, appearing from behind a clump of bushes.

Holden gave the tiny creature a disgusted look and tried to keep going on the run. He knew from experience that, in public, there were no guarantees that a paparazzo wasn't snapping photos somewhere.

"Don't walk away from me," Viève said. "I asked you a question."

"Busy," Holden said. "You know we've got a film starting tomorrow."

"I'm not the one going to premieres," Viève said, nipping at Holden's heels.

Holden stopped running. "Look, this thing, with us, it's over," he said. He was trying to be gentle.

"Over?" Viève screeched. "Over?! You think you can fuck me and then tell me it's over?"

"Hey, hey, hold it down," Holden said, looking around. "Viève, we haven't had sex in, like, three years."

"You think this is loud, just wait until I go to the press," Viève said. "How will your precious Mary Anne like knowing you've been seeing me since Toronto?"

Holden felt rage building in his chest. He didn't want this crazy girl to hurt Mary Anne. "Viève," he said, his voice low, "this doesn't have anything to do with Mary Anne."

"What? This has *everything* to do with Mary Anne."

Holden looked at the wicked creature standing before him. "You're crazy," he said. He watched Viève's expression change from insane to aroused. Her lips softened and her eyes grew wide. The transformation frightened him.

She stepped forward and pressed herself against him. "Baby, you want me to wait for you? At your truck?" Viève whispered. "I know how much you like me post-workout."

"Stop," Holden said. He grabbed her hand and pushed her away. "Don't you get it? We're done." He brushed past her and started running uphill.

"Oh no, we're not," Viève called.

Holden ran faster, then turned back and looked at Viève standing on the hiking path watching him. He felt a sinking sensation that he knew he couldn't outrun. Viève Dyson was insane, and she was vindictive. And for the next two months she would be his costar.

Rule 20

Act Like Their Friend, Even If You're Faking It

Jessica Caulfield-Fox, Manager-Producer

As per Hollywood custom, upon entering Worldwide's executive dining room, Jessica scanned the room for producers, managers, agents, executives, and celebrities. Pockets of people dined together. Jessica could determine what projects would go into production by the inhabitants at each table. A big star sitting with a big director? Green-light a film. A has-been dining with a wannabe? Not so much.

Jessica's nerves killed her hunger as she followed the hostess to the table where Terri Seawell sat waiting. Terri had built her reputation in Hollywood as a reporter who often exposed the unexposable. As Jessica approached, she surveyed the crusty old journalist in her orange pantsuit and unnaturally blond hair. *Don't let her appearance fool you,* Jessica thought.

Of course, Terri didn't print every nasty secret she uncovered. She hadn't remained an entertainment reporter for more than thirty-five years without knowing what secrets to keep. But Terri needed a story.

Mike had warned Jessica that morning before she left the house. "Babe, be prepared; Terri Seawell doesn't suffer fools," he'd said, picking Max up and swinging him around.

"Daddy," Maxi screamed, giggling.

"She ruined Jill and Brian's marriage. Terri printed the entire off-the-record conversation with Jill. They never recovered," Mike said.

"Lydia gave her total access," Jessica said and pulled on her cashmere top.

"Not sure what's up with Lydia. She's making some dangerous decisions."

"Such as?" Jessica asked.

"Giving a first-time director a sixty-million-dollar movie on a below-average script. Putting Viève and Holden on the same film set with Mary Anne," Mike said. "Should I continue?"

"No," Jessica said.

"So, what *is* going on?"

Jessica shrugged. She turned from the mirror and looked at Mike. She considered omission a type of falsehood, but she didn't want to tell him about Cici's sex tape.

"Come on, Jess, you've never been a good liar. And Lydia is no dummy. She knows something about the letters. Are you going to tell me or just keep me in the dark?"

"It's not my secret to tell."

Mike held up his hand, halting her. "Okay, if that's how you want to play it." He picked up Max and headed down the hall.

"Mike, I really don't—"

"Stop, Jess," Mike interrupted her. "I get that Lydia's your friend. And I understand if you need to protect her and can't tell me something. But don't lie to me. Okay?"

Jessica stopped short and stood in the hallway. A look of disappointment passed over Mike's face, and Jessica felt a twinge of guilt. "Okay," she said.

"You'll be careful?" Mike asked.

"Yeah," Jessica said.

"Because it's not just you anymore. You get that, right?" Mike said. Max sat on Mike's shoulders, ready to go downstairs.

"Go, Daddy, go!" Max yelled.

"Yeah, I get that," Jessica said. She watched as Mike bounded down the stairs with Max bouncing and giggling. Jessica needed to be cautious with Terri, and not just for her own sake.

"Terri, darling, I'm so happy you're here," Jessica now said. She gave Terri the obligatory two-kiss greeting.

"Jessica! I hear your movie is a mess."

"What? Terri, who's telling you these silly lies? We just started production, and everything is fantastic."

"The set must be awful if we're eating at the commissary and not with the crew. Trying to keep me away from the chaos as long as possible?" Terri asked.

"Nonsense," Jessica said. "Just thought this would be quieter, so we could talk."

"Bullshit. So Holden is dating Mary Anne Meyers," Terri said. "How does Viève Dyson like that?"

"Terri, surely you don't expect me to comment on the private lives of my clients and the stars of my film?"

"I have confirmation from his publicist," Terri said.

"About Viève or Mary Anne?" Jessica asked kiddingly.

"About both," Terri said.

Both? Jessica's heart sank. *He's dating both Mary Anne and Viève?*

"Well, his publicist confirms Mary Anne, but someone very close to Holden confirms Viève."

"I see. And do they confirm Santa Claus and the Tooth Fairy, too?" Jessica asked, trying to make light. *Both? Holden wouldn't be so stupid to sleep with both Mary Anne and Viève, would he? And while all three worked on the same film?*

"Is this the kind of set visit I'm going to have, Jessica? The kind where we play coy with each other?" Terri asked.

"I guess that depends," Jessica said. There was a lot at stake for everyone involved. All of their careers were once again on the line.

"On . . ."

"On your definition of discretion," Jessica said.

"I'm around, aren't I? For over thirty years. I think that gives you an idea about my ability to be discreet. Do you know I've attended Steven and Billy's New Year's Eve party every year for the last seven? Kiki and I have lunch twice a month."

"Steven's a huge star and a close friend of yours; as is Kiki," Jessica said. "But with other people there might not be so many reasons for you to be cautious."

"How about you and I be honest and I'll let you read what I write before I turn it into the magazine?"

"Keeping in mind that everything I say is off the record?"

"From an unnamed source," Terri said.

Jessica looked at Terri. She didn't know if she could trust her, but if she wanted to put their spin on any story Terri wrote, she'd have to give Terri some information. "Sounds good. So where do you want to begin?"

"Let's start with Lydia. What's it like working with her and producing for Worldwide?"

"Well, she grew up in the industry, so she's a complete pro," Jessica said as the waiter set her Cobb salad before her.

"You think that Lydia is doing a good job at Worldwide?"

"I think she's phenomenal," Jessica said.

"Really? I mean Arnold Murphy was incompetent, and Lydia is obviously much smarter and better qualified than he. But I question some of her recent decisions."

"Such as?" Jessica asked.

"I read *Vitriol* and, no offense, I still don't understand why she's making this film. The only way I can explain the rush is that Celeste Solange wants to make it. But even Cici wanting to star in the film seems a little weak. She's not the lead, and I find it hard to believe that she's dying to play mother to an actress Viève Dyson's age. So what is it, Jessica? What is the compulsion? Why *Vitriol*? And why now? Lydia has her thrillers for the year. Her slate is full."

Jessica paused. Terri, Jessica knew, spoke daily with Billy. The gossip that she believed Billy and Terri traded could fill *OK* magazine for a year. Terri's question provided Jessica with an opening, a soft pitch that Jessica desired, to begin a plan of misdirection. Did she swing or just sit and let this pitch go by?

"Funny you should ask," Jessica said.

* * *

If Jessica believed all the heist films that Hollywood produced, to catch a thief you needed to be cleverer than the criminal—which worried her. Because the man they suspected was one crafty culprit. Jessica stopped at the gate in front of Steven Brockman's estate.

"How may I help you?" a voice inquired over the speaker.

"Jessica Caulfield-Fox to see Billy."

"One moment, Ms. Fox."

Jessica waited while the phantom voice told Billy of her arrival. She tapped her hand on the steering wheel, trying to release her jitters. She wasn't an actress, and although she often told tender lies so as not to offend *(I loved your screenplay!)*, she entered unfamiliar territory when it came to convincing someone that she was scared and worried for his well-being when actually she believed he wanted to harm her and her friends. Jessica prayed that Cici's primer on conveying emotion worked.

She'd timed her arrival based on Steven Brockman's shooting schedule. By arriving at Billy and Steven's without an appointment, Jessica was arming herself with the element of surprise. She wanted Billy alone and unprepared for this meeting. Jessica watched the wrought-iron gates lumber to life. Showtime!

* * *

A gorgeous young man who could have been a Calvin Klein underwear model wordlessly ushered Jessica into the formal living room. Decorated entirely in chocolate browns and deep reds, with a hint of tiffany blue, the room appeared dramatic and expensive. Floor-to-ceiling windows framed Billy and Steven's view of their infinity pool and the ocean beyond.

"Jessica, my love. I had no idea you were coming by today." Billy entered the living room wearing a robe. "Please forgive me. I've just finished my swim."

"No, I'm so sorry to barge in on you. I would have called but, well, I needed to see you in person."

"Really? Are you all right?"

"Can we talk here?" Jessica whispered, making sure she wore a pleading look on her face.

"Of course, by the pool. Nelson!" Billy called. The Calvin Klein model reappeared. "Jessica and I are going to the pool. I'd like some juice. Jess, anything for you?"

"Pellegrino?" Jessica asked.

Nelson nodded.

Billy led Jessica through the back patio door and to a plush seating area by the pool. "Here is private. No extra ears." He settled onto an outdoor recliner, leaned back, and crossed his ankles. A demure yet powerful pose. "Now, what is it, Jessica? I've never seen you so agitated."

So far so good, Jessica thought.

"I don't know where to start," she said. "Or how to ask."

"Well, first, what's it about?"

"Everything. I'm worried. I mean this could be awful for Steven and you." She watched Billy lean forward.

"Tell me. You know I'll do anything I can to help."

"I'm worried about Lydia," Jessica said.

"Lydia?" A look of surprise formed on Billy's face.

"Her recent decisions? They just seem so, so . . ."

"Arbitrary?" Billy offered.

"For lack of a better word, yes," Jessica said.

"And you're concerned?"

"Very."

"Have you discussed this with Ted or Mike?"

"Ted? Please. Ted's biggest blind spot, aside from Celeste, is Lydia Albright. Billy, you're discreet and a realist. I mean, what is Lydia thinking, giving Nathan Curtis his first feature? Do you know him?"

"I met Nathan for the first time a couple of months ago, when he did some photographs of Steven for *GQ*."

Jessica felt her heartbeat quicken with Billy's lie. She knew Billy and Nathan were friends back in their swinging London days. Why would Billy hide his prior relationship with Nathan Curtis? Jessica and Lydia had a theory that Billy and Nathan were working together. Nelson arrived and placed their drinks on the settee between Jessica and Billy.

"What about Viève?" Billy asked.

You know her from London, too, Jessica thought. "Viève? I worked with her on *Collusion*. She is a complete nut. To put her on set with her former lover Holden Humphrey and his new girlfriend, Mary Anne? *Vitriol* is a powder keg waiting to explode."

Jessica watched Billy smile at her remark. She picked up her water and sipped. "But I know you wanted Viève in the role opposite Steven." she said. She wondered if Billy would mention that he knew Viève.

"I've not met Viève," Billy said, glancing down at his juice. "But her acting is superb, and her age helps Steven appear young to the public."

Another lie. From behind her Dior sunglasses, Jessica studied Billy's face. He didn't flinch. Lying took practice, and Jessica surmised that Billy had had plenty.

"And Cici . . . well, you know about Cici, right?" she asked.

"The DVD?"

Jessica paused, a little surprised by Billy's straightforward response. "Yes, the DVD."

"I've seen it," Billy said.

Jessica leaned forward. She wanted to appear calm, but her heart beat so fast it felt like it would pop out of her chest. "And?"

"Who knew Miss All-American Superstar could be such a naughty, naughty girl," Billy said.

"That DVD will destroy my movie," Jessica said.

"Maybe. Maybe not."

"Come on, Billy, once the DVD hits the mainstream media? You and I both know the press and public will have a feeding frenzy."

"Well, it might not ever go mainstream, right?" Billy asked.

Jessica shook her head. "Not possible. Whoever has the film knows they have a cash cow. Footage of Celeste Solange fucking? That's like a money tree growing in your backyard."

"What if a private collector has the footage?" Billy asked.

"Nathan Curtis saw it," Jessica said. "Whoever has it is showing it. The story will break." She watched Billy, needing to know what he'd say. Did he know who owned the DVD? Were he and Nathan in this together? *Spill something, Billy,* she thought. Instead Billy gazed out over the pool toward the ocean.

"Did you see the cover of last month's *Redbook*?" Billy finally asked.

"The one with Steven, Katherine, and Sylvan?"

"The perfect all-American family," Billy said.

Jessica felt envy oozing out of Billy. He lived the perpetual life of the other woman without the possibility of Steven's ever leaving his wife and making his relationship with Billy legitimate. Steven couldn't divorce his pretend wife and marry his gay lover, not even in California—not if Steven wanted to keep his fan base.

"No."

"*Redbook*'s circulation tripled because of the cover shot," Billy said. "Steven was thrilled." Jessica watched as Billy's cool exterior cracked. His brow creased, and his tone contained pain.

"I don't know how you do it, Billy, hiding your life for Steven's career," Jessica said softly.

"I guess my situation is much like being the other woman, except here, in L.A., where everyone knows I'm the full-time live-in."

"I'd never feel secure," Jessica said.

"Security is overrated," Billy said. "But you're right, I have to keep some things for myself."

Jessica saw a flicker of anger behind his eyes. She almost felt sad for him. The idea of loving someone the way she loved Mike and being unable to tell the world? The pain that repression caused? And all this while Steven pretended to be married to someone else?

"Ours is like any marriage; you never know what goes on in your spouse's mind." Billy stared at the infinity pool, his expression frozen in thought.

"Billy, do you know who has the DVD of Celeste?" Jessica asked gently.

Billy tore his gaze away from the view and looked at Jessica, hardening again.

"Jessica, I'm afraid that's a secret I'm unwilling to share."

Rule 21

You Get What You Pay For

Kiki Dee, Publicist

Kiki would pay for sex. Why shouldn't she? Men paid for sex. She was an older woman with a lot of dough and she'd finally found somebody who would provide. Capitalism 101: supply and demand. Kiki was merely helping the economy. She leaned against the plush pillows on the king-size bed at the Peninsula.

Working girls, aka actresses, constantly prowled the Peninsula bar looking for producers and agents. But where were the working boys? Kiki had finally asked Terri Seawell.

She and Terri went all the way back to their days in New York. In her twenties, Kiki had broken into entertainment as a dancer, while Terri struggled for a break as a singer. Back then, young, broke, and beautiful, they turned a few tricks to cover the rent. Of course, they didn't *call* them tricks. No, the girls were simply dating older men. Older men who wanted the girls taken care of. And in return for their male companions' generosity and concern, Kiki and Terri expressed their gratitude.

Now Kiki maintained a position on the heavy end of the economic scale. She had money, power, and connections. And yes, she was happy to give a little financial help, as long as she got some sexual satisfaction in return. She glanced at her Cartier watch with irritation: He'd said four-thirty and her watch now read ten after five. She had left the fake name at the front desk and gone to room 245 as he'd requested. Kiki looked down at her La Perla bra. Brand-new. Boom Boom had picked it up that morning at Barneys.

"I want the white satin with black pinstripes," Kiki had told her.

"Demi cup or full coverage?"

"Demi."

"Do you want a thong or boy-cut shorts?" Boom Boom asked.

"I'll take the thong. And make sure to get the garter belt and some black stockings."

"Got it." Boom Boom scribbled on her pad.

Kiki watched Boom Boom pick up her purse. The bag looked like something Boom Boom had purchased at Goodwill.

"What is that?" Kiki asked.

"My bag?"

"Yes, but who made it?"

"I don't know. I picked it up at Target," Boom Boom said.

"Did you just say that you picked it up at Target?" Disgust laced Kiki's voice.

Boom Boom looked at Kiki and then at the offending bag.

"You are working for KDP and walking around Beverly Hills with a bag from Target? Boom Boom, how long have you worked for me?"

"Almost five years."

"And have you ever seen me wear anything made by anyone other than a well-known designer?"

"No."

"Have I ever mentioned the word *Target*?"

"No."

"Do I go to Supercuts?"

"No."

"Have you ever seen me in anything other than heels?"

"No."

"Then why? Why do you torture me so?" Kiki asked. She could feel her heart rate rising and her blood vessels expanding. A lack of money didn't create Boom Boom's fashion faux pas—Kiki knew that Boom Boom and her entire family were rolling in dough.

"It all seems so superficial," Boom Boom said.

"Superficial? Superficial? You are in public relations! Of course it's superficial. Superficial is what we do. We specialize in superficial. We sell superficial. Our *whole business* is about image and presentation. Our world, our business, has nothing to do with substance or reality. If you want reality, go work for a nonprofit. But if you want glitz, glamour, and everything that is unreal, then movie publicity is the biggest game in town. Don't you get it? Have you learned nothing in five years?"

Boom Boom sighed.

"Do you want to work here?" Kiki asked.

"Yes," Boom Boom said.

"Do you want to be an assistant for the rest of your life?"

"No."

"Then get with the program," Kiki said. "If you want to be in public relations for entertainment, then you have to wear the uniform, walk the walk, and talk the talk. That includes clothes, shoes, bags, brows, and a mani-pedi twice a week. Got it? Have I spelled it out for you?"

The girl had received every conceivable advantage: money, a great college education, supportive parents, and now, thanks to Kiki, excellent hair. Why wasn't she more driven, moving faster?

Boom Boom nodded and threw her bag over her shoulder. "Fine, Kiki. But I won't like it."

"Then get a different job. You'd think after five years you'd figure it out," Kiki said. She clicked her computer icon for her phone sheet. "Go, go! I have my meeting this afternoon and I need that lingerie." She waved her hands at Boom Boom. "And don't forget my K-Y Jelly," she yelled as Boom Boom exited her office.

A wicked smile danced over Kiki's lips. She enjoyed the role of bitch and she liked being in charge. But maybe she wasn't in charge anymore, as obviously this young stud didn't feel the need to appear on time. She scooted down the bed, trying to adjust her thong, and heard the door open in the other room. What did he look like? She hoped he was tall with black hair. Maybe Italian or Spanish? Argentinean would be good. Or Greek? Her very best lover had been Greek. Oh, they were very bad, those Greeks . . . so bad but so good.

Kiki rearranged herself on the bed, trying to strike a sexy pose. Her body felt firm (Pilates and weight training) but her skin? Melnick could do only so much with her skin. Skin lost its elasticity. Melnick kept her face looking young-*ish,* but so far, even with all the miracles of modern medicine, he could do nothing to make the skin on the rest of her body appear as it did when she was twenty.

"Kiki?" Two candles flickered on either side of the bed, illuminating his perfect face.

"Yes," she said.

She looked at him from head to toe. She watched as he pulled his black T-shirt over his head. He couldn't be much more than twenty-five. A young man's body was heaven-sent. Why *was* youth wasted on the young? They had no idea the beauty and power they possessed until both slipped through their fingers. He looked like he worked out seven days a week. His pectoral muscles were firm and defined. A full eight-pack flexed across his abdomen. His skin glistened in the candlelight. The curved muscles around his hips made Kiki's toes curl. He slowly unbuttoned his jeans and slipped them over his bare ass, then stood and faced her. She smiled. *Hello, big daddy,* she thought. The last thing she wanted to see when he took off his pants while she was lying completely exposed on the bed was a flaccid penis, and he didn't disappoint her.

He leaned forward and placed his hands on the bed. "Where should I start?"

Kiki rested against the pillows. "Why don't you work your way up?"

* * *

"Fanfuckingtastic!" Kiki said as Boom Boom pulled the black leotard out of her Versace bag. "He made me come six times in two hours. Can you believe that? *Six times!* Completely worth the money. Completely! I need you to call and schedule another session for next week."

"His name?" Boom Boom asked.

"Who knows? Who cares? He gave me his number." Kiki tossed the piece of paper from the notepad in her hotel room to Boom Boom. "He wants room two-forty-five again. Who knows why? Just get me into his schedule. Weekly. And make sure I always have cash when I meet him. It's fifteen hundred for a two-hour session, plus tip. So two thousand. I feel so good. Boom Boom, you really should get fucked like that. Someone completely servicing your every desire? What woman ever had that? Right? I mean, come on, sex is almost always about the man. Have you ever been with someone who made the sex completely about you?"

Boom Boom remained silent as she pulled out the night-vision goggles and set them on Kiki's bed.

"I'm getting you a session. My gift to you. You'll love it," Kiki said. She dropped her Prada skirt to the floor and pulled on the black catsuit. "Nice bag, by the way."

"Thanks. I don't think I want a session," Boom Boom said.

"What? You have no idea what you're missing. It doesn't have to be the same guy if that's weird for you."

"No. I mean, I don't—"

"Don't tell me. You're a—"

"Please don't, Kiki. It's personal."

"You are! You're a virgin. Oh my God, do you know how rare that is in Los Angeles? I think you may be the oldest virgin I've ever met."

"I didn't say that I—"

"You didn't have to. Look at you. You're bright red."

"That's not it. I'm seeing someone. Or, kind of seeing someone."

Kiki looked at Boom Boom. Seeing someone? Her little frumpette had a friend? "Really?" She felt a pang of jealousy. Of course, Boom Boom had natural youth on her side. Even the dowdy one could find a date, while Kiki's age forced her to pay for pleasure.

"Kiki—"

"No, listen. I think this is fantastic. Believe me, I had my fun at your age. But when the newness wears off, you let me know. Because I am telling you, there is nothing as good as a man concentrating one hundred percent of his sexual energy on your pleasure." Kiki looked at the equipment lying on her bed. "Did Sherman give you the key card, too?"

"Here," Boom Boom said, handing it to Kiki.

"So we've got everything, then?"

"Everything that was on your list."

"Including the mini-camera?"

"Right here."

"Okay, so we're ready. Sherman's contact said she'd leave the file cabinets unlocked. We have the key cards to get into the building and then into Melnick's suite," Kiki said. Her sexual endorphin high fueled her. "And the rental car is out front?"

Boom Boom nodded. She was already wearing her black turtleneck, black pants, and . . . black *heels*?

"Are those Ferragamo?" Kiki asked, appraising Boom Boom's shoes.

"Yes."

"I haven't seen those anywhere," Kiki said.

"Next season."

Kiki gasped. "What? You have next season's Ferragamos?"

"I know a guy," Boom Boom said. She slipped her bag over her shoulder. "Shall we go?"

"You know a guy?" Kiki was impressed. Maybe Boom Boom had been paying attention. It certainly seemed so with the bag, shoes, and . . . was that a Chanel overcoat?

Boom Boom saw Kiki eyeing the coat. "It's Chanel," Boom Boom said.

"Very nice." Kiki reached out and touched the cloth. "Very nice."

* * *

The lights at the reception desk had remained on after hours, just as Sherman's contact promised. Excitement pulsed through Kiki. She hadn't stolen files in almost five years. When she started KDP, breaking and entering quickly became one of her favorite business tactics.

"It's got to be the next cabinet," Kiki whispered. She stood, turned to her left, and pulled out the top drawer. How did people do this all day? The file cabinet hit her at shoulder level. She stood on her tippy toes to see the names.

"Do you want the step stool?" Boom Boom asked from her post by the front door.

"I'm fine. I see it. If I can just reach over." Kiki stretched toward the file she wanted.

"Kiki! Someone is coming," Boom Boom whispered.

"What?"

"A man and a woman."

"Is it Melnick? Are they coming here?"

"I don't know. I've never seen Melnick."

"What does the man look like?" Kiki asked.

"He's got a big nose and—"

"That's him," Kiki said. She slammed the file cabinet drawer shut and turned toward Boom Boom. "Hurry, we need—" Kiki lost her balance before she felt the pain in her shin. Her right hand sank deep into the lowest file cabinet drawer, which she had failed to close. Her fingertips touched the bottom of the drawer as her head hit the metal edge. She bounced sideways and landed on her back.

"Kiki?" Boom Boom stood above her. "Kiki?"

Kiki looked up and tried to focus on her assistant's face. Two Boom Booms floated above her.

"You're bleeding," Boom Boom said, kneeling beside her.

"Why are there two of you?" Kiki asked. "I don't even want one."

Kiki heard a clicking noise. "What's that?"

"Kiki, shut up. That's the front door. The doctor is here."

Boom Boom shoved Kiki into the coat closet next to the file cabinets. They both huddled on top of a pile of shoes, sweaters hung over their heads.

"Who's he with?" Kiki asked. She could barely see into Melnick's first exam room where he and the tiny creature had disappeared.

"It's her," Boom Boom said.

"Who?"

"Kiki, *the one whose file we're here for*! It's her!"

Kiki squinted. She felt a warm trickle on her face and touched her forehead. *Blood? Her face? She'd cut her face?*

"I'm bleeding," Kiki wailed.

"Shh, I told you that. Shut up. Prison won't be kind to you," Boom Boom whispered. "He's got a needle. He's giving her a shot."

"It's not her," Kiki said. She pushed Boom Boom, trying to get a better view.

Boom Boom shoved her back. "Look, Kiki, get your fucking elbow out of my ribs, okay? I know what I'm seeing. Just sit back and listen to the commentary."

Kiki turned and looked at her assistant, ready to whip the girl with her words, but then she saw the cold look in Boom Boom's eyes. Boom Boom's expression said she'd knock Kiki out if she uttered another word. Kiki leaned back into the broom behind her. "Boom Boom," she said.

"I'm not kidding, Kiki," Boom Boom said.

"You're promoted."

Rule 22

Sex Sells

Celeste Solange, Actress

Cici disliked reporters; they rarely wrote good things about her. And that included Terri Seawell. As Cici stretched, she looked into her exercise mirror at Terri behind her, draped over a chaise lounge eating a buttered croissant, sipping a cappuccino, and flipping through *Variety.* Cici knew that her publicist, Kiki, relied on entertainment reporters like Terri to maintain Celeste's value in the marketplace. And the studios, Worldwide included, banked on the public's obsession with actors' lives to spur ticket sales. But even with this knowledge, she still believed that Lydia and Kiki's decision to grant Terri Seawell full on-set access during the filming of *Vitriol* was foolish. Cici knew Lydia had only struck the bargain to keep Steven Brockman on the film, but to have on set Terri Seawell, Hollywood's oldest and most notorious entertainment reporter, while a sex tape of Cici was floating about town? It sounded to Cici like a recipe for disaster.

Cici watched herself as she contorted her lithe body, doing post-workout stretches. She still looked good, though perhaps not as good as the barely eighteen girls on the DVDs she'd found in Damien's closet. She hadn't found any extra footage of herself on the unmarked DVDs from Damien's safe, just nubile young girls.

"So, is this how you start all your days?" Terri asked. Her eyes darted to Liam's tush as he bent over to pack up his workout gear.

"Most of them," Cici said.

"So what's next?"

"Shower, then Kiki, then the set. My call time isn't until after lunch today."

"And where are we lunching?' Terri asked.

"I don't have a lunch scheduled for today. I'm in production," Cici said.

"You don't eat when you're in production?"

"Not much." Cici watched Terri slather butter on her final bit of croissant and stuff it into her mouth. Cici guessed from Terri's ample bosom and derriere that the journalist enjoyed mealtime.

"How sexy is that?" Terri asked. "So tomorrow is the same setup? Workout and call time after lunch?"

"Yes," Cici said. "Exactly the same."

"Then I'll sleep in and have room service. Meet you on set, if that's okay with you."

"Of course. Whatever you want; whatever you need," Celeste said. "Kiki told you that after tomorrow I have a ten-day break in my shooting schedule, right?"

"What? No, I didn't know that," Terri said. She was visibly irritated.

"Lydia mentioned she wants you to follow Holden, if that's okay. I mean, I don't have any real plans. Ted and I are going to take a quick break at the house in Fiji," Cici lied. She hoped Terri bought it. Cici needed to be reporter-free for the next week and a half.

"Holden Humphrey? No, I'm happy to follow Holden around for a couple of days. Is he still sleeping with Mary Anne Meyers?" Terri asked.

"Now, Terri, isn't that a question for Holden or Mary Anne?"

"Whatever. I'll just ask Viève," Terri said.

"Yes, why don't you." Cici flashed Terri a cherubic smile.

"How do you like working with her?" Terri asked.

"Mary Anne? I love—"

"No, Celeste. I *know* you love Mary Anne. I mean Viève. How do you like working with Viève?"

"She's very talented," Cici said.

"Cut the crap. Is she as cuckoo as everyone says?"

"I really don't know what you're talking about."

"Cici, we've been through a lot," Terri said. "You know that I've always been close to Damien's wives. Or, I should say, former wives." She gave Cici a pointed look. "You know there are always so many *rumors* in town."

Cici felt the pinch of anxiety. Terri's innuendo made her uncomfortable. Could she know?

"Perhaps I should rephrase my question. Viève Dyson. Off the record, how is she to work with?"

"Well, as long as we're off the record," Cici said.

* * *

Cici disliked spending time with an entertainment reporter, but spending time with an entertainment reporter *and* a publicist was torture. Terri and Kiki, masters at spin, were having a conversation that made Celeste feel like someone had strapped her to the teacup ride at Disneyland without any speed control. She knew the two aging mavens' history: They'd been roommates years before in New York, when they were young, broke, and struggling. But prior to this meeting, Cici didn't realize the competitive nature of Kiki and Terri's relationship. For forty long minutes she listened to Kiki discuss all her superstar clients, instead of, as planned, discussing Cici's Oscar campaign.

"I told Holden he's a fool to have Mort as a publicist. Especially now, with this luscious little love affair? Such an opportunity! And Mort will completely waste it."

"I'm sitting down with Holden this week. I'll tell him he should be with you," Terri said. "So how was the Peninsula?"

"Fanfuckingtastic!" Kiki gushed. "The best experience of my life.

Thank you so much for passing him along. I'm weekly now. He's unbelievable."

"Who?" Cici asked, curious as to what, other than celebrity scandal, could elicit such an enthusiastic response from Kiki.

"What's his name?" Kiki was saying to Terri. "I didn't even ask. I was too busy screaming yes, yes, yes!"

"What are you talking about?" Cici looked first at Kiki and then at Terri.

"A special little service for women, of which I am sure you have no need," Terri said.

"At least not yet," Kiki said. Give it another fifteen years. Then, if you're unmarried, you, too, can become a client."

"A what?"

"It's a male escort service," Terri said. "For wealthy, older women."

"Speak for yourself," Kiki snipped. "It's for wealthy, *single* women."

"Kiki, you can fool some of the people, but we were born the same year. Just because I choose not to surgically deform myself doesn't mean that you are in fact younger. You just look stranger," Terri said.

"You bitch," Kiki said. "You know that I'm younger than you."

"By three weeks."

"Still."

"An escort service? You two use an escort service?" Cici asked.

"Well, don't look so surprised, Celeste," Kiki said. "You'll see. Once you hit forty, if you're not married, the dates dry up."

"Try fifty, and she's right," Terri said. "But the desire, the need?"

"That continues."

"And increases," Terri said. "But the supply of willing males . . ."

"Nonexistent," Kiki said. "Even thc ones who were begging for it when you were younger—"

"If they're still alive—"

"—are disinterested," Kiki continued. "Viagra killed it for us more mature—"

"Old," Terri interrupted.

"—ladies," Kiki finished.

"The men our age go after the girls your age," Terri said. "And why not? They have plenty of dough, and now, with Viagra, they have staying power."

"You two don't need an escort service," Cici said. "You're both smart, wealthy women. Men your age must go for women like you."

"Oh really?" Terri asked. "Just how old is Ted?"

Cici looked first at Kiki and then at Terri.

"He's almost sixty," Cici said.

"Try sixty-five," Terri said. "Women aren't the only ones who lie about their age."

"Ted isn't sixty-five," Cici said. "There's no way. His kids are only—"

"Get online and check," Terri interrupted. "I believe his daughter is almost your age, Cici, and his son is thirty-five."

Cici thought about Terri's words. *Ted? Sixty-five?* She was sleeping with a man older than her father would be? When Cici first met Ted, she believed him to be in his early fifties, but if he, too, like everyone else in entertainment, subtracted seven years from his age, then he *was* almost sixty-five.

"Seventy is the new fifty," Kiki cackled.

Cici tried to manage a smile. Did everyone in town lie about something? Kiki placed her hand over the younger woman's.

"Cici, you can't be upset about this? You're dating one of the wealthiest and most powerful men in the world."

"And he is absolutely mad for you," Terri said. "He was quite a whore for a while after his wife died."

"What?" Cici looked at Terri. A tremor passed through her. She wanted a monogamous relationship. She'd chosen Ted after Damien, in part, because she wanted someone to trust.

"How many models did he date?" Terri asked.

"I lost count after the crazy one from England."

"The one with the heroin addiction?"

"Right. But that came out after they broke up," Kiki said.

"You two must have the wrong guy," Cici said.

"Like there could be any mistaking Ted Robinoff," Terri said.

"Darling, I'm afraid they are all hounds," Kiki said. "Besides, what's to worry? You aren't married, you have your own money, and he's forking over a ton of dough for your Oscar campaign. Terri, you should see the money he's shelling out! The parties and the ads. I think he's going to personally shake the hand of every Academy member who's still breathing at the Ray Stark Villa."

"It worked for Harvey," Terri said.

Cici's heart beat faster thinking about Ted's devotion to her. But she loved him, and she didn't want him fooling around with models, actresses, or prostitutes.

"Oh Cici, stop," Terri said. "We shouldn't have said anything."

"Please, darling, it's obvious he's in love with you. It's not like he's still taking his Asian sex tours," Kiki said.

"Asia?" Cici whispered.

"Most of them go to Asia now," Terri said.

"Keeps everything private, you know," said Kiki. "They don't have to read about their fetishes in the tabloids."

"Really, who cares if you want a golden shower? Sexual preference is none of my affair. And I'm a reporter," Terri said.

"Sex sells," Kiki said. "So, Terri, since you're here. I want your opinion on these shots. I'm not very pleased with them, honestly, but which one do you think we should build the Oscar campaign around?" Kiki placed four publicity stills of Celeste from *California Girl* onto the table.

While Kiki and Terri prattled on about the Oscar campaign, Cici's mind spun. (She had already seen the shots, and her opinion seemed irrelevant anyway.) Ted had flown to Hong Kong two days earlier. He'd spent the majority of the last three months traveling between Malaysia, China, Japan, and Hong Kong. Celeste glanced at her reflection in the window. She could barely make out her face. Was it her age? Did he want someone younger? Was he bored? She had rescheduled her appointment with Dr. Melnick twice and was considering canceling altogether, but now she wondered if she needed to keep the appointment after all.

She looked at the two cackling old birds. Kiki's face looked overdone. One more procedure and any hint of normalcy would disappear. But Kiki treated plastic surgery like a weekly mani-pedi appointment. Meanwhile, Terri was the opposite. The jowls on that one! She could wrap the loose skin from her chin around her neck and use it as a scarf. Both were wealthy. Both were the definition of success. But lonely? Obviously. Married? Kiki twice, unsuccessfully. Terri, never. She had legendary affairs. She'd slept with every A-list male star through the sixties, seventies, and well into the eighties. But now? Children? None. No family. Cici watched Kiki and Terri riffle through the pictures of her. Cici didn't want a solitary life when she grew old. She didn't want to hire a male stud service to satisfy her sexual needs. She didn't want to rattle around in a giant house with only staff and assistants to keep her company. Where would she spend her holidays? And why hadn't she thought of any of this earlier?

"Cici." Kiki tapped her on the arm. "Come back to us, darling. Terri likes this one." She held up a midrange still of Cici's face. "What do you think?"

"I thought you wanted to go with a close-up?"

"Well, I did, but sweetie, you're not twenty-five anymore, and I want to at least keep the perception of youth for the public," Kiki said.

"Look, here," Terri said, pointing to a close-up of Cici's face, "under your eyes. It's the beginning of bags."

"Can't they touch up the photo?" Celeste asked.

"Oh, honey," Kiki said. "They already did."

* * *

Two days later, Cici lay on a gurney waiting for Melnick's nurse to wheel her into the surgical suite.

"You sure you want to do this? You don't have to," Mary Anne said, a concerned expression on her face.

"You'll wait for me?" Cici asked. She suddenly felt vulnerable without Ted.

"Of course."

Cici reached her hand to Mary Anne and tried to calm herself. She didn't have to do this; she knew that. The surgery was elective. But her public expected her to personify youth and to age gracefully. And Cici thought that aging gracefully, in the public's eyes, meant aging very little at all.

"Miss Solange? Are you ready?" Melnick's nurse stood waiting to push her to the operating suite. The vanity of the procedure made Cici feel that she had no right to be afraid, but suddenly her palms were moist.

"Cici." Charles Melnick rounded the corner wearing his scrubs, his hands raised to the heavens. "I do this every day; no worries."

Cici attempted a smile. She glanced at Mary Anne.

"I'll be here when you wake up," Mary Anne said.

Cici nodded her head and gave her a small smile as Mary Anne's fingers slipped away.

Rule 23

Never Panic

Lydia Albright, President of Production, Worldwide Pictures

Lydia almost erased the message when she saw the blinking light on her answering machine. Only solicitors called her home number; everyone else called her office or her mobile. But this time, for some reason, she pushed the button—and heard a cryptic message from Ted Robinoff, her boss, the owner and chairman of Worldwide Pictures.

"Call me from your landline at home as soon as you get this." That was it.

Lydia fished her BlackBerry from her purse. No messages, no e-mails. Ted, Lydia realized, wanted no trace of this call. Studio security monitored the landlines at Worldwide. Most offices, unbeknownst to their executive inhabitants, contained bugs, and some even had cameras. Security had the capability to listen to all the mobile phones Worldwide purchased for their executives. So, as Lydia dialed Ted's number in Japan, she realized this call from Ted was different from most of their conversations.

"Lydia?" Though it was deep into the night in Tokyo, Ted answered without a hint of fatigue in his voice.

"Hello, Ted."

"Where's Cici?" he asked.

Ted's question surprised Lydia. Ted lived with Cici. And since she and Lydia were close friends, Ted and Lydia maintained an unspoken agreement never to discuss Cici except as regarded film roles.

"I'm guessing either on her way to the set or at home," Lydia said.

"Then why did I just pick up a message from Terri Seawell asking me how Cici and I are enjoying Fiji?"

Lydia paused, trying to remember why Terri thought Cici and Ted had flown to Fiji.

"Oh, that's right," Lydia said, covering, "Cici's off the shooting schedule for a couple of days and she wanted to be Terri-free."

"What do you mean Terri-free?"

Lydia assumed Cici had shared with Ted that Terri Seawell was shadowing her during the filming of *Vitriol.*

"It's for the Oscar campaign for *California Girl.* Terri's shadowing Cici while we shoot *Vitriol.*"

"*Vitriol?* Terri Seawell is on set for *Vitriol*? Are you sure that's wise?" Ted asked.

Lydia felt anxious. What did he know? Why would he question Lydia's decision to allow Terri access to the set?

"Terri's article gets Cici and Steven Brockman the cover of *Vanity Fair* before the Academy votes," Lydia said.

"But where's Celeste? She hasn't been home in two days and she's not answering her cell. I don't want to appear like a jealous lover, but I haven't gotten a return call."

"Did you try Mary Anne?" Lydia remembered that Mary Anne had offered to help Cici after her surgery. Mary Anne would know the cover story Cici wanted to give Ted.

"I'll try her. And you'll see Cici today. Tell her to call me."

Today? Lydia glanced at the calendar on her BlackBerry. Of course, today. She'd blocked out two hours of her day for a lunch visit with Cici, and Ted had access to Lydia's calendar.

"No problem," Lydia said. She felt a squeeze in her chest.

"Any more letters?" Ted asked.

"So far no," Lydia said. She felt apprehensive. "I'd tell Briggs if I received more."

"I'm sure you would," Ted said and released the line.

* * *

"He knows," Lydia said. She looked at Cici enjoying her second day post-surgery in a bed at the Peninsula, surrounded by pillows and flipping through *Vogue*. Mary Anne sat beside Celeste while, across the room, Jessica spoke with Mike on the phone.

"About the face-lift?" Mary Anne gasped.

"He doesn't know," Cici said, still turning pages.

Lydia paced in front of the window. She felt trapped. She was convinced that Ted's tone had meant that he knew something. She looked across the suite to Jessica yapping on her phone. *Vitriol* was already a mess. Mike had arrived on set that morning to find Viève locked in her trailer.

"And it's an eye-lift, by the way," Cici said. "Not a face-lift."

"Not the eye-lift, the sex tape," Lydia said, exasperated.

"Sex tape?" Mary Anne looked confused.

"I'm bored," Cici said. "Where is Melnick? He's late, and I want to go home."

"This is the Peninsula, Cici," said Jessica, now finished with her call. "Anything you want, they can find. Besides, we can't smuggle you out until later. If Terri finds out you're in Beverly Hills and have ditched her, this face-lift won't remain a secret." She picked up the room-service menu. "Anyone else hungry?"

Lydia felt frustration rise inside her. Had they heard her? Did they even listen? She'd risked her career for these three, and all they wanted to discuss was plastic surgery, shopping, and lunch? She had ditched her security detail to attend this meeting. Why weren't her friends more alarmed? Was this a game for them?

"*He knows,*" Lydia said. She wanted them to stop chatting. To stop pretending everything was fine. To begin to feel the fear she experienced almost every day. But their chatter continued.

"Lydia, he can't know," Cici said. "Don't worry. Oh! I didn't tell you? Terri and Kiki go to hookers."

"Hookers? But they're so old," Mary Anne said.

"What? Old people don't do it?" Jessica asked. "You think Mitsy and Marvin haven't been like rabbits since they renewed their vows and went to Miravel for their couples' weekend?"

"Are you and my mom still e-mailing?" Mary Anne asked Jessica.

"Occasionally, but not about you," Jessica said playfully. "Never about you. Or Holden. Or anything like that."

"Ted knows," Lydia said again. She could feel her irritation turning to anger. But the other three continued prattling. "Ted knows about the sex tape!" Lydia didn't realize she'd yelled, giving voice to her anxiety, until she saw the looks on her friends' faces. Lydia never yelled. Not even during *Seven Minutes Past Midnight,* with Arnold clawing down her back. But now, at this moment, the overwhelming sensation that she might drown in fear had consumed her. She watched her three friends give her placating looks.

"What did he say?" Jessica asked softly.

"It's not *what* he said, but *how* he said it." Lydia watched her friends exchange looks.

Cici finally broke the awkward silence. "I know what you mean. Ted conveys information he doesn't want to verbalize through tone."

"Exactly. I'm telling you, Cici, he knows. And I need you to tell him about the footage, because if we don't—"

"What about Sherman?" Jessica interrupted.

"Sherman doesn't matter if Ted knows," Lydia said. She heard the desperation in her voice.

"He still matters if the goal is to get the DVD," Jessica said.

"Right. Isn't Howard negotiating with Sherman?" Cici asked.

"Besides, if we get the DVD, all Ted has is speculation," Jessica said.

"Wait, I'm still back on the sex tape," Mary Anne said, a look of shock on her face. "Your sex tape got out? I thought you destroyed it."

"So did I," Cici said. "But it seems Nathan Curtis saw the footage at some sex party. Then Sherman Ross, this very questionable private investigator who works with both Howard and Kiki, gave the DVD to Kiki."

"Your publicist?" Mary Anne asked. "But why?"

"To let Cici know he had the tape," Jessica said. "So she can make an offer to purchase the DVD."

"Right. Seems he's brokering the sale for whoever owns it," Cici said. "I've got Howard on it—he's attempting to buy it from Sherman."

"But who stole the footage?"

"Mary Anne, if we knew who stole the footage, do you think we'd still be having this conversation? Do you think I'd be this upset?" Lydia asked, her tone harsh.

"Sorry," Mary Anne whispered.

"Jessica and Lydia seem to think Billy has something to do with it, and maybe Viève and Nathan," Cici said. "Viève and Billy have been friends for years, but they're keeping that a secret, and we don't know why."

"And Lydia's been getting crazy stalker notes and phone calls," Jessica added.

"So Worldwide put a security detail on Lydia," Cici said.

"And Ted doesn't know any of this?" Mary Anne asked.

"Ted knows about the notes and the stalker," Jessica said.

"But not about my sex tape. Or my eyes," Cici finished.

"He knows everything," Lydia said. "Cici, you're in denial if you think Ted doesn't know about the DVD."

Cici gave Lydia a sour look. "Excuse me, Lydia. You said yourself that Ted didn't mention the tape. If we get the DVD, then all Ted has is groundless rumors, and all of us know how many rumors float around Hollywood."

"And audiotape," Lydia muttered. "Ted might be monitoring your home phone and your cell."

"Then why would he call you? He'd know I was staying at the Peninsula. He'd know about my eye-lift. I used the home phone and my mobile for those calls."

"Unless he's just that smart." Lydia leaned forward and looked at her friends. "He wants us to *believe* he doesn't know." She watched them exchange a glance. They thought she'd lost her mind. She could see it on their faces. These three women, for whom she risked her career, questioned her sanity.

"Okay, Lydia, you're really starting to sound paranoid," Cici said, giving her a weak smile.

"Paranoid? Paranoid?" Lydia heard her voice become shrill. "Cici, I've got a wack job sending me notes, the wealthiest man in America, my boss, only wants to speak to me on an untapped line, you have a sex tape about to be auctioned, Arnold Murphy shows up at a Worldwide premiere . . . and I'm paranoid?" Her head pounded. "I can't do this. I feel like I'm doing this alone. Why aren't any of you concerned? The fate of our careers and the future of Worldwide rides on this, and all you three want to do is order lunch and have mani-pedis!" She grabbed her purse and headed for the door. "You give me a call when you get serious." She heard the door slam behind her as she walked down the hall.

Rule 24

Never Ignore a Threat

Mary Anne Meyers, Screenwriter

Mary Anne lounged in a cable-knit sweater on the chaise next to her swimming pool while her niece and nephews splashed one another. The underwater pool lights had come on ten minutes earlier. The wind had picked up when the sun set.

"Aren't you guys cold?" Mary Anne called. She watched her niece, Lauren, climb onto her cousin's shoulders.

"We're good," Gavin, her older nephew, called to her.

It was the final night before her family, excluding Mitsy and Marvin, returned to St. Paul, and Mitsy had decided that tonight she wanted to cook a big family meal. Mary Anne could smell Mitsy's meat loaf from inside. She looked through the kitchen window and watched her mother standing at the sink. Steam outlined the glass, so she guessed Mitsy had just dumped the boiled potatoes in preparation for mashing. Michelle and Sue had gone shopping at The Grove, while Michael and Marvin drove to the Valley to check out some commercial real estate they'd found for sale.

Mary Anne leaned back and watched her nephew dive into the pool. The first scream she heard sounded as if it came from her neighbors'. But the second scream was louder and definitely came from the house.

"What was that?" Mary Anne bolted up and jumped for the door. She wondered if Mitsy had cut herself, but she'd never heard her mother make such a horrifying sound, not even when she required seven stitches after her blender accident.

Mary Anne burst into the kitchen. Mitsy stood motionless and Michelle shook.

"What?" Mary Anne asked, looking first to her mother and then to her sister. "What is it?"

"Your . . . the front door. There's a—" She looked past Mary Anne to the three kids shivering and dripping water on the kitchen floor.

"Mom, what is it?" Gavin asked, his voice fearful.

"Go back outside and dry off," Mitsy said, her tone stiff. "I'll come with you."

"Mary Anne," Michelle whispered, watching the children leave. "There's a dead cat outside the front door."

"What?"

Mary Anne rushed to the front door and stopped in the doorway. A white Persian cat lay limp on her doorstep.

"Oh my God." Mary Anne knelt down and peered closely at the furry body.

"Is it?" Michelle pressed her fingertips to her lips.

Mary Anne nodded. "I think so." She bent her face close to the cat to see if she could hear her breathing.

"What happened to her?" Michelle asked.

Mary Anne reached down and carefully touched the cat's chest, trying to feel for a heartbeat. She stroked her. "Poor kitty," she said. Slowly, the cat opened her blue eyes. Her lids appeared heavy, as though she were drunk.

"She's alive," Mary Anne said. "Let's go. We'll take my car."

* * *

"You found her unconscious in your front yard?" the vet asked as she felt the cat's stomach.

"That's right," Mary Anne said.

"She's groggy, but I don't feel any internal injuries." The vet shone a light into each of the cat's eyes. "I want to take her in back and have our tech draw some blood. See what caused her to pass out on your front step. Toxicity or something else going on. Who knows. Maybe she was napping."

"She really didn't look like she was napping," Mary Anne said. "I thought she was dead."

"You don't know who the owner is?" the vet asked, picking the cat up.

Mary Anne shook her head.

"Okay, wait here. I'll be right back."

* * *

"Vicodin? Who would give a cat Vicodin?" Mary Anne asked as she held the cat in her arms.

"Who knows," the vet said. "She might have gotten into it accidentally; maybe someone left it out?"

Mary Anne looked at Michelle. The cat had really looked dead on her doorstep. Was she supposed to die there? Was Mary Anne meant to find her? Who would put a drugged, semi-dead cat on a doorstep and drive away?

"She doesn't have any identification. Do you want us to take her?" the vet asked.

Mary Anne glanced down at the cat curled up and purring in her arms. "What will you do with her?"

"She's not microchipped. So we'd keep her for twenty-four hours, and if no one claimed her, we'd send her to the pound."

The pound? Mary Anne didn't want the kitty to escape death only to be put down.

"Or, you could keep her for a while—see if any of your neighbors claim her."

Mary Anne smiled. "I think that's the best idea."

She and Michelle walked through the waiting room toward the door. "What are you going to call her?" Michelle asked.

"I can't name her; her owners might come get her."

"You have to call her something."

"I'm not sure." Mary Anne stood waiting for the receptionist to print up her bill. She glanced at the counter. Magazines lay across the front desk. *People, US, Star,* and *OK!* She glanced at the cover of the newest *US*. Was that—? She felt her heart drop to her knees. The blood rushed out of her face, and a clammy sweat broke out across her forehead. She picked up the *US Weekly.* The headline read REIGNITED ROMANCE and underneath was a grainy picture of Holden with *Viève*. The magazine had printed a smaller picture of Mary Anne toward the bottom right of the cover. MARY ANNE'S HEARTBREAK was the title above a horrible shot of Mary Anne walking in her neighborhood alone, wearing sweatpants and an oversize jacket.

"What is that?" Michelle breathed over Mary Anne's shoulder.

Mary Anne fought back the tears that popped into her eyes. She knew they filled the tabs full of lies. But a photo? A photo of Viève and Holden together?

"That picture has to be old," Michelle said.

Mary Anne glanced at the date on the magazine cover. No, this was the most recent issue.

"There's no charge," the receptionist said.

"Excuse me?" Mary Anne tore herself away from the photo of Holden bent over to listen to Viève. Were they kissing?

"No charge for today." The receptionist reached out and stroked the cat. "Lucky kitty, seems someone nice found you."

"Thanks," Mary Anne said. She waited until the receptionist had turned away before stuffing the magazine into her purse.

She and Michelle drove home in silence. Mary Anne pulled to a stop in the drive at her house. "I have something I need to do," she said without looking at her sister.

"What do you want me to tell Mom?" Michelle asked, climbing out of the car.

"Tell her that I went to get cat food."

Michelle pushed open the car door and grabbed the cat carrier the vet had given them. "Mary Anne," Michelle said, and paused. "You know the pictures they use . . . they have to sell magazines."

"I know," Mary Anne whispered. She stared out the windshield. She wanted to believe Holden had accidentally bumped into Viève. But Mary Anne also knew from her history with Viève that there weren't any accidents.

* * *

Mary Anne didn't want to cry. Crying made her feel weak. She handed the magazine to Holden. "When did it *really* end?" Mary Anne asked.

"I don't love her," Holden said. He glanced at the photo.

"Holden, answer me," Mary Anne said.

"We ended years ago, before *Collusion*," Holden said. "I told you at Shutters."

"But that wasn't the last time you were with her, was it?" Mary Anne asked.

Holden hung his head. Deny until you die, was the mantra he'd recited throughout his life. But now Mary Anne stood before him holding a copy of *US Weekly* with a picture of him and Viève.

"We broke up, like I said, after our thing. That picture is of her stalking me. She's been breaking into my house, leaving me notes, chasing me around town."

Mary Anne felt her knees wobble. "Why didn't you tell me?"

"Look, she just showed up and climbed into my bed. I didn't want her to come over."

"I don't know what to say," Mary Anne whispered.

"I ended it. I told her to leave me alone. That picture is of me ending it. I told her I want you," Holden said, walking toward Mary Anne.

"Don't touch me." Mary Anne backed away from Holden. She

felt unsure about his story. She'd caught Viève with a boyfriend of hers once before; plus, Holden's reputation wasn't built on monogamy and long-term relationships. No, Holden's reputation rested on bedding supermodels and starlets.

"Look, the relationship thing? It's pretty new to me," Holden said. "I wasn't even sure we were in a relationship until I met your family."

"Until you met my family? Are there others?" Mary Anne asked. "Have you been seeing other women this entire time?"

"No, no, no. I mean, for a long time I thought you were still seeing Adam." Holden sat on the couch and slumped forward with his hands in his lap. "She didn't mean anything. Not like you."

"And that's supposed to make me feel better?" Mary Anne whispered.

"I—" Holden wanted to answer, wanted to say whatever would make Mary Anne see that he hadn't done anything wrong, that he'd only done what he'd been asked. "Look, I was only doing my job. When Jessica asked me to pretend to be interested in Viève, I knew this would happen. I knew she'd get completely crazy in the head and think we were a couple again," Holden said.

"What?" Mary Anne looked at Holden. "You were leading her on? This entire time?" Suddenly Mary Anne's sadness felt like rage.

"No, not the entire time, just while we were on set for *Collusion.*"

"But after our thing?" Mary Anne asked. "At Shutters, after we . . ."

Mary Anne watched Holden squirm. He couldn't look her in the eye.

"I can't belie—"

"But we didn't do anything!" Holden exploded. He jumped from the couch. "We didn't do anything. I watched her get off and that was it."

"You watched her what?" Mary Anne felt a sick sensation in her stomach.

"For the film, Mary Anne, for the film. Jessica asked me to pretend I wanted her, and part of the pretending was watching her diddle herself, okay?"

"I've heard enough," Mary Anne said, raising her hand to halt his words. She walked toward the door. How was it okay for Holden to lead Viève on, crazy or no? It definitely wasn't okay for him to keep all these little secrets to himself.

Holden jumped in front of Mary Anne. She took a step back as he reached his arms out to her.

"Mary Anne, please. I am . . . I am so sorry."

Mary Anne looked into Holden's perfect blue eyes. Eyes that entertainment reporters dedicated entire paragraphs to. How many women in America would trade places with her, this very instant? How many women would forgive Holden Humphrey any indiscretion just to be near him? Mary Anne guessed most, maybe all. But not this one.

"Sorry? All you can say is you're sorry?" She brushed past him and pulled open the front door. "Holden, you need to do better than that."

She turned toward the front door. Her anger felt small next to her pain. She wanted him to reach out, to stop her. She wanted him to explain his actions, to make the hurt go away. She wanted him to turn back the clock and erase what he'd done. But instead she pulled open his front door and walked away.

Rule 25

Contain Your Disappointment

Jessica Caulfield-Fox, Manager-Producer

"We got it," Howard Abramowitz, Cici's attorney, chirped into Jessica's car. He sounded giddy with excitement.

"You're sure?" Jessica asked. She zipped along Mulholland toward the Valley.

"As sure as I can be with Sherman. He said there was one other bidder, but Cici's offer was the highest and the DVD is ours. I set up the wire transfer."

"And I'm meeting him—"

"At Nat's on Burbank, in Van Nuys," Howard said. "So we've dodged a bullet."

"This time," Jessica said. She hoped there were no other tapes of Cici having sex.

She pulled up to Nat's on Burbank and Hazeltine. No one in the industry would see her here, deep in the Valley and miles away from Worldwide, Summit, and Galaxy.

Sherman's blue Porsche pulled into the strip mall parking lot. Jessica waited for him to park, then hopped out of her own car. She pulled open the passenger-side door of his 911 and got in. Sherman gunned the car out of the parking lot and zipped west on Burbank Boulevard.

"So you have something for me?" Jessica asked. She couldn't contain her smile. Of course there were no guarantees for the future, but at this moment she felt as though they'd won.

"Something," Sherman said and nodded his head toward the dash.

Jessica opened the glove compartment and pulled out a folder—it contained paperwork and no DVD.

"What's this?" she asked, suddenly apprehensive. She had expected a DVD in a DVD case, not a file folder full of medical paperwork.

"*That* is second place," Sherman said.

Jessica's mouth fell open. Second place wasn't good enough. "I just spoke to Howard. He said we had a deal."

"And we did. Until five minutes ago."

Jessica felt her heart plummet. "What happened five minutes ago?"

"Bigger bidder," Sherman said.

Jessica looked out the windshield at the countless Valley strip malls racing by the car. "We can get more money," she said.

Sherman shook his head no. "I said bigger *bidder,* not larger price. This isn't about dollars."

Jessica reeled. To go from victory to defeat in seconds. "Who is it?"

"You know I can't tell you," Sherman said.

"If you can't tell me the buyer, then where'd you get the DVD?" Jessica asked. She looked at Sherman. "Come on, Sherman, you have to give me something." She heard the pleading in her voice.

"I just did. Take a closer look at that file."

Jessica opened the file and skimmed the medical documents, starting with the patient's name. A few moments went by as she shuffled the papers. "Is this . . . ?"

"Yeah, it is," Sherman said.

"Amazing. But how does this help me?" Jessica asked.

"Turn the page," Sherman said.

"Billy paid for this surgery?"

"It seems so," Sherman said.

"And nobody in town knows about the procedure?" Jessica asked.

"I've never heard about it before," Sherman said. "And I'm sure all those hot male stars she's slept with don't know, either."

"This is some deadly proof," Jessica said. "Where did you get it?"

"A combination of places. L.A., England, Asia, Kiki Dee."

"Kiki knows about this?" Jessica continued to read the file. Sherman was right: This information's going public could destroy multiple careers and marriages.

"Kiki acquired the L.A. file."

Jessica wondered how Sherman had managed to snag the information from Kiki but thought better than to ask. "So does this mean that Billy gave you Cici's sex tape?" she asked.

Sherman let a smile slip onto his face. "Jessica, without naming names, it would appear so."

"But why?" Jessica mumbled as she continued to read the file. The name on the front of the file was Viève Dyson's, but it looked like her original name had been Keith Tinkler.

"I'm thinking revenge," Sherman said.

"For what? Celeste never did anything to Billy."

"Oh, no, no, no," Sherman said. "Celeste and her status as A-list superstar is merely a pawn in this power play."

"What?" She gave Sherman a confused look.

"Jessica, I like you and I feel bad for snatching the DVD from you, so let me share with you my theory," Sherman said.

"Which is?"

"The revenge, the payback, is for Lydia. What better way to destroy Worldwide and Lydia Albright than to destroy their five hundred-million-dollar investment in Celeste Solange films?"

"What did Lydia ever do to Billy?" Jessica asked.

"Not what she *did* but what she *covered up*. Ask Lydia. She's helped to cover up Steven Brockman's affairs with other men, several of them. I think the men, the lifestyle, and the drugs may have pushed Billy over the edge."

"Billy did all this for revenge?" Jessica asked.

"Yeah, and just wait, there's more."

* * *

"We need Lydia," Jessica said. She watched Cici read the contents of the folder. The two sat on a park bench nestled next to a magnolia tree in Holmby Hills Park. "She'll know what to do."

"Have you talked to her?" Cici asked.

"Not since the Peninsula," Jessica said.

"She was an ugly man," Cici said, holding up a picture of Viève, aka Keith, prior to his surgery. "Looks much better as a woman, don't you think?"

Jessica glanced at the before and after photos. "Did you suspect? I mean, she looks completely like a woman."

"We could destroy her," Cici said. Jessica heard a hint of anger in Celeste's voice.

"Or we could simply keep the contents as an insurance policy. For future use. I mean, it's not difficult to determine all the names of everyone she's slept with; it's not like she's been very discreet. And then, if we needed something from any of them in the future . . ."

"We have this," Cici finished. "Does that include Holden?"

Jessica sighed. "I heard. Mitsy e-mailed me. Have you seen Mary Anne?"

"This morning. I got the feeling it's over."

"Maybe," Jessica said. "Maybe not."

"They don't change," Cici said.

Jessica ignored Cici's careless comment. Prior to their second time as a couple, Mike, now her husband, was a horrible womanizer. And perhaps Jessica was in deep denial, but she truly believed that once they started dating the second time and then eventually married, he was devoted to her and their family.

"Even the good ones have secrets," Cici said. "It's over. Lydia was right about everything. My entire career is over." Cici put her head in her hands. "I can't believe that after all this someone else got that tape. Ted will find out, America will see the sex tape, and I'll end up homeless and out of work."

"Cici, most of that isn't true. You'll never be homeless if I have a place to live."

"Thanks," Cici said.

They stood and started to walk. "So I guess there's only one thing left for me to do," Cici said.

Rule 26

Give Good Gossip

Kiki Dee, Publicist

Terri, I have the most luscious bit of gossip for you," Kiki purred into the phone. She looked away from the *Enquirer* she was paging through and across the hall at Boom Boom, now ensconced in her own office and wearing the latest Vera Wang creation. Kiki watched as Boom Boom's newest assistant, the third in three weeks, and probably about to be fired, too, jumped up from her desk and trotted into Boom Boom's office. Since her promotion, Boom Boom had become quite a dragon lady. Plus, lately she seemed absolutely consumed with a relationship. Kiki noticed the multiple bags of La Perla and Agent Provocateur. Plus the long lunches and flowers. Kiki didn't know who the suitor could be. A young actor? A casting director? Perhaps a musician? Those musicians could be so naughty. Kiki smiled.

"About?" Terri asked, pulling Kiki back to their conversation.

"Not over the phone," Kiki said.

"I'm on set today, tomorrow, and the next day. Friday, they're shooting the love scene with Viève and Steven, the one where Cici's character catches them together."

"Isn't Holden in that one, too?" Kiki asked.

"The gang'll all be here," Terri said. "Can't miss that."

"This will be quite an article," Kiki said.

"Mm-hmm. The male supporting actor schtupping the writer *and* his costar, the male lead schtupping the production photographer. I'd say it's about average. And nothing I can put into the article and keep my job."

"Sounds like a Fleetwood Mac tour."

"Fleetwood Mac? Kiki, you are old," Terri said.

"I think I smell a dead movie," Kiki said.

"And some dead careers. After this stinker there won't be a live one left," Terri said. "I've seen the dailies; it's pretty fucking bad."

"Bad enough for a new studio head?" Kiki asked.

"I guess that depends on Ted," Terri said, "whom I haven't seen since this film began."

"New girlfriend?"

"Mmm, don't think so. My sources say something is going on in Asia. Besides, Cici seems too happy for Ted to be fucking around. But then, maybe Cici's just happy about her new eyes?"

"She *went* to Fiji," Kiki said, switching over to client-protection mode.

"Yeah, right. There should be a revolving door at Dr. Melnick's office," Terri said.

"You didn't hear it from me," Kiki said. "You know, she's got publicity for *California Girl* tomorrow. Want to sit in?"

"No. But I need to for the article."

"Come on, love. You'll get to be around your own kind," Kiki said, referring to the reporters who would each get four minutes alone with Celeste to land their interviews and sound bites in preparation for *California Girl*'s release. "I want your article in the issue of *Vanity Fair*, before the Academy ballots are due."

"Don't you think you'd better read it before you say that?" Terri asked.

"Why?" Kiki looked up from her newspaper. "Should I be worried?"

"There are a lot of rumors floating around your two biggest stars right now, Kiki. You can't expect me to ignore *all* of them for this article."

"Such as?"

"Well, the first one, which I confirmed, is the eye-lift," Terri said.

"You wouldn't!"

"And the second rumor is that there is a nasty little sex tape of Celeste floating around town."

"Terri, you wouldn't dare," Kiki said.

"Break the story? Probably not, but if someone else does, I have to respond, don't I? And then there's Steven and Billy, of course. And the list goes on."

"Stop," Kiki said.

"But of course if there were a bigger and better piece of gossip . . ."

"Bigger?"

"And better," Terri repeated.

"Why do you think I called?" Kiki asked. "But you have to come by to see it."

"Tomorrow."

"Tomorrow then." Kiki pushed release on her phone. "Jilly!" She yelled for her new assistant.

"Yes, Miss Dee?"

Kiki watched as Jilly scurried into her office. She looked at the girl from tip to toe. *Good cut, nice highlights, good skin, cute nose, Diane Von Furstenberg dress, Louboutin shoes, new mani-pedi . . . excellent, just exactly right.*

"Tell Boom Boom I need the Spice file," Kiki said.

"The what?" Jilly asked.

"The Spice file." When Jilly left, Kiki continued reading the *Enquirer.* She heard her phone ringing. "Get that, please," Kiki called. When the phone continued to ring, she looked up at Jilly's desk, but her fashionista was gone. "For fuck's sake." She pressed her headset. "This is Kiki."

"Why did you send your assistant to my office for a spice rack?" Boom Boom asked.

"What?" Kiki looked across the hall at Boom Boom sitting in her office.

"Your assistant came over, walked into my office, and said you wanted a spice rack from me? Is that supposed to be a joke?"

"The Spice file, I need the Spice file," Kiki said. "Where is the idiot?"

"The store, I guess," Boom Boom said and released the line.

Kiki shook her head. You could dress up smart, but you couldn't fix stupid.

* * *

What do you mean you can't find it?" Kiki whispered. She sat in a suite at the Four Seasons, across the room from Cici but close enough to hear every question each reporter asked. Sure, they had guidelines, strict ones, but every once in a while you got a rogue reporter from some Podunk market trying to ask Cici about Damien or her dead mother or absentee father or anything else that was completely irrelevant to the film and the press junket but would make a nice clip for the reporter's local news and perhaps launch the reporter's career.

"I can't find it," Boom Boom said. "You took it."

"I did not take it," Kiki said. "I gave it to you in the car after we stole it from Melnick's. You've had it this whole time."

"Kiki, you are losing your mind. I don't have the file."

"I handed the file to you when we got back to the car, along with the photos. I told you to get the film developed and put it in a safe place."

"You bumped your head," Boom Boom said. "You don't remember."

"Look, I do remember, and I expect *you* to remember where you put that file. Do you understand me?" Kiki clicked off her phone.

"Trouble in paradise?" Terri asked as she sat down on the sofa next to Kiki.

"New assistant."

"How awful, especially with awards season around the corner."

"Better now than after the holiday break," Kiki said.

"Speaking of the break, where are you going?"

"Maui. I go every year. Why?"

"Well, our friends Robert and Carlos mentioned that they like to travel."

"Do they?" Kiki asked.

"And that they love, love, love Fiji," Terri said.

"Really." Kiki looked at Celeste. "Well, I just happen to know someone who owns a private island not far from Fiji." She nodded toward Celeste.

"Exactly," Terri said. "Why don't you work your magic, and we'll have an especially delicious two-week break?"

"That really does sound like the perfect way to ring in the New Year." Kiki watched Celeste's stylist put the final touches on her hair before the next reporter came in. "You don't think it's too pouffy, do you?" she asked Terri.

"Not for this crowd," Terri said. "So when do I get to see this special little tidbit of gossip you've been tantalizing me with?"

"Soon," Kiki lied. She felt a rush of panic go through her. If Boom Boom failed to find Viève's medical file, it could be never.

"I thought you'd bring it with you," Terri said.

"So did I. It's not quite ready."

"Fine, but I'm writing my article during the break. So if this new material you have has any effect on my article, I need the information before we get back."

"Don't you worry," Kiki said, "you'll have it before then."

* * *

This was bad. Very, very bad. Kiki sat on the floor of her home office, dread rapidly replacing her excitement about her two-week vacation with Carlos. They were scheduled to leave tomorrow.

She had checked every one of her super-secret hiding places, all the places she hid things so she could remember where they were.

She even went to her bank and looked in her safety-deposit box. Nothing. She had nothing. How did she have nothing? Boom Boom swore that Kiki had taken the pictures and the file when they got out of the rental car, but Kiki couldn't remember. Actually, she remembered very few details about the night she and Boom Boom broke into Charles Melnick's office. She remembered pulling the file, and she knew that Boom Boom took pictures, but once she hit her head, her memory became fuzzy. She had to think. Where would she have put it? The file was perhaps the most important piece of dirt she'd ever acquired. Where would she, bleeding and with a nasty bump on her head, have put the file?

She was peering into the secret hole in the floor of her bedroom when her cell phone rang.

"Kiki?"

"Sherman," Kiki said. "Thank God."

"How can I be of service, my love?" Sherman asked.

"I can't find my file," Kiki said.

"Your file? Can you be more specific?" Sherman asked. "I've done a lot of work for you over the years."

"My most recent file. The one you helped me get. Remember?"

"Oh, that one. But you had it," Sherman said.

"I did?"

"Don't you remember? You called me and told me that you and your assistant—what's her name?"

"Boom Boom?"

"Yes, Boom Boom. You told me that you two got the file out of Melnick's office."

Kiki heard the faint, soft sound of female laughter in the background. "I did? I remember calling you and telling you I gave it to Boom Boom," Kiki said. She was losing her mind.

"No. Kiki, come on. You would never let someone else have something that dangerous. Not you. You're too much of a pro for that. You told me that you kept the file and hid it."

Kiki sighed. Of course, he had to be right, no matter what her memory said. She would have trusted only herself with a file that important. "Did I tell you where I hid it?" she asked.

Sherman laughed. "If only you had, I might be a very rich man."

Damn. Damn damn damn. She'd lost it. "Where are you? You sound very far away," Kiki said.

"Just getting a jump on my end-of-year vacation," Sherman said. "I'm in Saint Kitts for the next two weeks."

"I guess Saint Kitts is a hot spot this year. My former assistant is there."

"Really? Do I know her?" Sherman asked.

"Boom Boom," Kiki answered, a bit annoyed. Weren't they just discussing her? "The newest publicist at my company. She was short and dumpy, but now she's just short. I had such a tremendous influence on her. She's seeing a trainer and wearing all the best clothes. Quite remarkable. I think she wants to be just like me."

"Oh, I'm sure she does," Sherman said.

Kiki heard another giggle over the phone. "Sounds like you're not alone."

"No one should go on holiday alone," Sherman said.

"You're correct," Kiki said. "No one should go on holiday alone."

* * *

Kiki, this is fabulous," Terri said. "They look like they could be our grandsons."

"Absolutely." Kiki forgot to pretend she wasn't old as she eyed Carlos and Robert. The international terminal at LAX was hopping. Everyone in entertainment was finally free for the two-week end-of-year vacation.

"Did everyone decide to leave town today?" Terri asked. "I just saw Demi and Ashton."

"Oh no, dear, that can't be right," Kiki said. "They never fly commercial."

"What did you bring to read? It's a long flight."

"I have three scripts, a copy of Ally Carter's latest book, and a bagful of magazines. You?"

"Writing, the whole way. I want to get this article finished. That way I have the entire fourteen days to work on him," Terri said, looking at Robert standing two feet from her holding her bags.

Kiki looked at Carlos. She felt a warm sensation between her legs. He wasn't cheap, but he was worth every cent.

"Where is the material you promised me?" Terri asked.

"I have it in the bag I checked," Kiki lied. "I didn't know you'd work on the plane."

Terri sighed. "Fine, I'll read it there."

"Have you decided on the slant of your article?" Kiki asked.

"That all depends on the material you have," Terri said. "And if anything breaks over the holiday."

"Breaks? What's going to break?" Kiki asked, her pulse increasing.

"Relax. I hear nothing. I don't think anyone will find this sex tape, and as for Billy and Steven, their secret is safe with me."

Maybe everything would be okay. Of course Kiki didn't have the file. The loss of it brought her to tears; the value of that secret was incalculable. Every male celebrity the little vixen had bedded would be ripe for the picking. Holden. She would finally have landed Holden Humphrey as a client and really been back on top.

"I hope so," Kiki said. "I'd hate to miss anything important while I was away."

"What could happen? Everyone is out of town," Terri said.

"Well, everyone who isn't in production."

"Right. So everyone but Lydia, Jessica, Cici, and Mary Anne. And from the dailies of *Vitriol* that I've seen, those girls will get a nice long holiday once this film gets released!"

"Really?" Kiki asked.

"After this piece of crap, the stink will be all over those ladies for a very long time."

Rule 27

Every Story Needs a Climax

Celeste Solange, Actress

Cici paced on set. She wanted to be in her Star Wagon listening to Lydia and Jessica give Billy their hard sell, not out here. They were confronting him with the evidence that he'd paid for Viève's surgery. Hopefully, he would be so eager to keep that scandal under wraps that he'd tell them everything he knew. If he admitted to stealing the DVD and told them to whom he sold it, she'd still have a chance. Cici's heart beat fast. She felt her career and her relationship with Ted slipping away.

"Celeste."

She knew that voice. Excitement, followed by fear, rushed through her. She turned, and there stood Ted. It felt like years since she'd last seen him.

"Oh, my . . . ," Cici whispered. Her head felt light. Briggs Montgomery stood behind Ted with Jay and half a dozen men in suits.

"Ted? What are you doing here? I thought you were still in Hong Kong." She forced herself to breathe and smile—the things people did when they weren't terrified.

"I came back early. Have you seen Lydia? Toddy said she was on set."

"She's in my trailer," Cici said. She leaned forward to give Ted a quick kiss, but he put his hands on her shoulders.

"Alone?" Ted asked.

"She's with Billy and Jessica," Cici said.

"Okay." Ted started to walk across the soundstage.

Cici jumped in front of Ted and his entourage. "Ted, sweetie, you can't go in there now," she said quickly.

"Cici, this is important." He tried to walk around her.

She needed to make him stop, or at least slow him down. Who knew what they were discussing in there? "But, darling, aren't you happy to see me? Don't you want to hear about the film and how I'm doing?" she asked.

Ted stopped short and looked down at Cici. "You know that you are always my priority, don't you?"

"Yes, I do," she said. She reached out and touched Ted's lips with her finger. "Always."

"So trust me when I say it's in your best interest if you let me go speak to Lydia."

Cici looked past Ted and saw Billy storming back onto the set with Lydia and Jessica behind him. "No need, darling. It looks like they're coming to you."

"There they are," Ted said to the men behind him. Cici watched as two of the men walked swiftly toward Billy.

"Billy Gerard?"

"Who are you?" Billy spat, giving both men a fierce look.

"FBI, sir. We're going to need you to come with us."

"Is this a joke?" Billy glanced around the soundstage with a smirk plastered on his face. "First I'm accused of financing a sex-change operation for a transsexual, and now I'm under arrest?"

"Sir, you're charged with violation of the DMCA."

"The DMC what? Is this some kind of prank?"

"You're charged with DVD piracy and intellectual property theft, a felony and violation of the Digital Media Copyright Act."

Cici looked up at Ted. "Are those guys for real?"

Ted nodded as the Feds snapped the cuffs onto Billy's wrists.

"You have the right to remain silent . . ."

Cici looked across the soundstage at Nathan, who was getting the same treatment from two other officers. "Nathan, too," Cici whispered. Jessica and Lydia stood silent beside her.

"Billy, what are they doing to you?" Steven wailed, running toward Ted. "What's going on?"

"Steven, calm down. Call your attorney," Billy said as the Feds pulled Billy and Nathan toward the soundstage door.

"But Billy?" Steven called.

"Just call Howard!" Billy yelled. "This is a mistake."

Cici watched the Feds lead Billy and Nathan away. She looked at Steven, who now stood motionless next to Ted.

"Just call Howard," Billy yelled. "Steven, do you hear me? Go get your cell and call Howard now."

The FBI led Billy off the soundstage. Once the door slammed shut, Steven's expression changed from fearful to satisfied. He looked over at Ted and nodded his head. Then he looked at Lydia. "You'll call me when we have a new director," he said, turning away from them and walking calmly toward his trailer.

Cici was stunned. "Did Billy and Nathan just get arrested by the FBI?"

"Piracy and theft," Ted said. "Billy was trafficking in pirated DVDs in Asia. Some of them were Worldwide films. I've been working with the FBI, trying to persuade the Chinese government to release evidence, so the U.S. Attorney could file criminal charges in federal court against Billy's bootleg movie business."

"And Nathan?" Jessica asked.

"Nathan got in on it," Ted said. "As far as I can tell, he copied movies in theaters, transported cash. But Nathan definitely wasn't the brains behind the operation; that was Billy."

"And the letters were from Billy," Lydia said.

Ted nodded his head. "The letters convinced Steven to help me. Once we traced the paper—"

"You knew who sent the letters?" Celeste asked.

"For a while now," Ted said. "Steven was fed up with Billy's illegal activities—and, quite frankly, scared. Billy had become a huge liability to him."

Cici felt her insides wobble. Was she a liability to Ted? "That's all?" she asked, looking at Ted.

Ted looked at Cici, his lips set in a hard line. "As far as we can discuss here, yes, Celeste, that's all."

* * *

Cici lay in her bathtub soaking. *Vitriol* had wrapped for the day—what else could they do? Their director waited arraignment in a federal jail and their female star was an undisclosed transvestite. Ted and Lydia had disappeared together after the Feds escorted Nathan and Billy off the soundstage.

Celeste closed her eyes. When would she learn that business and love never mixed? She thought that, with Ted, it wouldn't matter that they were both in the film industry. But in Hollywood, business and your personal life always got tangled. Your friends were your business partners, your bosses, your colleagues, your confidants, your codependents, and your enablers. Why had she believed it would be any different with Ted?

"Cici?" Ted came in and stood over her bath. He looked out of place in his suit and tie standing next to her tub.

Celeste sighed. She saw it in his eyes. He knew. He knew everything. She wondered how he had found out. Celeste looked down at the bubbles in her bath. Her insides felt as fragile as the soapsuds that surrounded her.

"I tried to take care of the problem."

Ted sat on the edge of the marble tub. "I know. Lydia told me. You girls are very crafty—if Billy and Nathan hadn't already sold the DVD out from under you, I'm sure they would have handed it over to Jessica and Lydia this afternoon, in exchange for the file on Viève."

"But how did Billy even get the DVD in the first place?"

"Hollywood is a small town," Ted said. "I hear Damien's divorce attorney traded it to Billy for drugs. I'd be surprised if Janice isn't disbarred."

"How did you find out about the tape?" Cici asked.

"You mean what was you ladies' biggest mistake?" Ted asked with a tiny smile on his face. "Lydia gave Briggs Montgomery the letters before she knew about your film, and before you met Nathan. So she didn't have any idea the letters were connected to it."

Cici sank deeper into the bubbles. "And the letters were from Billy."

"So it seems. Sherman told me his revenge theory as well. Once I read the letters, I became concerned for Lydia's safety and, tangentially, yours. So I upped the security on Lydia. And, well, you guys may be secretive with the rest of the world, but when you're together you jabber, jabber, jabber. And Jay may be Lydia's security guard, but he works for me."

"I see."

"And the house." Ted pointed around the room.

"Cameras?" Cici gasped, sinking farther into the tub.

"No cameras, Cici. Not in the bedrooms or bathrooms. But on the outside of the house, the entrances. And microphones in all the public rooms."

"The phones?"

Ted nodded. "The landlines."

"There is no privacy in this world," Cici said. Her heart felt heavy.

"No, honey, especially for an international superstar. But listen to me: I promise, I do these things to protect you, not to exploit you."

Celeste looked into Ted's eyes. She felt the truth coming from him. He wanted to keep her safe. She loved Ted, but didn't yet want to cede all her privacy to him. "No more tapping the phones," she said.

Ted hesitated. "Fair enough." They sat in silence for a moment.

"This isn't Lydia's fault," Celeste said.

"I know, but she's not staying at Worldwide."

Cici looked at Ted. "You can't fire her. She was doing what was best for the company, for you, for the quarter of a billion dollars' worth of my films that you've invested in."

"Celeste, you misunderstand," Ted said. "She doesn't want to stay."

"What?"

"Look, I said the exact same thing you did," Ted said. "I would have handled it almost the same way. In fact when I found out about the DVD, I became just as paranoid and secretive as you two."

"Four," Cici said.

"Four?"

"It was four. Mary Anne, Jessica—"

"Right, right." Ted held up his hands. "I know the usual suspects."

"So what do you mean Lydia isn't staying?"

"She wants to leave," Ted said. "After awards season she'll announce her departure. She's keeping her overall deal at Worldwide, and of course I'll make any film she brings me. But she's finished as president of production."

"You're kidding?"

"No. I offered to raise her salary. She declined."

"I thought she loved making movies," Cici said.

"She does love making movies. But, Celeste, the job of president of production isn't about making movies. That job is about politics and steering the ship. As president, the success or failure of every film rests on your shoulders. The entire future of the studio. Lydia loves movies, but she loves *making* them. Being on set with the director, the actors, the writer—that's making movies. That's the part she misses."

"So what about *Vitriol*?"

"What about it?" Ted said.

"That's a pretty hefty loss."

"No loss. We've got a new director."

"Who'd direct a film with only five shooting days left? And Nathan's coverage is shitty."

"What director would do that for Lydia?" Ted asked.

"Zymar," Cici said.

"Exactly. And you're now employed for another four weeks. Zymar thinks he can salvage the film if he has another twenty days."

"That takes us right up to the nominations," Celeste said.

"Almost," Ted said. He loosened his tie and started to unbutton his shirt.

"So," Cici began. She was nervous. "I need to ask you about Hong Kong."

"What about it?" Ted asked.

"Why do you go?"

"For business."

Cici watched him from behind the bubbles. She wanted to believe him. She wanted to trust him so badly. But she'd spent the last three months attempting to do damage control on embarrassing footage of her that her first husband had filmed. She realized that Ted and Damien were completely different, but she also remembered Kiki and Terri cackling about Ted and his sex trips to Asia. It was so hard to trust anyone in this town.

"Celeste, come on. We both have a past. But do you think those two old birds really know anything about my business?" Ted said. "I go to Asia for business and business only. I know about the sex tours. Billy went; he used to go for sex tours, and that's how he got started with the DVD piracy, meeting shady characters over there. I know what goes on. But the only reason I've been going a lot recently is because of this piracy investigation."

"So you've known—"

"Almost the entire time."

"And you never told me?"

"Like I said, Cici, I kept tabs; you were watched." He gave her a sly smile. "Nice eyes, by the way."

"I'm not sure how I feel about your finding out that kind of thing without my knowledge," Cici said, frowning. She watched as Ted dropped his pants to the floor.

"Then I guess we're even, because I'm not sure how I feel about being lied to."

"I didn't lie," she said, sinking deeper into her bath. "I just omitted some details." She watched as Ted climbed into the tub.

"Hey . . . why so glum?" Ted asked. "Seems like you four came out virtually unscathed."

"I guess," Cici said. Her insides felt raw. "Are you sure you want this? I mean us? Because this isn't going away."

"What are you talking about? The bad guys are in jail. And I got the girl," Ted said.

"Right, but we never got the DVD," Cici said, close to tears.

"Who told you that?" Ted asked, settling into the tub and wrapping his arms around her.

"Sherman Ross," Cici said.

"Oh, you mean, *you* never got the DVD," Ted said.

"Yeah, I mean me. Me and the girls. Who else?" She looked at Ted. A smile slipped onto his face. Her heart thumped. "You got it," she whispered. "Ted, you got it, didn't you? *You* bought the DVD from Sherman." She felt tears forming in her eyes.

"I told you, Celeste, you are my priority, and I want you to feel safe."

She held Ted's face in her hands and looked into his eyes. He'd spent millions of dollars and countless hours cleaning a mess she had made long before they'd met. "Thank you," she said. It was the only thing she could think to say. "Thank you."

Rule 28

Take a Vacation Whenever You Can

Lydia Albright, President of Production, Worldwide Pictures

Lydia felt a weight lift from her shoulders. Finished. Her chest relaxed and she could finally breathe. In eight short weeks, the weight of Worldwide and its slate of films would no longer be her concern. She still wanted to make movies, just one picture at a time. She stood on her front drive waiting for Zymar. She had given everyone on the production of *Vitriol* a short break. All the agencies and production companies closed a week before for the end-of-year break, and Zymar had promised he could rework the script in two weeks, with only minimal reshooting. Lydia believed him—she'd seen him work magic before.

Ted had asked her to stay on as president, and Lydia was thankful he wasn't bouncing her out on her ass. He could have. She'd lied to him, even if it was a feeble attempt to protect Cici. Instead, Ted had offered to keep her on as president of production *and* raise her salary. But she'd come to realize over the last months that she was better suited for the intricacies of a film set, not an executive suite.

The job had changed her. Changed her in ways she thought

nothing ever would. She had felt fear and bitterness and anger and rage—feelings she'd experienced at times, of course, but never as strongly as she did as head of a studio. Perhaps it was because of the responsibility and lack of control—she was responsible for every film Worldwide made, good or bad. She could say yes to a movie and have Worldwide cut the check, but she couldn't pick the scripts (the producers brought her those), she couldn't control the actors (she was a slave to their whims), and she couldn't force anyone to do good work. And yet, at the end of the year, when all the receipts were counted and ticket sales added up, it was her career that was judged based on the numbers. Lydia was willing to cast her lot with the stories she loved, the directors she respected, and the actors she wanted to work with. But she wanted to work with all that enough to feel ownership over it . . . one film at a time. She simply was not an executive.

"Hey, pretty lady, ready to take a ride?" Zymar called from his Harley.

"Where are we going?" Lydia took the helmet he handed her. She tucked in her brunette locks and straddled the back of the bike.

"Lady's choice," Zymar said. "Seems this is your last-minute trip. I'm just the driver."

Lydia clasped her arms around Zymar's waist and pressed against him tight. She felt good. She felt free. And for the first time in a long time, she felt calm. "How about anywhere but here?"

"The open road then. Sounds fantastic to me," Zymar said, revving the engine and zipping down the drive. "A little non-destination-oriented for an overachiever such as you. But I can roll with it." Zymar laughed.

Then let's roll, baby, Lydia thought. *Let's just roll.*

Rule 29

The Good Guy Gets the Girl

Mary Anne Meyers, Screenwriter

Mary Anne walked into her dark house. She dropped her keys and purse on the table just inside the door. When production began again on *Vitriol* next week, she'd finally see Holden and Viève. She'd dodged Holden's calls and e-mails, and so far he'd sent flowers only once. He'd yet to stop by the house, but Mary Anne thought she'd seen his pickup turn the corner on Wednesday evening as she pulled into her drive.

E.B. hopped up onto the table and meowed at her. No one had claimed the cat, so Mary Anne kept her and named her E.B. after her favorite children's author, E. B. White. She and Mary Anne had settled into an easy existence. Mary Anne kicked off her shoes and headed down the hall. The house felt quiet. She flipped on the lights in her bedroom, walked into her closet, where she dropped her skirt to the floor, pulled off her shirt, and slipped on her robe. She then headed toward her bathroom and turned on the water for her spa tub. She was so tired. Part of her was thankful that production had halted for two weeks.

She sat on the edge of the tub and tested the water with her fingertips. Almost right; just a little too warm. She turned up the cold water. She wanted a glass of red wine and a book. She used to sit for hours in the tub reading and drinking wine. Why had she stopped?

She padded back down the hall toward the kitchen. Half a bottle of Cabernet sat on the counter. She pulled the cork and poured herself a glass. E.B. walked across the kitchen island.

"Hey, you, you're not supposed to be up here," Mary Anne said, running her hand over the top of E.B.'s back. The cat's only bad habit she'd discovered so far was walking on the countertops.

She glanced out the kitchen window toward the illuminated pool. The corner of the house was lit up by the motion-sensor lights her brother had installed before returning to Minnesota. As Mary Anne gazed out on her backyard, she heard E.B. hiss and then saw something dart behind her in the window. Adrenaline shot through her. *Who was in her house?* She didn't want to turn around. She glanced at the cat from the corner of her eye. Mary Anne still held the wine bottle in one hand and her glass in the other.

"Put them both down."

Mary Anne felt her heartbeat quicken. She set both the glass and the bottle on the counter.

"Now turn around."

Mary Anne slowly turned. She held both her hands in the air, a Pavlovian response to an intruder. She looked at the crazy gnome holding a revolver in her right hand. She took a deep breath and stared at the gun. "Viève, what are you—"

"Shut it," Viève said. She moved toward E.B. The cat hissed again as Viève inched closer. "What did you do to her?" Viève asked.

"What did *I* do to her?" Mary Anne asked. "This is your cat, isn't it? You tried to kill her."

"You're exaggerating."

Mary Anne felt a bubble of rage rise in her chest. How easy for Viève to be brave standing in her kitchen holding a gun.

"Come here, Priscilla," Viève called, reaching for the cat with her right hand. The cat backed between the refrigerator and the wall, hissing. She swiped at Viève.

"Fucking cat," Viève said. "Come here." Viève reached out and yanked the fur behind the cat's neck, causing the kitty to go limp.

"Hey, you're hurting her," Mary Anne said, taking a step forward.

"Are you forgetting I have a gun?" Viève asked, pointing the revolver at Mary Anne again.

"No, not forgetting," Mary Anne said. She stepped back.

* * *

"So, how do you want me to do this?" Viève asked. "I mean, obviously we want your death to look like a suicide. Broken heart, that kind of thing. And don't worry, I'll do my best to console Holden." Mary Anne winced. Viève continued, "I'll give you the choice. I can hit you on the head with this"—she pulled a bat from the black bag she'd brought with her—"and then put you in the tub so it looks like you fell and drowned. Or, you can take all of these"—Viève held up a prescription bottle and gave it a gentle shake—"get into bed and fall asleep. Personally, I think it's incredibly kind of me to give you a choice. Because what I really want to do is crack you in the skull with the bat. But I am civilized. I'm guessing you'll go for the less painful of the two."

Mary Anne stood next to her bed. Was this really happening? In her head she ran through the people who knew she was home. She had spoken with Cici much earlier in the day, and her mother wouldn't call tonight—Mitsy called on Tuesdays and Thursdays. She glanced at her clock: ten P.M. No one was coming by.

"I've done the math. You'll be long gone before anyone notices."

"Viève, why are you doing this? You don't have to do this. We broke up. Holden and I aren't together any—"

"I know that. You think I don't know that? I know everything."

"Then he's yours," Mary Anne said.

"Mine? You're kidding, right? Have you seen him? Have you talked to him?"

Mary Anne shook her head.

"Of course you haven't, because you don't love him like I do. I tolerated you. I knew he was fucking you, and I tolerated you. Because I knew he'd figure it out. I knew he'd figure out that he really loved *me*."

"And he did," Mary Anne said. "He figured it out. He fucked you. I let him go. He's yours now."

"Fucked me? Ha! He hasn't fucked me since we broke up three years ago—because of you. No. He's certainly not mine. He's despondent."

"Despondent?" Mary Anne asked.

"What, you didn't know? He can't eat, he can't sleep, he doesn't even work out. Holden Humphrey is getting pudgy because of you! You bitch."

Mary Anne felt a tiny bit of pleasure at the idea of Holden's being lost without her.

"Obviously I have to do this. Don't you understand? You have to die. This is the only way he'll ever get over you." Viève walked to Mary Anne and opened the pill bottle. "If you're dead, he can't sit alone in his room staring at a blank wall anymore." She thought for a moment. "Or, at least, not forever. Here, take these." Viève counted out ten pills. "And I'm keeping count."

* * *

Holden pulled his pickup to a stop outside Mary Anne's house. He knew she was home; her car was parked on the drive. It was time for him to make his big play for her forgiveness. He'd tried to call before he came over, but she never answered his calls, and had returned his flowers to the store. But he had to see her. He had to try.

He was embarrassed about sneaking around, following her home, feeling a bit like Viève, the stalker. Holden walked toward the front door. He'd try one last time, and if it didn't work, he'd take his lumps like a man. Who was he kidding . . . he'd fall on his knees and beg if he had to.

He reached out his hand to ring the bell and noticed that the front door was ajar. A jolt of anxiety passed through him. Mary

Anne's front door was open? And she was home? He gave the door a gentle nudge. The kitchen lights were on, but no one was there. He stepped quietly down the hall toward the bedroom, pausing by the den. He heard voices coming from Mary Anne's bedroom. Was she seeing someone already? He leaned forward to listen. No, both voices were too high-pitched for one of them to be male. One was Mary Anne and the other was . . . *Viève*? What did that psycho want with Mary Anne? Holden pressed on toward the bedroom, until he could peek through Mary Anne's door. He watched as Viève handed Mary Anne a glass of water.

"Now swallow," Viève ordered. Mary Anne grimaced. "Good, just three more." A wicked smile danced across the actress's face. Mary Anne started to gag. "Stop that or I'll have to use the bat," Viève said.

The bat? Was that a gun? Viève was holding Mary Anne hostage in her bedroom and feeding her something? He needed to call the cops. Holden turned and quietly tiptoed down the hall toward the front door.

"And where do you think you're going?"

* * *

"You people are not making this easy for me," Viève said. She stood in the bedroom while Mary Anne and Holden sat on the bed. "I was doing this for you," she said, pointing the gun at Holden. "You've lost your mind, okay? You're completely going to pot over her." Viève made a horrible face and nodded her head toward Mary Anne. "I mean, come on! A little exercise couldn't hurt you, Holden, even if you're heartbroken."

"Hey," Mary Anne said.

The overdose hadn't yet kicked in, because when Viève turned toward Holden, Mary Anne spit out most of the pills and threw them under the bed.

"So, lover," Viève purred. "As much as I adore you, since you've stumbled upon my little homicide, I'm afraid I need to rework my plan. Let's see." Viève tapped the revolver against her lips while she thought. "Oh, I know, let's make it a Shakespearean tragedy, shall we? You, Holden, can be our Romeo. You stumble upon your Juliet having overdosed because of her broken heart. Completely bereft, you shoot yourself in the head, splattering your brains on the wall. Only in this one, Juliet never wakes up again. Oooh, I like it. You two will be in entertainment heaven forever. You may become legends. Thoughts?" There was a wild look in Viève's eyes—wilder than normal, Mary Anne thought.

"Viève, you can't kill Holden," Mary Anne said.

"And why not?"

"You love him, and he loves you. Right, Holden? Don't you love Viève?" Mary Anne looked at Holden, willing him to go along with her.

"Right, yes," Holden said. "I do."

"He told me that when he broke up with me," Mary Anne said.

"He broke up with you?" Viève asked. She paused her pacing and looked at Mary Anne. "No, Mary Anne, you broke up with him. Just as I planned."

"No, he broke up with me. I went and begged him not to. But when he saw the cover of *US Weekly,* he knew he loved you."

"You did?" She turned her fierce gaze to Holden. He nodded. "Then why have you avoided me?"

"Uh, I needed to—"

"He didn't want the tabloids to blame you for our breakup. He knows how important your image is, and he wanted to let things settle. At least, that's what he told me when we broke up. Right, Holden?"

"Yeah."

"Oh lover, that's so sweet. That makes me almost wish I didn't have to kill you."

"But you don't," Holden said. He stood and walked slowly toward Viève. "We can be together. Now that she's gone. We don't have to worry about anyone coming between us again." Mary Anne watched Viève's face grow softer with each step Holden took toward her. Viève obviously wanted to believe Holden. *Surrender to it, just let go,* Mary Anne thought. Holden held out his arms toward Viève. Viève's eyes got wide; she looked hypnotized by the thought of reuniting with him. *Almost,* Mary Anne thought. She started to stand, ready to grab Viève when Holden grabbed the gun. Mary Anne glanced at Holden just as the gun exploded.

Rule 30

Remember What Sustains You

Jessica Caulfield-Fox, Manager-Producer

Jessica watched Mike lift Max and toss him high into the sky. Max squealed and Mike laughed. This was her life. This was the important part of her life. Not film, not drama, not fighting on set, not Viève. Not even Jessica's close friends. The moments with Mike and Max eclipsed Hollywood and filmmaking and everything else. Jessica pressed her BlackBerry to her ear as she took one final look in her closet.

"Blanks?" Lydia asked from the other end.

"Blanks. She stole the gun from set," Jessica said.

"Mary Anne is so lucky," Lydia said.

"They didn't even take Mary Anne to the hospital. You know how she hates hospitals. Seems that Mary Anne swallowed only two Vicodin. Nobody dies from two Vicodin."

"And Holden?"

"Saved the day. Once they discovered the gun held blanks, Holden grabbed Viève just as she was lunging at Mary Anne. He held her while Mary Anne called the cops. They've already committed her," Jessica said. She glanced across her room at Mike zipping up their suitcases. "So we're leaving town for the next seven days. Thought you should know," Jessica said.

"Go and enjoy," Lydia said. "I think everyone needs a break after this fiasco."

"*Vitriol* really took it out of us, didn't it?" Jessica asked. "Where are you? It sounds so loud."

"That's the wind. We're in Sedona," Lydia said.

"You guys rode Zymar's bike all the way to Sedona?" Jessica asked.

"Yeah, but I think I'm renting a car for the trip back. Either that or hopping on a plane. I'm not nearly as hard-core as he. Enjoy your trip," Lydia said. "Once you get back you might get really busy."

"We're always busy," Jessica replied.

"You and Mike might get even busier."

"You've got another film for us?"

"Ted may have an entire slate for you two."

"What?"

"He wants to talk to you and Mike about heading up the studio together," Lydia said.

"Together?"

"Yeah, kind of like Walter and Laurie did at DreamWorks for a while."

Jessica paused. She and Mike running a studio? Together? Co-presidents of production?

"You two always succeed. Mike is magic and you're amazing. It's really a no-fail situation for Ted," Lydia said. "If you want it."

Jessica couldn't decide now. Her emotions felt raw with all the insanity lately. She needed a vacation. Right now the industry, with all its intrigue and politics, just made her tired. "I don't know. After watching everything you went through, Lydia, I don't know if I want it. And that's even with Mike as co-president."

"Think about it while you're gone. Talk to Mike. I know Ted wants to have a conversation with you both once you're back."

"Okay," Jessica said. "You know how to reach me—"

"Go," Lydia interrupted, "enjoy."

"Jess, come on, are you ready?" Mike called from their bedroom. She clicked off her BlackBerry and set it on her dresser. "You're not taking your BlackBerry?" Mike asked, raising an eyebrow.

"This is a family vacation, and I've got everyone I need for a family vacation with me," Jessica said.

She pulled the front door shut as Mike waited for her in their Range Rover. She hadn't yet mentioned Lydia and their conversation to Mike. She knew he'd want the job, and he would be great as president of production at Worldwide. And she suspected that should she decline, Ted would give Mike the job without her as copresident. She needed to think. She needed this time alone with her husband and son to decide. To determine if she wanted to dive into Lydia's job or maybe sit on the sideline, producing a film a year, repping clients . . . and being a mom.

"Ready?" Mike asked as Jessica fastened her seat belt.

"Ready."

Rule 31

Old Friends Make the Deadliest Enemies

Kiki Dee, Publicist

The sun, the surf, the sand, and the sex. Kiki's body felt relaxed and refreshed. She'd spent the entire holiday break indulging her every desire. Looking out the bedroom window of Ted and Cici's house in Fiji, she turned her lustful eyes toward the beach below, where Carlos lay on a towel. *Yummy!* Why had she waited this long to acquire a friend like Carlos? He satisfied all her fantasies. And she knew. She knew that Carlos and Robert were lovers. They weren't fooling anyone, wandering off every night down the beach for their post-dinner stroll. Those two boys were way too beautiful and way too close. Try as they might to fool her with their butch lingo and cigar smoking, Kiki knew the boys were a little light in the loafers. And she didn't care. She didn't care what or who Carlos did in his off-time. She didn't ride bareback. As long as he was hard and attentive when he was with her, and she was well satisfied, then forget it! He was worth every penny.

"Kiki?" She heard Terri wandering down the hall toward her room. "Kiki, are you in there?" Terri knocked on her door. "I'm going to the beach, but I'm almost done with my article and I need that file," she said.

Kiki rushed into her private bathroom and turned the shower on full blast. She'd avoided this moment for the last ten days. She didn't have the file. She peeked out the bathroom door and saw Terri retreating in her two-piece toward the beachfront deck. She knew that once she told Terri that she had lost the file, Terri would write whatever she wanted. And Terri had enough ammo to blast *Vitriol,* Cici, and all of Worldwide.

Kiki left the shower running and slipped into the hallway. She wanted to read Terri's article, and now was the best time. Terri was being more than a little cagey about what she was writing, alluding to all kinds of possible story lines and bits of gossip—bits of gossip that although tolerable within Hollywood, were unacceptable if outed to the general public. Kiki glanced toward the beach; she could just make out Terri lying between the two beautiful boy toys. Now or never.

Kiki opened the door to Terri's room. The woman was a slob. When they were roommates, Terri threw her clothes around, and even now, forty years later, her floor was covered with pants, shirts, lingerie. Hadn't Terri ever heard of a hanger? Kiki glanced at the desk on the far side of the bedroom. There, like manna from heaven, sat Terri's laptop. Terri wrote everything on her MacBook Pro . . . and it was still open. The screen saver was a fantastic Annie Leibovitz photo of Terri with David Bowie, taken two dozen years earlier. Kiki pulled the door to Terri's bedroom shut and walked to the desk. She sat and touched the finger pad. The screen sprang to life. There was Terri's yet-to-be-filed *Vanity Fair* article on *Vitriol.* Kiki sat, inhaled, and began to read.

* * *

"You bitch!" Kiki screamed.

She ran down the hall toward the beach as fast as her knobby knees would carry her. "How could you?" She burst onto the sand where Terri reclined on a chaise lounge. The boys were nowhere in sight.

"Kiki?" Terri looked up, shielding her eyes from the sun.

"You've always been envious! Just admit it, you fat cow. Ever since I did Mick and you were stuck with Keith."

"What are you talking about?" Terri asked.

"Your fucking article, that's what I'm talking about."

"You read my article?"

"Of course I read it. What are you trying to do? Destroy me?"

"That article is my private property," Terri said. "You broke into my room and read my article!"

"You traitorous bitch. I got you that gig. I gave you that information—all of it off the record, I might add—and you've put it into a piece that is going out just before the Oscars?"

"I have confirmation."

"From whom?'

"An anonymous source," Terri said, a wicked gleam in her eye.

"Bullshit," Kiki said. "You've never used an anonymous source in your entire career. Who told you?"

"I'm not saying. Now sit down and enjoy the rest of our holiday."

"I will not enjoy anything. I'm not kidding, Terri, you tell me right now who tipped you or I will—"

"What? What will you do? Hmm?"

"Our friendship will be over," Kiki sputtered.

"Oh, Kiki, don't be silly. We both know too much about each other for our friendship ever to be finished," Terri said. She lay back on the chaise to soak up the sun.

"I'm not kidding, Terri. You tell me now."

"I'm not telling you anything, you crazy old broad," Terri said. "No matter what you say."

"Fine." Kiki turned back toward the house and headed back to Terri's room. She knew what she needed to do.

***

It felt like a giant Frisbee slipping from her fingertips. A five-pound Frisbee. The sun glinted off the computer's silver top as it arced up over the Pacific's waves, sailing through the air, much farther than Kiki thought she was capable of throwing it. But Pilates and yoga had made her stronger than she'd anticipated. She felt joyful watching the computer fly. That bitch. That horrible bitch of a woman whom she had pretended to be friends with for the last forty years. Terri had no idea what true friendship was, or how to keep things quiet. Discretion? Fuck, no. Terri wasn't discreet. She was manipulative, she was mean, she was cunning. Terri was nothing like Kiki, a solid friend with true loyalty.

Kiki turned back toward the house. There'd be no way that Terri would ever file her story now.

"What did you just throw into the ocean?" Terri stood five feet from Kiki, her tree-trunk legs planted firmly in the sand. "I am a writer, and you just threw my laptop into the ocean," Terri said. "A writer, Kiki, do you understand? And you threw my *laptop* into the ocean." Terri walked slowly toward her. Kiki had never seen Terri's eyes look so crazy, not even when they were dropping acid in the Haight with Tom.

"A writer, Kiki. Do you know what that means?" Terri asked.

Kiki shook her head, glancing to her right and left for an escape route. Terri outweighed her by at least fifty pounds.

"It means I hope you've said your prayers, because I am going to kill you," Terri said.

Kiki backed into the surf trying to get around Terri. She bolted to the left, making a quick dash for the house, but Terri's arms wrapped around Kiki's knees. Kiki's chin hit wet sand and she swallowed salty water as a wave crashed over her. She choked and spat as Terri grabbed her shoulders and pushed her under another wave. Her lungs burned; she couldn't breathe. Blackness grabbed her as she sucked in saltwater.

* * *

Kiki choked and heaved. She rolled onto her side and vomited seawater.

"I am a writer!" Terri screamed. "She threw my laptop into the ocean!"

Kiki looked up at Carlos, leaning over her. "Kiki, you okay?" Carlos asked. Kiki felt another wave of nausea and she leaned to her right again and puked.

"A writer, do you understand? My laptop! My laptop in the ocean!"

Kiki slowly sat up and looked to her left. Terri strained against Robert's well-muscled arm, trying to get to her. "You! You're dead, do you hear me? Dead! I may have missed this time, but I know you, Kiki Dee. I'm coming for you."

"Hey, stop," Robert said. He pulled Terri toward the house.

"It was one laptop, Kiki," Terri yelled. "I still have it all up here." She tapped her head. "I'll get another computer. I'll file that story, and when I do, you and your clients, all of them, are dead. Dead! Even Steven. I'm not scared. It's all coming out."

Robert pulled Terri up the stairs.

"Do you hear me, you anorexic bitch? All of them, dead!" Terri screamed.

Kiki watched Robert push Terri into the house. She looked at Carlos and inhaled fresh air. "Thanks for saving my life," she said.

Carlos pulled her slowly to her feet. "Glad we were here. Robert and I were on our way out for a walk. Two minutes later and it would have been just you and her," he said.

Kiki shuddered. Her dead body could be drifting out to sea, never to be recovered. "Did you see the whole thing?" she asked.

"Oh yeah, from you walking down the steps with the computer to her tackling you in the ocean. Quite a scene. That old lady is strong. It took both of us to get her off you," Carlos said. "Whatever was on that computer must have been pretty intense."

Kiki looked toward the house. "Intense? Yes, I guess *intense* is the right word."

***

The end-of-year holiday wasn't quite over, but Kiki sat in her office and waited for Celeste. She assumed Cici wanted to meet with her so that she could have the pleasure of firing her in person. Kiki's right eye was a bright purple seen only on exotic birds and horrible bruises. She had phoned Cici from the maid's quarters on the island and told her everything, including the slant of Terri's *Vanity Fair* story. Kiki then boarded a plane, alone, and returned to L.A. She figured she had a forty-eight-hour lead time (if that) to try to do some damage control before Terri filed her story.

"Kiki, darling," Cici said, breezing into the office. "Oh my. You weren't lying. You two really did have a go, didn't you?"

"The best of friends make the worst of enemies," Kiki said.

"So true," Cici said. "Our friends know all our dirty little secrets, don't they?"

"Every single one," Kiki said. "And I'm afraid this time it's going to spill everyone's blood. Cici, I am—"

"Not another word," Cici said. She glanced at her watch. "What's your new assistant's name?" she asked.

"Jilly."

"Jilly," Celeste called out. "When Miss Seawell phones, put her through."

"Celeste, I am the last person Terri will call," Kiki said.

"Oh no, darling. She's going to call."

"What? Why do you think—"

"I sent her a note asking her to," Cici said.

"Celeste, darling, I know you are a very big star, but this tiff between Terri and me, you aren't going to fix it with a note."

"Miss Solange," Jilly called from her desk. "I have Terri Seawell on one."

"Put her through, please," Cici called back. "Kiki, put her on speakerphone." Kiki pushed the button on her phone. "Terri? Are you there, Terri?" Cici asked.

"Cici, darling, yes of course I'm here. Thank you so much for your note," Terri said.

"Oh Terri, my pleasure. Did you enjoy the house?" Cici asked.

"Loved the house. It's absolutely divine."

"You liked it then?" Cici asked. She looked up at Kiki and smiled.

"Adored. So I've rewritten my article," Terri said. "I don't know if you heard, but I had a terrible accident with my laptop while I was on your island."

"No? What happened?" Cici asked.

"Some water got on it. Scrambled my hard drive, absolutely destroyed the entire thing."

"Oh Terri, I'm so sorry. I can only imagine how horrible that was for you."

"Well, being a writer, one does become inordinately attached to one's laptop. But fortunately for me, I back everything up. So the only thing that was lost was my article for *Vanity Fair.* Are you with your publicist now?"

"Kiki? Yes, she's right here."

"I'm e-mailing you a copy of the article." Cici looked at Kiki, who glanced at her own computer screen.

"You should get it in just a few minutes," Terri said. "The article is lovely. I hope it helps your Oscar campaign, and maybe ticket sales for *Vitriol.*"

Kiki opened the e-mail from Terri with the attached article. Her jaw dropped as she scanned Terri's story. *How had Celeste managed to get Terri to write this?* "It's fantastic," Kiki whispered to Cici.

"Kiki loves it," Cici said. "I'm sure I will, too."

"Thank you again for the house," Terri said. "And the pictures, too."

"Not a problem. Let me know when you want to go again."

"I will, darling. Ciao," Terri said, and the line went dead.

Kiki looked up from her computer screen and over at Cici. "How did you do this?"

"Do what?"

"This! This article! How did you get her to write this article?"

"Maybe it was the gift I sent her," Cici said.

"Gift?"

"Some pictures, of Terri. From the house."

"Pictures?"

"Last year Ted had security cameras installed in all our houses," Cici said. "I had no idea about Terri's fascination with black latex, did you?"

Kiki swallowed.

"Cameras? In *every* room?" Kiki asked.

"Every room," Cici said. She stood, picked up her Versace bag, and walked toward the door.

"Oh, Kiki, Pilates looks very good on you," Cici said. "And so does Carlos."

Epilogue

Dreams Do Come True

Mary Anne Meyers, Screenwriter

"Mary Anne, wake up," Holden said. He nudged her gently in the ribs.

"Uhhh. What time is it?" Mary Anne rubbed her eyes and turned toward her bedside clock.

"Six o' clock. They're announcing the nominees."

Mary Anne pulled herself up in bed and looked over at the plasma screen on the far wall. The two celebrity announcers looked way too perky for this early in the morning.

"Have they announced Best Actress yet?"

"No. Screenplay is next," Holden said.

"Mmm . . . wake me up when they get to Cici," Mary Anne said sleepily. She turned over and snuggled into the covers, letting the warmth of the down surround her. Mary Anne heard "And the nominees . . ." as her eyes fluttered closed.

* * *

"Mary Anne, wake up, wake up!" Holden shook her. "You missed it! Did you miss it?"

Mary Anne opened her eyes and watched Holden jumping over her on the bed. "Cici got nominated! I knew it!" she said.

"*You* just got nominated for an Academy Award!"

"What? You mean *Cici* just got nominated."

"No! You! *You* just got nominated for *California Girl.*"

"But how?"

"You *wrote* it," Holden said. "Wait, that's the phone. And there goes your BlackBerry. Are you ready for this? You'd better get up and get showered because this is a big day. You're going to the Academy Awards."

Mary Anne looked at the television. There was her picture plastered on the screen beside the other nominees.

"Hi, Jess. Yeah, she's right here. No, she missed it! I woke her up, but she fell back asleep." Holden held out the phone to Mary Anne. "It's Jessica for you. And your BlackBerry keeps buzzing."

Mary Anne placed the phone to her ear. "Hello?"

"Congratulations!" Jessica said. "Little Miss Academy Award Nominee."

"Thanks. Have they announced Best Actress yet?" Mary Anne asked.

"They just did."

"Cici?"

"Not this year," Jessica said.

"She's going to be so disappointed."

"But *you.* You are going to the Academy Awards! How great is that?"

"I never even thought about it. I knew they were pushing the film, but I didn't think that *I'd* get nominated," Mary Anne said.

"Well, you have been! So get up and get showered and dressed. I want you to come over to the office today. Let's sit down and talk about how you want to capitalize on this."

"Capitalize?"

"What projects you want? Long-term goals? What script ideas you have? Now is the time to get all those favorite ideas of yours going at the studios," Jessica said.

"Okay. What time?"

"How about ten?"

"See you then," Mary Anne said. She pushed the off button on the cordless phone and glanced at the television screen. Her insides started to tickle and she broke into a smile. She was going to the Academy Awards. She, Mary Anne Meyers from St. Paul, Minnesota, would forever be known as Academy Award nominee Mary Anne Meyers. Her heart began to beat fast. She looked at Holden. He was typing a message on his BlackBerry. "I'm awake, right? This isn't a dream?"

He looked at her and smiled. "You're awake. It's all real, baby. It's all real. There's the phone. You want to get it, or shall I?"

"I got it," Mary Anne said. "I'm sure it's my mom." She reached over and grabbed the ringing phone from the bed. No, she was awake. Right now her life just felt like a dream.

Acknowledgments

As an author, to write the stories I'm given I sit alone at my computer, but for my stories to become books takes much work and dedication by many talented and wonderful people.

First, thank you to my über-agent, the amazingly talented Andy Barzvi. Next, thank you to the rest of my team at ICM: Janet Carol Norton, Nick Reed, Josie Freedman, and Eric Reid. Thank you to Langley Perer, Jill McElroy, Alex Kerr, and everyone else at Benderspink. Thank you to my attorney, Paul Miloknay, who continues to give me brilliant advice.

Thank you to my talented, patient, and all-around wonderful editor, Lindsey Moore. Thank you to the entire team at Crown for your hard work and support, especially Kristin Kiser, Philip Patrick, Christine Aronson, Annsley Rosner, Sarah Chance Breivogel, Tina Constable, and Donna Passannante.

Thank you to my publicist (not anything like Kiki), Leslie Ferguson. Thank you to my Web maven, Madeira James.

Thank you to my family: Margaret Marr, Elizabeth Leahy, Paula